TANGLED WEBS

SHEILA KENDALL

Beaten Track
www.beatentrackpublishing.com

Tangled Webs

First published 2019 by Beaten Track Publishing
Copyright © 2019 Sheila Kendall

All rights reserved.

No part of this publication may be reproduced, stored in a retrieval system, or transmitted, in any form or by any means, without the prior permission of the publisher, nor be otherwise circulated without the publisher's prior consent in any form of binding or cover other than that in which it is published and without a similar condition including this condition being imposed on the subsequent publisher.

The moral right of the author has been asserted.

ISBN: 978 1 78645 388 4

Beaten Track Publishing,
Burscough, Lancashire.
www.beatentrackpublishing.com

TANGLED WEBS

Charmaine, John & Hype,

    Thank you for allowing us to stay in your wonderful home. Have had a wonderful time here and would love to return!

    Best wishes

        Sheila

Chapter One

Mike bit his lip anxiously as he watched the horses approaching the finish line. This was it. His big break. His horse was two lengths in front, couldn't possibly lose. This time tomorrow, he would be a—*Damn.* Disbelievingly, he watched as the horse stumbled and fell, the jockey rolling to safety, the horse scrambling to its feet.

Mike groaned, dropped his head into his hands. How could he have been so flaming stupid? He'd risked everything on that accumulator, not least his marriage. Melinda would go mad when she saw how much money he'd taken out of their account. His only hope was to stop her finding out. But how? She always drew money out when they went to do the weekly shopping; she'd know instantly there was £200 missing, would want an explanation, a reason.

Mike racked his brains for a way out of this. He couldn't transfer any money into the account until Monday, and by then it would be too late. She'd already threatened to leave him if he didn't stop gambling, and in his heart, he sometimes feared she meant it. Granted, her threats in the past had been empty ones, but when she saw what he'd done this time…

If only he could get her away for a week, stop her going anywhere near that account until he could get the money back into it.

***

Melinda turned in surprise when her husband put his arms around her, spun her and kissed her soundly on the lips.

"Pack your bags, my darling wife, we're going on holiday."

She gasped. "What? Where? We never said anything about holidays," she protested when she finally got her breath back.

"Call it a special treat. You deserve a break. You haven't been right since the miscarriage, have you? And I haven't been helping much with being so flaming selfish."

Melinda looked at him suspiciously. Yes, he'd been a bit preoccupied lately, but she couldn't accuse him of neglecting her since she lost the baby. If anything, he'd been a little too attentive, always asking her if she was all right, fussing over her, refusing to be fazed even when she snapped at him to leave her alone.

Which meant, by a process of elimination, that he'd done something else wrong or he wouldn't be suggesting a holiday *for her*. Something he didn't want her to find out about—it didn't take a genius to realise it was probably to do with gambling.

Melinda knew she should just ask how much he'd lost, refuse to go anywhere until he told her, but she wasn't feeling strong enough emotionally to cope if it was a large amount. She was prepared to ignore it for the time being, take his offer at face value, get away from the house and the memories for a while. Maybe it was what she needed—a break from everything. It certainly wouldn't do her any harm.

"So where are we going for this holiday?" she asked with an attempt at enthusiasm.

"I thought we'd go to Chester. You've always wanted to go to Wales, haven't you? And what better place to stay than Chester?"

"Er, Wales?" she suggested with a wry smile.

"Now, come on. You know how I feel about the countryside. This way, we'll be able to have a look at Wales at the same time."

She shrugged, her brief flash of humour gone. These days, it was harder and harder to cope with Mike and his incessant need for excitement. It was okay while he was at work, but the weekends were a nightmare, with him always wanting to be doing something or other. Could she cope with being on holiday with him for a week? Still, if it kept him away from the bookie's, maybe it wouldn't be such a bad thing.

"Okay, I'll go and pack," she said with false brightness.

***

Mike breathed a sigh of relief as she went out of the room. He'd done it! There was no way she was going to find out about the £200 now, and she hadn't even realised there was a race meeting at Chester—another bonus. With any luck, he'd be able to win back what he'd lost and more besides. With the optimism of a true gambler, he was still convinced the big win was waiting for him, that his luck would change and change soon.

***

"You're late," Stella Cox accused as her husband walked through the front door of their home.

"I know, love. I got called into a meeting at the last minute."

"You should have told them you were going on holiday and couldn't get tied up at the last minute like that. Honestly, Graham, I do wish you'd stand up for yourself more, stop letting people walk all over you."

He hid a smile as he looked at her standing there, the one person he actually did allow to 'walk all over him', as she put it.

"Anyway, I've left you a suitcase on the bed. You'd better get packed or we'll never get there. Oh, and I thought we'd stop for lunch on the way, although I know it'll be more like afternoon tea now, but still, it can't be helped."

Graham frowned at the three suitcases already in the hall. *Surely those aren't just her clothes? We're going for a week, not a month!*

"Can't I put my stuff in one of these?" he asked. "I won't be taking much."

"Of course you can't. They're all full."

"And you need three suitcases, do you?"

"We're going to the races tomorrow, aren't we? I can't go there without a suitable outfit."

His eyebrows rose slightly. Anybody would think they were going to be in the Royal Box, not the paddock, listening to her. And he'd just bet she'd been out and bought something new for it to add to her vast collection of clothes. God knew she could probably keep the entire Third World clothed for a year from her wardrobe alone.

Despite all his efforts, Graham couldn't fit four suitcases into his car boot, and his own ended up on the back seat.

"I thought we'd stop off in Ironbridge on the way. We can go to that little tea room we found there," Stella decided as she settled herself in the passenger seat.

"We won't be stopping off anywhere, not even at the motorway services with that case on the back seat," Graham retorted. "You know how I feel about leaving anything on view in the car when it's parked."

"Oh, for heaven's sake, you can be such an old woman sometimes," she trilled with her silly little laugh which so irritated him.

"No. I can be cautious," he corrected her.

"The car was broken into *once*, Graham. It's not as though it's happened since."

"It's never happened because I don't take the same chances I did back then. If you want three humping great suitcases with you, we go straight to Chester."

She didn't reply, and he smiled to himself. Stella in a sulk was preferable to her incessant chattering, and he had plenty to think about after that meeting he'd been called to—a meeting he'd known he couldn't afford to miss.

***

All Graham's problems had begun when he first met and fell in love with Stella Markham. Back then, she'd been as glamorous as she was now, and he'd been stunned that this girl was interested in him; he couldn't believe his luck when she accepted his proposal. His friends had warned him against it, could see through the veneer, but Graham hadn't listened to them. He'd married her without a thought for the future. And what a future it had proved to be.

Stella, like they'd said, had no intention of working once they were married and had given up her job without a qualm, intent on being a 'society wife'. It wasn't cheap. Not working gave her more time for shopping and entertaining, and Graham struggled to make ends meet for the first five years of their marriage until he began to climb through the company ranks.

He still wanted more, career-wise at least, but he was struggling with the job he had, not from the point of view of being able to do it; rather, it wasn't what he'd wanted from a career, from his life. What he'd originally taken as a stopgap until he could take on the job he wanted had soon become essential to fund Stella's lifestyle. Until today, he hadn't ever seen a way out of the mire he'd got himself into when he said "I do" to the woman sitting beside him in silence in the car.

Rumours had been flying for a while about problems with the company, and they'd all known there were going to be cutbacks at some point, so it hadn't come as a surprise today when they were called together so management could ask for voluntary redundancies.

Graham had worked there for twenty years and would get a good deal. This was his chance to do what he wanted. All he had to do was take the offer and he could go into business with Darren Welch. They'd talked about it on and off for years. They would set up their own employment agency. For Graham and Darren, it would be a chance to help people, get them into their dream jobs. But it would take money to set it up, and whilst Darren had been in a position to do it for three years, Graham hadn't had the money available for his half of the investment. Until today.

Stella wasn't one to sulk for long, and by the time they left the motorway, she'd recovered enough to begin making plans for their future as she saw it. Evidently, she'd decided the meeting Graham had been called to that afternoon meant promotion despite him saying nothing of the sort to her.

"You know, I think we'll have to consider moving house," she said as she looked at the luxurious properties they drove past. "I mean, once you're at management level, we can't be entertaining your clients where we live now, can we?"

"But I won't be at management level," he said quickly. "If anything, I'm going to be made redundant."

It was as well he was driving rather than Stella or they'd have ended up in the nearest ditch if her cry of dismay was anything to go by.

"Oh, no. Surely not? They can't afford to let you go, can they? Financially, I mean, apart from the job you do."

He should have known he wouldn't get away with it so easily, that she'd know exactly how much it would cost the firm to let him go. So much for doing this without having to tell her the truth: he was going to volunteer for redundancy.

"It won't be the end of the world, you know," he assured her. "I thought it was time I set up in business on my own anyway."

"Doing what, for heaven's sake?" Her eyes narrowed in sudden suspicion. "This hasn't got anything to do with that stupid idea of Darren Welch's, has it? I won't have you gambling our futures on a whim, Graham!"

"It isn't a whim. We've looked into all the pros and cons—"

"Oh, so you've been planning this all along, have you?"

"We've been talking about it, yes. It was just a matter of me getting a chance and the money to put into the idea. If I get a redundancy offer, I'll be taking it while I'm still young enough to do this."

"And what about me?" she demanded. "What happens if we decide to have a family? You'll need a steady income then, to support me and a child. You can't expect to have that if you go into business on your own, can you?"

"You won't have a child, Stella," he replied with a sigh. "You've said all along you don't want kids. You can't change your mind now just because I'm threatening to do something you don't approve of."

"This is a marriage, Graham. I have as much say in what you do as anybody else would—more even. I will not have you throwing in a perfectly good job because you want to play at being your own boss."

He laughed harshly but didn't say anything. As far as he was concerned, there was no marriage left let alone equal rights in it. He was going to do what he wanted to do for once, and Stella could like it or lump it.

***

Melinda sighed as she stirred her by-now lukewarm coffee and gazed around the motorway services restaurant at the couples and the families breaking their journeys and sitting together, talking to each other, bound for destinations only they knew about while she sat in solitude waiting for her husband. *How much longer is he going to spend on the gaming machines?* She'd been waiting more than an hour for him to come back to her, the only saving grace being that he hadn't actually ordered any coffee for himself.

Idly, she wondered why she wasn't fretting more about the amount of money he must be feeding into the machines, but somehow, it didn't seem that important today. Sometimes she wondered if it was losing the baby that had made her less concerned about his gambling, or was it that she knew she could walk away from the marriage now there were no children involved?

Melinda gasped as the thought struck her. Did she really want to leave Mike? Had she reached the end of her tether with him? She knew in her heart that she was tired of fighting with him over his gambling, wanted him to choose between it and her. It wasn't that she expected him to just stop. He'd need help, to accept he was addicted, but it was so hard persuading him to go for that help. She had enough emotional problems of her own to cope with, without having to worry about Mike's as well.

As if he'd realised where her thoughts were going, Mike came back to stand at her table, glancing at his watch and asking if she was ready to leave yet as though she'd been the one delaying them for the last hour.

Silently, she followed him out to the car, climbing in beside him, forcing a smile on her lips as he told her he'd managed to win 'a few pounds' on the machines.

"I suppose it makes a change for you to actually win anything," she muttered.

"Hey now, come on. The averages are pretty good, you know," he retorted, conveniently forgetting how long it was going to take to recoup a certain £200 he'd lost.

"I hope you enjoyed it. You won't have a chance to do any more gambling this week, will you?"

"No, I don't suppose I will."

She flung him a questioning look. Why had he sounded hesitant? Why was he so insistent on them coming to Chester, for that matter? And why— *Oh, no...*

"It's Chester races this weekend, isn't it?" she asked flatly.

"I thought you knew it was."

"No, Mike, I didn't. There again, I'm not the one who turns straight to the racing pages in the newspaper, am I?"

"I thought you might enjoy a day at the races. It's a long time since we've been."

"You mean a day at the races on my own while you go from tout to tout putting bets on horses that fall at the first hurdle?"

"They'll not fall at any hurdles," he said smugly. "It's a flat race."

"It can be as flat as it wants, I'm still not going," she snapped. "If you want to go, I'll spend the day in Chester."

He shrugged and patted her arm. He knew her too well, knew when it came to it, she'd be at his side tomorrow. She didn't like shopping on her own anyway.

***

Peter Clarke looked around the hotel dining room at his motley group of staff. Of them all, only one didn't look keen on being present at this weekly meeting and that was his own daughter. Tina could always think of better things to do than attend 'team meetings'. It was a shame one of those things wasn't finding herself a job other than waitressing here, but as his daughter, she seemed to think she was a level above the rest of the staff, ordering them about, refusing to do the more menial tasks which were required of the waitresses and generally making herself more and more unpopular.

"You'll probably have guessed we're completely full this weekend, I've even had to let out Room One, for which, I don't mind telling you, I'm going to be in trouble about when Val finds out."

"I hope you haven't given it to any complainers," Carol, their chef, muttered.

"No. It was a chap who was desperate for somewhere to stay. He'll be more grateful than annoyed."

"And you warned him how small it is?" she persisted.

"Yes. Anyway, Carol, can you sort out some specials for the board tonight? I know you don't usually do any on a Friday, but I think we should give them a try."

"You do know it's my night off tonight, don't you?" Tina asked. Her father shook his head and smiled at her.

"Not this week, it isn't. I'm sorry, Tina, but we're going to need all the staff in this weekend."

***

Tina's face darkened, and Carol's heart sank like a stone. She was difficult enough when she was in a reasonably good mood, but if she was being denied her night off, she was going to be hell to work with. Maybe it would be worth her while having a word with Peter after the meeting, see if she could persuade him to let Tina off after all. Surely Valerie or Peter could stand in for just one evening?

The door opened to admit Shona, their other waitress, and Peter smiled and indicated a chair.

"Sorry I'm late," she panted.

"That's fine," he assured her. "You get your breath back. You haven't missed anything."

"No, just the time she should be here for," Tina muttered. Carol glared at her.

That was the main problem. For some reason which nobody could explain, Tina had taken a dislike to the other waitress as soon as she'd started, and it led to a terrible atmosphere in the kitchen. It never ceased to amaze Carol that Shona didn't turn put Tina in her place once and for all, but the other girl didn't seem to notice what was going on half the time, at least, not at work.

By the time the meeting broke up, Tina's face was like thunder, and Carol didn't waste a moment asking Peter if she could have a quiet word.

"Office?" he said, and she nodded, glad he hadn't suggested a more public place. The last thing she wanted was for Tina to overhear them.

Valerie was already in there and looked up with a weary smile when her husband and the chef walked in.

"Hi, Carol. Sorry I missed your meeting, Peter, but the phone hasn't stopped ringing all morning."

"I know. It's at times like this I wish we had twice as many rooms as we have."

"When you say things like that, I worry you've done something stupid like letting out Room One again." Valerie winked at Carol.

"Oh, don't worry, he has done." The chef laughed.

"I knew it! You can't accept it should be a single, can you?"

Peter shrugged. "Tell you what—as soon as we've got through this week, I'll start advertising it as a single."

"And we'll have a single bed put in there so you can't 'accidentally' let it go as a double, shall we?"

"Look, you two," Carol interrupted, anxious to get her point across, "while I could chat about Room One all day, we need to decide what we're going to do about your daughter."

Valerie looked like she'd been slapped in the face. She'd put off a confrontation with Tina for as long as she could, but they had no option now. She needed pulling into line.

Tina walked around with a gigantic chip on her shoulder, believing the world owed her a living or, more specifically, her parents. She could have done well for herself. She'd sailed through her GCSEs, but when it came to the sixth form, she didn't have the self-discipline to manage her study/leisure time and, not surprisingly, failed her AS Levels in spectacular style.

The waitressing job in the hotel was supposed to be a stopgap until she decided whether she wanted to go to college or not, but that had been almost three years ago, and now it looked as though Tina intended staying on in the hotel forever more. Staying on and causing trouble for the staff.

"What do you want us to do?" Valerie asked wearily.

"I'd like you to give her the night off—"

"No," Peter interrupted. "I can't have her getting her own way over this. It's going to look as though I'm favouring her over the rest of you because she's our daughter."

While Carol could see his point, she still didn't want Tina and Shona working together that evening. She looked to Valerie for help.

"I'll have a word with Tina, make sure she knows she can't mess you about," Valerie promised.

"It's not me I'm worried about. It's Shona. The poor girl struggles as it is without Tina undermining her with the customers all the time."

"What do you mean, undermining her?" Peter asked.

"She deliberately mixes the orders up to make Shona look bad, and then it appears that she's the one who's sorting it all out…"

"Oh, now, come on, Carol!" Valerie protested. "You're making her out to be some sort of ogre. I know Tina has her faults, but I don't think for one moment she'd deliberately try to do any harm to the hotel."

"No, but she doesn't think things through before she does them, love," Peter demurred.

"That's typical of you. You never see any good in her!"

Realising she'd opened a can of worms between husband and wife, Carol held up her hands and edged towards the door. "Just, please, make sure she behaves herself tonight however you do it. Okay?"

***

There was silence for a moment after the chef had left, closing the door quietly behind her, until Peter finally defended himself.

"If Tina wasn't our daughter and was an ordinary employee, what would you be saying right now?"

"Well, of course I'd be saying we should look into the allegations Carol has made…"

"Exactly. So why is it any different because she's our daughter? I'm not saying Carol's right, but I do think we should find out what's going on between her and Shona."

"And I suppose by 'we', you expect me to do it."

"No. I think it's about time I had a chat with her," he replied grimly.

He knew Valerie. The girl could wrap her around her little finger, and on this occasion, he intended to treat Tina as what she was: an employee. There'd be no chance for her to throw the 'I'm your daughter' card at him like she would with her mother and get away with it.

Chapter Two

STELLA THREW THE hotel a disparaging look as she got out of the car. It wasn't the type of place she was used to staying in. For one thing, where was the valet parking, the uniformed doorman?

"Thought we'd go a bit downmarket for this trip," Graham offered in cheerful explanation as he opened the boot. "We're going to have to learn to cut our cloth a bit tighter when I start up my own business."

"Even though you didn't actually know about this change when you booked the hotel?" she retorted. "I must say, that was very forward-thinking of you, darling."

"You know me, I like to be prepared," he replied glibly, admitting to nothing.

"No, you like to take every opportunity to save money," she snapped.

He bit back another retort. This wasn't the time or place to point out that Stella didn't know what saving money actually was about. Not if he wanted to keep her calm while they were here. Stella in a temper was something best avoided, at least until they were booked into the hotel, otherwise they'd be going straight back home again. He wouldn't blame anybody for refusing to let her stay if she threw a tantrum on their front doorstep.

As it happened, it wasn't Stella having a problem when they walked inside. She looked at Graham with raised eyebrows when they heard argumentative voices coming from what they assumed to be the office.

"This gets worse by the minute," Stella muttered as he rang the bell on the desk.

The argument stopped for a moment and then resumed, although they couldn't hear what was being said.

Usually, it was Peter who booked guests in, not Valerie, but on this occasion, she was the one who came out of the dining room, flustered and trying to ignore those raised voices.

"I assume we've arrived at a bad time?" Stella drawled.

"Oh, no. It's just the radio that's on too loud," Valerie assured as though she genuinely expected them to believe that.

Before Stella could say any more, Graham stepped into the breach, booking them in, asking where their room was—anything to keep his wife quiet. He wouldn't put it past her to accuse the poor woman of lying to cover up for whatever was going on. Better to allow her to keep a dignified approach to problems within the hotel as long as they were nothing to do with the guests.

It was some consolation that Stella nodded her approval of the room they were given: a four-poster bed could always be guaranteed to smooth his wife's ruffled feathers. Thank God he'd checked they had one before he booked them in. Nevertheless, Stella sniffed disparagingly as Valerie left them to unpack.

"God alone knows what sort of service we can expect this week if they're having problems with the staff."

"I'm sure it'll be absolutely fine," Graham replied absently as he checked his mobile.

"What are you doing?" she asked sharply.

"I need to get hold of Darren, tell him what's gone on today."

"Why? I haven't agreed to you doing this yet."

"You don't have a say, Stella. If I don't take the offer, I'll end up losing the chance and the money involved. That's the way it is. Darren and I are going into business, and I'm sorry if you don't like it, but after all, I'm the one who brings the money into the house."

She gasped at that, even paled slightly, but didn't speak, slamming her way into the bathroom. He shrugged, made his call to Darren and put her reaction out of his mind. It wasn't his fault if she didn't like the truth when she heard it.

***

Tina glared at her father as he relayed Carol's complaint about her attitude and her attempts to get Shona into trouble. She'd come into the office at his request on the assumption that he'd thought twice about letting her have the evening off, only to be told off for undermining the rest of the staff.

It wasn't good enough. What right did he have to lay into her like that? She was his daughter, for God's sake, not an employee.

"You do see what I'm saying, don't you?" Peter asked finally. "We all have to work together, and it isn't good practice for one person to be shown as not competent enough to do her job."

"So you think I'm undermining her, do you? The same Shona who couldn't give a damn about the hotel because she walks around in a daze half the time? I mean, is she the one who's complained or is it someone else?"

"I'm not telling you who's said what, I'm asking you what it is about Shona you dislike so much," he replied as patiently as he could manage.

"I don't *dislike* her, as you put it. If you want the truth, I feel a lot more strongly about her than just dislike."

Peter stared at her in bewilderment. "Why? What has she ever done to you to make you hate her? Do you have any idea what that poor girl is going through?"

"Oh, here we go." Tina sneered. "Everybody feel sorry for Shona, forget about what anybody else has gone through, just bend over backwards for her."

Peter sighed. This wasn't the way they'd brought up Tina. How could she be so cynical about a girl who'd gone through what Shona had for the past few months?

It had broken his heart when the girl first arrived on their doorstep in response to an advert they'd placed in the local paper. It was clear from her expression how desperate she was for the job, but he'd still insisted on a proper interview, tried not to delve too deeply into her reasons for wanting the waitress position. It had been almost a month before Valerie finally found out what the problem was for Shona, and once she did, all the staff immediately wanted to help her, make her feel welcome. Everyone except their daughter.

It hadn't made any sense at all to Peter and Valerie. The two girls had been at school together, but where Shona went on to university, Tina fell by the wayside. Seeing her old schoolmate reduced to working as a waitress seemed to delight Tina, as if she couldn't care less about the circumstances which had led to the situation the other girl was in.

Up until then, Shona's life had been on track. She was loving university, getting consistently good grades, making new friends everywhere she went, until the day her mother rang to tell her that her father had walked out on them. Just like that. Gone. Shona hadn't thought twice; her mother needed her. She couldn't possibly stay at university, not when her mum was so upset, and besides, she wouldn't be gone for long.

She'd been home a month when she'd realised there was no way her mum could cope without her, and suddenly all Shona's hopes and dreams for her future were gone. She was forced to find a job close enough to home to keep an eye on her mother, desperate to get out of the house at least for a few hours each day, and she'd found that at the hotel.

Now, Tina, Peter's *own daughter*, couldn't find it in her heart to befriend the girl. Where had they gone wrong? Was it the way he and Valerie had allowed her to leave school, drift into this job with them, hadn't forced her to look for anything else, sort her life out? Had they been too soft with her?

"So is there anything else?" Tina asked, sharply breaking the silence.

"Not at the moment, but, Tina, if I hear one more complaint about you, I'm going to tell you to look for a job somewhere else. I won't have the rest of the staff undermined. We need a good solid team to keep this hotel running smoothly—"

"Oh, you and your stupid team," she snarled. "Why can't you accept that *we're* the employers and they all need to do as they're told, keep in line, if they don't want to lose their jobs. God knows there's enough people out there looking for work, we could replace the whole lot of them with no trouble at all."

That was when Peter finally lost his temper with her.

"And why can't *you* accept that you're the one who's messed up your life? Nobody here, certainly not me or your mother, is responsible for that. You could have been at university like Shona, except you wouldn't have had to give up your course. You could've had the world, but you decided it was more important to have a social life, to throw your chance away. So don't you dare sit there and bad-mouth the business your mother and I are running here. So far as I'm concerned, if anybody goes, it'll be you, *not* a member of this staff who works their socks off. Now get out before I say something I'll really regret."

"I could save you the bother and walk out right now, you know," she yelled back.

"You know what, Tina? Right now, I wouldn't try to stop you. It's up to you—either pull your weight here or find something else, but don't for one moment think you'll be living here rent-free."

He had her over a barrel, and she knew it. She could walk out of the job but she couldn't walk out of her home. There was nowhere else for her to go.

"Well, of course I'm not going to walk out. But I might look at the Job Centre, see if there's anything else I can do…"

"You do that, but not until Monday if you don't mind. We've got a busy weekend ahead of us."

He smiled, suddenly the genial father again, but Tina wasn't fooled for a moment. He'd laid it on the line for her all too clearly: shape up or get out, and as she had no intention of kowtowing to the staff, out she'd go. Just as soon as she found herself a decent job that paid proper money. Hopefully enough money for her to move out altogether.

***

Shona jumped like a startled rabbit when her mobile bleeped. She knew before she opened the message that it was from her mother. Nobody else would send her a text during the day.

"Check it," Carol urged her. "You'll only worry about it if you don't."

"It's ridiculous. I've only been here for half an hour."

"Check it anyway."

Reluctantly, Shona opened the message, sighing again when she saw what it said. "She wants to know where I am. I told her I was coming to work. She can't have forgotten already."

Carol frowned, wondering how best to say what she felt she needed to without upsetting the girl.

"Is she taking those antidepressants the doctor gave her?" she asked.

"As far as I know, yes. Well, she says she is, but I can't be sure unless I stand over her while she takes them, and it doesn't feel right somehow, doing that with my own mother."

"You don't think she could be suffering some memory loss due to the side effects, do you?"

"Oh God, I hope not. She didn't say if the doctor had mentioned any, but…well, now you've said it, she does seem to be a bit spaced out most of the time."

"I think you need to have a word with the doctor yourself, love," Carol suggested quietly. She didn't want to say any more, but she was genuinely worried about Shona at the moment. The girl was out of her depth with everything going on in her home life. It wasn't fair that she had nobody to help her through this emotional maelstrom, which, after all, was none of her making.

"So what are you going to do?" Carol persisted.

"Send her a reply saying I'm at work. There's nothing else I can do, is there?" Shona replied wearily.

Carol could have offered to let her go home and reassure her mother, but for once she put Shona's interests first. The girl was better here than scurrying round after her mother all day. And anyway, she was needed here if they were going to be busy.

Shona had barely put her 'phone back in her bag when Tina stormed into the kitchen, glaring at her, and stopped in front of Carol, demanding to know who'd said what to her father.

With deliberate calm, Carol sent Shona to put the specials on the blackboard before she answered Tina.

"Right, young lady. Firstly, you never, *ever*, come into my kitchen like that. It's a dangerous enough place anyway, and I'll not have you putting yourself or the staff at risk. Do you understand me?"

Tina nodded sullenly.

"Secondly, it was me who told your father. I can't cope with you and Shona at each other's throats all the time."

"For her to be at my throat she'd have to get a bit of a backbone first," Tina retorted.

"All right then, I'll rephrase that. You at her throat all day long. I won't have it, Tina. It's bad enough coping with a hotel full of guests without you trying to upset the apple cart all the time."

"God, how old are you? Upsetting the apple cart? You sound like my grandmother!"

"Don't change the subject. You know exactly what I mean. Now, are you going to pull yourself together or do I need to get tough with you?"

"Okay, okay, I'll be all sweetness and light with Shona. How does that suit you?"

Carol sighed. "If I believed it even for a moment, it would suit me just fine."

"Oh, you can believe it. I can be a little angel when I put my mind to it," Tina promised airily.

Carol was no fool. Tina knew how to convince people she'd turned over a new leaf. Whether Shona would notice Tina was being nice to her was another matter.

Chapter Three

Mike was the sort of guest Peter liked best. He breezed through the door with a ready smile on his face and an attitude that said he worried about nothing and nobody. His wife Melinda, on the other hand, was quiet, didn't quite meet Peter's eyes when he greeted them both, and he sensed immediately there was something on her mind.

"If you'd like to follow me I'll show you to your room."

Peter heard Melinda's gasp behind him when she saw the size of that room, guessed what was wrong before either of them spoke.

"Bloody hell, mate, I know you said it was small, but this is ridiculous," Mike blustered, making it all too obvious his wife hadn't known anything about it.

"We can't stay in here," Melinda said, a catch in her voice that tugged at Peter's heartstrings. "I mean, it isn't even a full-sized double bed, is it?"

Looking at the room through their eyes, Peter had to acknowledge Valerie's point about it being more of a single than a double, but there wasn't a lot he could do about it now. Unless…

"Look, if you can cope in here until Sunday morning, I've got a couple here for only two nights. I can move you into a better room after that."

"Well, now that sounds fair enough, doesn't it, Melinda?" Mike asked, his good humour immediately restored.

"And, of course, we'll adjust the charges accordingly," Peter added when she didn't answer, hoping that would be enough to settle her mind.

"We could try somewhere else," she suggested.

"Like where? Everything in Chester's booked up this weekend."

"We could go to Wales, like I said originally."

"Oh, no. I've driven all this way, I'm not driving again tonight."

Knowing he'd won Mike over, Peter left it to him to talk his wife into staying and didn't doubt Mike would succeed because Peter had picked up on the desperation in the man's eyes. The races were the attraction—the driving force that would make him persuade his wife to stay. Many gamblers had come and gone in Peter's time at the hotel, but this man was one of the worst he'd ever seen.

***

Stella's eyes swept around the lounge, coming to rest on Mike and Melinda where they sat in the window with their drinks. She summed them up instantly in her mind: second wife and much younger than him, although he was rather pathetically trying to compete with her from an age point of view. They certainly weren't the sort of people she expected to come across in the hotels they usually frequented, and it didn't bode well for Graham that they were here.

"Hi, there. Please, come and join us," Mike called over.

"Don't even think about it," Stella warned in an undertone.

Her husband threw her an amused look and shook his head. "Oh, I think it's rather a good idea. At least we can't argue about our future if we join them, can we?"

As far as Stella was concerned, their future was already sorted out. Graham wasn't going into business with Darren Welch and that was an end to it.

Mike was the type of person who could befriend anyone, and Graham, who looked beyond the tattoos and the gold chains, saw a chap who was quite likeable. They were soon deep in conversation about the racing, Mike more than happy to give tips to anybody who wanted them.

"Are you a regular race-goer?" Stella asked Melinda, feeling she had to at least make an effort to speak to this...this child bride.

"If I had my way, we wouldn't be here in Chester, let alone going to the races tomorrow."

"I can't see the point in coming to Chester unless you're going to the races." Stella eyed the other woman up and down and found her sadly lacking in the fashion stakes. "I assume you won't be eating in the hotel this evening?"

"We haven't decided yet."

"Personally, I prefer to dress for dinner when we're staying in a hotel."

Melinda hastily hid a smile. She wasn't going to be cowed by a woman who—judging by the outfit she was wearing and the profusion of diamonds about her person—seemed to think she was staying at the Ritz, not a small hotel on the outskirts of Chester.

The two women were silent for a while, Stella sipping her drink with every sign of boredom and Melinda not wanting to talk to anybody, especially not this woman.

Graham, on the other hand, having decided this couple were okay, suddenly declared they should all go to the races together the following day.

"I don't think so, darling," Stella said quickly before the other couple could agree. "You know we like to go into the winners' enclosure..."

"And that's a problem because...?" he asked, a definite twinkle in his eye.

"Well," she floundered, "one has to dress properly for such things, you know."

"Now don't you worry, my love, we'll not show you up," Mike assured her, and she raised delicately arched brows at him.

That look said it all, but while Melinda flushed, Graham only grinned at her and winked at Mike.

"Don't worry about Stella. She's always had ideas above her station."

"My station, as you put it, is as wife to a successful businessman and don't you forget it," Stella snapped.

"A self-employed businessman even," Graham added.

Melinda watched them mentally squaring up to each other, thinking to herself it must be good to have an equal relationship between a couple. She and Mike never discussed things properly like a normal married couple. He frustrated her, treating her like an irritating child if she tried to discuss anything with him. Apparently, she hadn't lived long enough to have an opinion on anything.

Was that why he didn't take her seriously whenever she asked him to stop gambling? Was it that he didn't regard her as an equal because she was so much younger than him? If that were the case, she didn't see how there could be any future for them. Even when they did have children he wasn't going to change. To him, she was a trophy: the young wife other men would have liked and couldn't get. Bitterly, she wondered if she'd been the answer to some sort of mid-life crisis he was going through when they first met. When she'd fallen in love with him. Because she had loved him once, no matter how she felt now.

The evening was destined to get worse. Graham and Mike were getting on so well together that they arranged to go out after dinner.

"We're going into Chester ourselves, of course," Mike said, "but we'll be back here before the bar closes for the night. We'll see you then."

"Not if I have anything to do with it, they won't," Stella muttered as they went out of the door.

***

Mike didn't notice Melinda was quieter than usual that evening. There again, apart from sitting and eating his meal, he didn't spend a great deal of time with her, off on the games machines for the rest of the evening. She was relieved when he finally decided they should go back to the hotel—at least there she could leave him talking to Graham and Stella and take herself off to bed if she wanted to. She could always feign a headache or something. God knew she'd had enough practice at that over the last few months.

"You've been a bit withdrawn tonight. Anything wrong?" he asked as they crossed the bridge next to the racecourse, throwing her for a moment with his perceptiveness.

She was more used to him not noticing her at all.

"Not really. I just…well, I wonder why we can't talk to each other like that other couple at the hotel do," she murmured. "Don't you think it's a bit odd that we never do?"

"Talk? It struck me the poor bloke was being ruled by his wife." Mike grinned.

"At least she's allowed to have an opinion," Melinda muttered just low enough for him to pretend he hadn't heard her.

"Don't you worry about it, love. We've got one of the best marriages going, and I should know. I've already been through one of the worst ones, but then I met you."

She bit her lip, trying not to react to the patronising tone in his voice, but she couldn't, had to say something.

"If we had a good marriage, you'd listen to me about your gambling, give it up when I ask you to. You wouldn't leave me sitting alone in bars while you were on the machines."

"Don't be silly. Nobody said you had to sit on your own. You could have kept me company, you know."

"Oh, yes, and how would that have looked? As though I was condoning what you were doing. That's what I mean, Mike. You don't listen to me. You have no idea how I feel or what I want out of this marriage. You've got yourself a trophy wife and you expect me to behave like one, be content with that."

He stopped walking abruptly and stared at her, trying to see her face properly in the shadows thrown by the hedges they were passing.

"Are you serious?" he asked incredulously. "Do you really see yourself as a trophy wife?"

"I'm twenty years younger than you, Mike. What else am I supposed to think?"

"But, well, you're my wife. That's all. Just my wife."

It was the 'just my wife' that did it. Suddenly Melinda's numbness since she lost her baby was gone. The fog of grief cleared, and she looked at him with new eyes. Saw him for what he was: a gambler who wanted nothing more than a young wife to show off, one who would let him carry on with his own life. One who would be pliant—one who wasn't like his first wife had been.

Melinda knew full well why that marriage had broken down. Catherine had been nothing like her, had been the stronger character of the two, had refused to allow Mike to do what he wanted, and he couldn't cope with that. When it came to choosing between his wife and his gambling, he'd chosen the latter, unable to face up to his faults.

So what would happen if she, Melinda, gave him that same ultimatum? Which would he choose, her or the gaming tables? How much did he really love her? Did he even respect her? And was she strong enough emotionally to find out? Could she cope if he chose the gambling, left her to fend for herself? It was bad enough now, when he left her alone if they went out together. How would she cope if he wasn't there at all? If she had to live the rest of her life alone with no baby and no husband to love her?

***

Stella had made her mind up long before they sat down to eat that there would be something badly wrong with the meal, if not the food then definitely the service. It was, therefore, an almost inevitable twist of fate which led to Tina being their waitress for the evening.

In an effort to prevent any more trouble, Carol had given the girls one half of the dining room each to deal with, something she'd never tried before, but tonight, she was desperate.

"And I don't want to see either of you approaching the other one's tables," she warned. "Let's try and get through this evening without any complaints, shall we?"

And then Stella and Graham had sat at one of Tina's tables.

That young lady may have decided to turn over a new leaf as far as her attitude towards Shona was concerned, but it didn't mean she was going to work any harder than usual. She took Stella and Graham's order and returned to the kitchen looking bored to death.

Carol sighed and shook her head. "I hope to God you're not showing that face to the customers."

"What face?"

"The 'bored don't really want to be here' face."

"Well, I don't, do I? I should be out clubbing with Kelly and Tracey tonight, not doing an extra shift here."

"But you *are* doing the extra shift, and you could at least pretend to be enjoying your work."

Out in the dining room, Stella drummed her fingers impatiently on the table, watching Shona serve her customers, smile at them, chat, bend over backwards to make sure they were happy.

"You girl!" she finally called.

Shona had been given her instructions not to approach Tina's tables, but she couldn't ignore the call from one of the guests, especially when there was no sign of the other girl.

"We need to see the wine list."

"I'll ask your waitress to bring it for you."

"You will not. You can bring it yourself. You're not exactly rushed off your feet, are you?"

Shona smiled pleasantly but didn't reply, heading for the kitchen instead.

"Tina, the couple sitting near the window want to see the wine list," she reported.

"Oh, for God's sake. Why didn't you give it to them?" Tina snapped.

"Your table, Tina, not Shona's," Carol pointed out quietly. She frowned as Tina went off with the wine list and looked at Shona. "Do you reckon they could be complainers?" she asked.

"The woman probably is. He seems okay, but she's a right sour-faced madam."

"I wish I'd known before they sat down. We could have nudged them to your side of the room. You're so much better at looking after that type,"

"Do you want me to take them over?"

Carol hesitated for a moment. That would be the ideal solution, but then she was the one who'd decreed they attended to one half of the dining room each. It would only put Tina's back up if she changed the rule now.

"No. Let's just hope Tina manages to cope with them."

By the end of the meal, Stella had notched up another black mark against the hotel, complaining to Graham about the service, the food—everything she could think of. He didn't reply, instead following her into the lounge for their coffee and hoping Mike and Melinda would get back soon. Anything to take the pressure off him!

"And as for that waitress...well, I don't see how they can even think of employing her," she continued as he poured the coffee. "I mean, she should be doing this, not us. It isn't good enough."

"You won't be leaving her a tip at the end of the week then." He grinned in a feeble attempt at defusing the situation.

"I don't want her serving us again. I'm going to make sure we get that other girl for the rest of our stay."

He opened his mouth to ask how she intended to do that but then changed his mind. It might keep everyone else amused, watching her try to manipulate the staff to suit herself, but not him.

It was obvious as soon as Mike walked into the lounge that something was badly wrong. Melinda trailed behind him, and Graham watched her intently, wondering what had happened while they were out. She looked close to tears, and as for Mike—Graham had thought him a nice chap before but began to change his mind. How could he upset his wife and then breeze in and join them as though nothing had happened? He made a point of smiling at Melinda as she sat down, asking if she'd had a nice evening, and she shook her head, tried to smile back at him.

"Not really. We had a bit of an argument on the way back."

"I'll still bet you've had a better evening than us," Stella retorted before Graham could say any more, then launched into an account of the dreadful service they'd received in the restaurant. Melinda nodded at the appropriate moments, but Graham was pretty certain she wasn't listening to a word Stella was saying. Not that he blamed her; he didn't particularly want to listen either.

Once Mike had brought their drinks over, Stella had a fresh audience and seemed to forget her previous dislike of him, happy to compare their evenings and the meals they'd had. Mike was pointedly ignoring his wife, and as seeing as Graham was so quiet, he seemed only too happy to give Stella his full attention.

"So what went wrong with your evening?" Graham asked Melinda quietly.

"Oh, just general things really. Mike and I don't always see eye to eye about his...about his hobby."

"Sounds odd. What is it, some sort of fetish?"

She smiled and shook her head. "I almost wish it was. It would make it a lot more bearable in some ways, or less worrying, at least."

Graham was aware he was treading on dangerous ground. He didn't know the woman, had no right to probe, but he couldn't sit here and make small talk for the sake of it.

"You know, I sometimes worry about Stella's hobby as well," he mused wryly.

"Go on, what's her hobby?" she asked, notably glad he hadn't asked her any more questions.

"You already know. Living above her station. Well, that and complaining about everything she possibly can as she goes through life."

"I don't think I could cope with somebody like that."

"I don't know how much longer I can," Graham admitted grimly.

Melinda laughed, and it was as though the sun had come out for a moment. Graham gasped slightly as he felt something, he didn't know what, pull at him at that sound, at the sudden life in her face. Sure, he'd had enough of Stella, but this was ridiculous. He couldn't go around being attracted to every other female he met.

"I'm sorry," she apologised. "I know it's not funny, but we are a bit of a pair, aren't we? Both here on holiday and both wishing we weren't."

"Never mind. You and Mike are coming to the races with us tomorrow, aren't you? We can sympathise with each other, let them get on with it, whatever it is they want to get on with."

Melinda knew she should say no. Should refuse to go, make Mike go on his own, but why cut her nose off to spite her face when he'd go anyway? She might as well see if she could have a good day with…with this couple.

She really had to remember they were a couple. She was married and so was Graham. They were just two people sympathising with each other over a bad evening. Nothing more.

Chapter Four

SHONA DAWDLED ALONG the road, giving every impression of being near exhaustion. It hadn't been an especially busy evening, but she was weary and dreading going home. For some reason, Friday always seemed to be the worst day of the week for her mother, perhaps because her dad had walked out on a Saturday morning. Shona wasn't even sure, given the fog of despair she lived in, her mother realised it was the end of another week without her husband. Either way, it was always a difficult night to get through.

As soon as she walked through the door, her mother padded out of the lounge to meet her, still in her dressing gown and slippers, hair uncombed, crumbs from the sandwich Shona had left her for lunch down her front.

"Where have you been?" she demanded querulously, "leaving me on my own all day and on a Friday as well. You know there's a lot to do on a Friday ready for the weekend."

Shona didn't answer, her gaze going instead to the kitchen table where the mail from that morning lay, still unopened.

Up until today, that was the one thing she could have trusted her mother to do: open the mail, deal with whatever it contained. It was one of the things which Shona believed helped her mother keep a tenuous grip on reality.

"You haven't opened the post, Mum, and it looks as though there's a bill with it."

"Oh, leave it be. Just put it in the drawer with the rest of it. Your father'll deal with it when he comes home."

She turned and headed back to the lounge as Shona picked up the little pile, gasping when she saw what looked ominously like a final demand. It wasn't the only one. Apart from the demand for the 'phone, there was a letter from the building society asking why neither of her parents had contacted them about their previous letters. What previous letters?

"Mum, which drawer do I put these in?" she called as casually as she could through her rising panic.

"The one next to the cutlery."

Slowly, Shona approached the drawer, opened it, gasped when she saw the pile of unopened letters.

Oh God. Why hadn't she ever thought to check her mother was actually doing something with the mail? She should never have assumed—the contents of this drawer were proof her mother hadn't dealt with anything. But why on earth had her father stopped paying the mortgage? Surely he knew they couldn't afford to pay it. Had he had some sort of breakdown as well?

The nightmare Shona's life had become suddenly coalesced into downright fear. She couldn't do this anymore. She had to contact her father, get him to come and talk to them about what they did next.

***

On the day Terry Jackson walked away from his marriage, he felt as though the weight of the world had been lifted off his shoulders. He'd known for years he couldn't cope any longer with his wife's mood swings, her continual worrying about silly little things nobody could do anything about. For some reason, it didn't occur to him that his departure would have any impact on his daughter. Shona was away from home now; he'd done his duty, had stayed with his wife until Shona went to university, and it was time for him to move on. Unfortunately, when he went, he set aside *all* his commitments, not just the emotional ones.

He'd had every intention of contacting Shona, maybe at Christmas or on her birthday, but never in his wildest dreams had he expected to get a text from her. She'd made it obvious how she felt about him, and he'd decided to leave it for a while before getting in touch, arranging to meet up with her. Yet he had to admit Shona's text sounded absolutely desperate. If it had come from Mary or even mentioned her name, he may have ignored it, but this was a definite cry for help from his daughter, and he couldn't possibly ignore that. He was going to have to go and see them both.

***

Shona hadn't said a lot in her text, just enough that he'd know she was at home with her mother and she really needed to see him, to talk about some of the problems with the house. She suspected that if she mentioned her mother, he wouldn't come, and after all, it was household problems that she had. Mainly the fact that he clearly hadn't paid a single bill since he left even though he knew his ex-wife had no income of her own and his daughter was only working part-time. It beggared belief that he could do that to them after all the years of marriage, of supporting them both.

Shona woke on Saturday drained and still tired. She'd spent hours tossing and turning before finally falling into a fitful sleep that left her feeling out of sorts and unrested. There was no sign of life downstairs, and she assumed her mother would stay in bed for most of the morning. Usually, Shona took her a cup of tea, but today, she was too fed up with both her parents to do even that for her, so instead sat at the kitchen table with the unopened pile of mail in front of her.

She stared at it for a moment unsure how to tackle it, then, with a sigh, she began to place it in separate piles—official-looking envelopes in one, letters to her parents in another, circulars ready for the bin—not that it looked any less daunting when she'd done that. There was no way of disguising the fact that the official pile was much higher than the other two. With a heavy heart, she opened the first one, read it carefully, laid it aside as something to be dealt with later. Trying not to think about what she was doing, what she was finding, she carried on opening and sifting until she ended up with a pile of bills and letters which needed looking at urgently, including the ones from the building society. And then finally, inevitably, she cried.

It was the first time she'd allowed herself to really grieve over this whole situation. To cry for the parents she'd lost, the future which had gone, the sheer futility of what she was trying to do now.

That was how her father found her. Weeping at the kitchen table surrounded by paperwork which she couldn't do a thing about.

***

Tina flicked idly through a magazine as the cleaners worked around her. She shouldn't have been in the residents' lounge, but anything was preferable to sitting in the family's quarters where her parents could nag at her. She'd pulled her weight this morning at breakfast, hadn't uttered a single word about the fact that Shona had rung to say she couldn't come in. She hadn't even complained about Stella when she'd demanded a refill of coffee before Tina had had time to take anybody else's orders. No, she'd stayed calm, served people, run after them until she was exhausted. She deserved a break. Deserved it and was determined to get it.

Unfortunately, her father didn't share her point of view, judging by the way he stood in the doorway of the lounge, arms folded, glaring at her.

"What do you think you're doing?" he demanded.

"Having a break. Why?"

"Carol and your mother are running themselves ragged in the kitchen, trying to clear up after breakfast. So get off your backside and go help them."

"Tell Shona to come in and do it," she snapped back.

He didn't even acknowledge that dig, instead advancing into the room.

"Kitchen. Now!" he roared, and the cleaner jumped, turned startled eyes on them both. "Sorry, I didn't mean to scare you," he apologised, all sweetness and light even as he took Tina's magazine and frog-marched her into the kitchen.

"Here, I've found her," he announced as though she were a stray dog he'd picked up off the street.

"Mum, he's just shown me up in front of the cleaner," Tina wailed, but Valerie didn't answer.

Carol hid a smile. *Good for her.* Usually, Valerie bent over backwards for the girl. Maybe she was finally learning her lesson, realising Tina needed a bit of tough love if they were going to get anywhere with her.

"Right, can you start on the pans, please?" Carol asked briskly.

"Do I have to? I've just done my nails."

"Then you can do them again this afternoon when you're officially off duty, can't you?"

"It's not fair."

"You know what, Tina?" Valerie sighed. "Life isn't fair, and if you've only just realised that, then you've been flaming lucky."

It was the closest her mother had ever come to swearing at her, and it had far more effect than anything Carol or Peter could have said or done.

Valerie was the one person who always defended Tina, was on her side, and Tina couldn't cope without her as an ally. Silently, she walked across to the sink, blinking back sudden tears, determined not to let them see they'd got to her. Pride was the only thing she had left at that moment.

***

Terry tried to hide his shock at finding his daughter so upset. Pulling a chair out and sitting down next to her, he slipped his arm around her shoulders as though nothing had changed.

"Where's your mum?" he asked gently.

"Still in bed. She doesn't get up early these days." Shona snuffled. "Dad, why have you left us in such a financial mess?"

"What mess? I haven't. I wouldn't do that to you both."

"But look at all this. There's bills and the mortgage and everything, and I can't cope with it all on my own."

Terry picked up the most recent letter from the building society, read it, swore roundly. "I don't believe this…"

"Why not? You haven't paid it, Dad. Of course they were going to write to us."

"Do you honestly think I'd have left your mother with no money to keep you both going? I transfer enough money to her account to cover everything and more besides—every month."

"You mean she hasn't bothered to pay anything at all?" Shona asked weakly.

"It looks that way, doesn't it? You'd better get her up, love. I need to talk to her about this, see what's going on here for myself."

Shona could have prepared him for the shock of seeing what his wife had become, but she chose not to, warning her mother instead that he was there.

"So how is she coping?" he asked as they sat and waited for her to join them.

"She isn't. She walks around in a sort of fog all the time. She's seen the doctor and been put on antidepressants, but they seem to be affecting her memory as well now."

"Well, she was never particularly good at coping with life, was she?" He sighed.

Moments later, Mary joined them, and Shona gasped when she saw her. She'd tried to make some effort for Terry, but it was a strange result.

The dress she'd put on hung on her, revealing weight loss her daughter hadn't noticed before. Her hair, which hadn't been washed in weeks, hung loosely around her face, but at least she'd brushed it for once. Her skin was sallow, and to her daughter's eyes, she'd turned into an old woman overnight.

Where Terry had felt sympathy for Shona, he could only feel irritation with his wife.

"You see, Shona, I told you he'd be coming home today, didn't I?" Mary said cheerfully, choosing to ignore the pile of bills and letters on the table.

"I'm not here to stay, Mary," he corrected her. "I'm here to try and sort out this mess you've got yourself into."

"I didn't get myself into it. You walked out on me," she snapped, belying Shona's words about her having memory problems.

There was no way this woman standing in the doorway was losing touch with reality; she knew exactly what she was saying, what she'd done. For the first time, Shona saw things from her father's point of view; it was her turn to be confused.

"Put the kettle on for us, will you, love?" he suggested. "And you, Mary, come and sit here. We don't want to be upsetting Shona with this."

"Why not? You've left her as destitute as me."

"You know full well I was transferring the money into your account to pay these bills every month. It's not my fault if you chose to ignore them."

"Well let's face it, I *knew full well* you'd come crawling back once you discovered your precious daughter couldn't cope without you," she sneered.

"Don't you dare have a go at her," he warned, turning to Shona. "You have to realise, love, this is all an act. Your mother can manipulate things to work exactly as she wants. For that matter, how did you convince the doctor to give you antidepressants, Mary? Tell them you couldn't cope, did you? Turn on the waterworks? Tell them how your evil husband had walked out on you? Or did you dare to tell them the truth?"

"But you did walk out, Dad," Shona protested. "What else would she say to them? It was you who went, not Mum."

There was silence in the kitchen for a moment, then Terry sighed and shook his head. "Look, have you got somewhere you can go? I don't want you to have to be involved with this lot. Come to think of it, shouldn't you be at uni?"

"I had to leave. Come home. Get a part-time job waitressing. I couldn't leave Mum on her own, the state she was in."

"Bloody hell, there's no flaming end to it with you, is there?" he snarled at Mary.

"Shona love," her mother said calmly, "why don't you go in to work? Me and your dad need to talk about things."

Shona wanted to know what was going on but didn't feel she could cope with it. She nodded and went to get changed, leaving them to snap and snarl at each other.

She would get to the bottom of it at some stage, but right then, all she could think of was that there might be a glimmer of hope for her, a faint chance she'd be able to take up her education again if only her father could see that he had to come back home. Her mother might have been putting on an act as far as the depression went, but surely that showed how much she loved and needed him?

Chapter Five

THE HOTEL WAS quiet when Shona arrived, most of the guests already off out for the day, and Carol was about to go home, but she froze when she saw Shona's face.

"Good grief! What on earth's the matter? Is it your mum again?"

"You could say that," the girl replied bitterly. "I've left her at home with my dad. He's come to try and sort the bills out for me."

Carol sucked her breath in sharply. What bills? It was months since Terry Jackson had left his wife—why was he only sorting the bills out now? Did that mean they hadn't been paid since he left? Whatever, Shona was a mess.

"Don't take your coat off," Carol said, "you're coming home with me. You need to talk to somebody."

"I thought I could help out here."

"And I think you need to be well away from Tina. She's spoiling for a fight, is that one. Come on, no arguments," Carol ordered briskly.

In the car, Shona sat quietly, and Carol was grateful it was she who'd intercepted her at the hotel rather than anybody else. As the daughter of divorced parents herself, she knew exactly what Shona was going through, although, for Carol, it had been easier. Her parents had divorced when she was only a child, and her mother had been left with little choice but to pull herself together and get on with it. To Carol's mind, it was atrocious what Mary was doing to her daughter. She should have sent her straight back to university, allowed her to live her own life. There was plenty of support out there these days for women in Mary's position. She didn't need to rely on Shona, ruining her future career and any other chances that came her way. Still, Carol thought with a sigh, it wasn't her place to judge people. All she could do was be there for Shona when she needed somebody to talk to, a sympathetic ear to hear her out.

It wasn't until she was sitting at Carol's kitchen table, a warm cup of tea in front of her, that Shona spoke. In fits and starts, she explained about her father arriving and the row between her parents. She looked up at Carol with tears in her eyes.

"The thing is, Mum was different all of a sudden. She practically admitted she hadn't paid those bills because she knew I'd contact Dad and he'd come back and sort it all out. The daze she's been walking around in was gone as soon as she knew he was there. To Dad, it looked like there was nothing wrong with her at all."

Carol ignored the last sentence, guessing Shona's father knew exactly what the true situation was. "So now you feel as though you've given everything up for nothing?"

"I suppose so...sort of. Yes."

"What will you do? Go back to uni, leave her to get on with it?"

"That's just it. For a moment, I really thought there was a chance I could go back, but, well, it's not going to make any difference, is it? I mean, all right, I know now she's been exaggerating things a bit, but I still can't leave her on her own. She still needs somebody with her, and Dad won't stay. I see that now."

"But Shona, love, why you? She isn't ill, you know. Yes, she's upset, maybe even devastated that your dad's gone, but it isn't as though you being there can help her. She has to pull herself together. Lots of people out there are divorced or separated, and they don't demand that their kids put their lives on hold to be with them. Surely she can see that as well, can't she?"

"I don't know what she sees or doesn't see anymore, Carol." Shona sighed.

"Well, I suggest you stay here with me for the rest of the day. We'll go in to work together, and then you can see how the land lies when you go home tonight, can't you?"

Shona bit her lip anxiously, reluctant to stay away for so long and already wondering what was going on back there, but Carol was firm. There was to be no going home for her today. Today she was having a day to herself.

"So what are we going to do?" Shona asked. "Only, I don't think I can sit and do nothing for the entire day. I'll worry if I do that."

"Then we're going shopping. It's what normal people do on a Saturday, and Chester'll be quiet with everyone at the races."

"It's ages since I've been shopping," Shona admitted.

"I thought it would be. Come on, drink your tea. Time's passing by while we sit here."

***

The atmosphere between the two couples was ominously frosty, considering they were going for a day out at one of the major events in the racing calendar. Melinda was deep in her own thoughts, Stella was refusing to speak to Graham after a 'phone call he'd taken from Darren that morning, and Mike was anxious to arrive before the first race.

Fed up with his wife's stony expression, Graham dropped back to walk beside Melinda, smiling at her ruefully. "Looks like it's going to be a stormy day," he remarked.

Melinda looked at the blue, cloudless sky and frowned. "It looks quite nice to me."

"Even though you and Mike aren't talking to each other and Stella and I are at loggerheads again."

"Oh, I see what you mean now. Sorry, I wasn't thinking."

"Graham, what do you think you're doing?" Stella called sharply.

Graham made a rueful face at Melinda and went back to his wife's side.

Melinda watched them as they walked in front, a significant gap between them. There was something about the set of Stella's head, the rigidness of her back, that told Melinda there was something badly wrong with their marriage, probably more so than her own. It just went to show that there was always someone worse off; if not worse off then having their own difficulties.

"I'm not going to be doing much betting today," Mike said out of the blue.

"Don't you mean *gambling*? We might as well have the proper word for it, Mike, not the one you think you should be using,"

"Oh, for God's sake, Melinda. Have you always got to be so pedantic?"

"I'm being honest. The sooner you realise your problem is gambling, not just an odd bet here and there, the sooner we can move on."

"There's nowhere to move on to. Come on, love, you're just in a state because of the baby. You and I both know there isn't a problem here. Look, I'll tell you what—why don't you try and find yourself a hobby of your own? You know, take up sewing or something."

"Sewing? How old do you think I am? My grandmother used to sit sewing when she was too old to go out of the house. And anyway, your gambling isn't a hobby, it's an addiction. I'm hardly likely to get addicted to sewing, am I?"

"For the last flaming time Melinda, I am not a gambler. A gambler is someone who can't go a day without betting on something or other. A gambler is someone who thinks about nothing else from one day to the next. A—"

"In other words, exactly like you," she interrupted speeding up so he couldn't answer her without being overheard, and smiling at Stella and Graham as she drew level with them. "We've got a lovely day for it, haven't we?" she said brightly.

"Let's hope we get some good racing to match," Stella replied.

"Any tips from you, Mike?" Graham asked, glancing over his shoulder at the other man.

"Oh, you know, just throw your money away. In fact, you don't need it on a horse at all. You can just chuck it in the nearest bin."

"My, my, we really did get out of bed on the wrong side this morning, didn't we, darling?" Stella drawled.

"She's not the only one, is she?" Graham retorted sharply, temporarily silencing her, before smiling at Melinda. "Look on the bright side. At least you've got someone to keep you company today."

"And believe me, I'm going to need it," she replied with an answering smile. "They can be long and lonely days at the races with Mike."

Stella looked at her curiously, but Melinda wasn't going to elaborate for her. Whilst she'd felt comfortable confiding in Graham, she was quite sure Stella wasn't about to become her best friend—or any sort of friend, come to that.

***

Terry took his time walking to the hotel, thinking about what he was going to say to his daughter. How much could he really tell her about the past? It wasn't his place to reveal the truth to her, but somebody had to do it, and soon, before she threw the rest of her life away. It wasn't fair that she was suffering for something which was none of her doing.

He hadn't said anything before to protect himself as much as Shona. He'd been tempted to call her—he didn't want to see her face when he told her the truth—but at that moment, he was scared he'd lose her. Then he'd be left with nothing at all.

***

Tina stubbed her cigarette out and turned to go back into the hotel, halting when the man walking along the road called out to her.

"Hi. I'm looking for Shona Jackson. She does work here, doesn't she?"

"When she feels like it, yes."

"I wonder if I could have a word with her?"

"It depends. Who are you anyway?"

"I'm her father."

Tina's interest piqued at that. As far as she was aware, Shona's father had walked out on her mother, which was why she was back home and working at the hotel. So why had he come back looking for her now?

With a bright smile, she indicated the door of the hotel. "Come on in and I'll see if I can find her for you."

"You're sure I'm not putting you out?"

"Not at all. I'm off duty myself now."

That was when Terry made his first big mistake of the day. He looked at Tina and guessed she was round about the same age as Shona—the same age and probably quite a good friend to her, especially as she'd been so welcoming to him.

Tina knew full well that Shona wasn't in the hotel; she'd seen her leaving with Carol, and it hadn't pleased her at all. The chef seemed to bend over backwards to look after that girl, and Tina couldn't see any reason why she should. At the end of the day, Shona was only a waitress, and Tina was the daughter of the owners. If Carol was bending over backwards for anybody, it should be her.

"We might as well go into the lounge," she said. "There aren't any guests in to disturb us."

"Right. And Shona?"

"Oh, don't worry, I'll go and track her down for you," Tina assured him and left.

She gave herself enough time to make it appear she'd searched high and low for Shona before going back with an apologetic smile. "I'm ever so sorry. She's not here. Apparently, she's gone out for the day with the chef. Can I give her a message? Or at the very least offer you a cup of coffee, seeing as you've come all this way to see her?"

Terry nodded and relaxed. "I'm glad Shona has a friend here. Coffee would be great, thanks."

Tina left again, frowning to herself as she prepared the coffee. How could she get this man to tell her what he wanted with Shona? It was a golden opportunity to find out what was going on—why Shona hadn't turned up that morning, and why she'd gone off with Carol like that. With any luck, Shona and Carol wouldn't be back for a few hours, which gave Tina plenty of time to convince Mr. Jackson he could trust her.

***

Having accepted Tina's explanation and the cup of coffee she brought him, Terry was worried about his next move. He had to let his daughter know he was leaving again, somehow; he couldn't just go. She needed to know what he was doing about those bills. He looked at Tina doubtfully as she smiled at him. Could he trust her to pass a message on to his daughter?

Almost as though she'd guessed his thoughts, the girl sat back in her seat and sighed. "You know, we all worry about poor Shona," she said. "It's such a shame she had to give up university and everything. But you're back now, aren't you? So presumably she can pick up where she left off—it's good that she can. I mean, she wouldn't want to throw her whole education away, would she?"

"I'm not back. I only came over this morning to sort out the bills and things for her."

"Oh, I'm sorry. Of course. I forgot she was having trouble with those."

"So she's told you what's been happening?"

"Yes. We're good mates, are Shona and me. We were at school together, so I suppose in some ways it was lucky she came here for a job. It meant I could put in a good word for her with Mum and Dad, with them being the owners."

Terry completely relaxed then. This girl was the ideal person to talk to about his daughter. She knew everything that was going on anyway, so there couldn't possibly be any harm in it, could there?

***

Tina wasn't a girl who shocked easily. Life had prepared her for all sorts of knocks, but even she was stunned when Terry left the hotel. For the first time in her life, she wished she hadn't lied, hadn't allowed the man to think she was Shona's friend, and had sent him on his way. But she *had* lied, and she'd ended up with knowledge she had no right to—knowledge which would devastate Shona and cause repercussions Tina couldn't even begin to imagine right then.

The trouble was, once Terry started talking, he hadn't seemed able to stop, mistakenly thinking if Tina knew the truth about Shona, she could be trusted to keep it to herself.

"I don't want Shona to hear this from anybody but her mother. It isn't my place to tell her, is it?"

"I don't know," Tina had muttered, but somebody had to tell Shona she wasn't Mary and Terry's child, that she wasn't officially adopted…that her parents had lied to her all her life.

And now Tina was supposed to keep the secret until either Terry or Mary decided to tell Shona the truth? Could she do it? Could she find a grain of decency inside herself?

For Shona's sake, she had to try.

Chapter Six

Graham winked at Melinda as his wife headed for the winners' enclosure.

"She's always had ambitions to own a racehorse," he whispered. "She'll not get in there, but she'll get pretty damn close."

"That's okay. Mike just wants to put his shirt on one," Melinda replied with a hint of bitterness and a glimmer of tears in her eyes.

Graham flung her a compassionate look. "You fancy a drink?"

"Shouldn't you be going with your wife?"

"Shouldn't you be looking for your husband?" he parried. "Come on. They won't miss us."

Melinda didn't take much persuading. Stella hadn't spoken to him once they'd arrived, and Mike had disappeared as soon as they were through the entrance. Maybe the pair of them would think twice about their behaviour when they realised Melinda and Graham had disappeared as well.

For Melinda, it was all too easy spending time with Graham. He listened to her, allowed her to express her opinion about things, and she, in her turn, was eager to hear all about his proposed new venture. Time passed as they sat chatting, and it wasn't until the third race was announced that they guiltily decided they'd better go and find their respective spouses.

While Mike hadn't noticed his wife was missing, Stella had certainly missed both her husband *and* Melinda. She glared at them furiously when they eventually joined her, still near the winners' enclosure, trying to appear far more important than she was. Her eyes swept over them both as they stood in front of her like a pair of naughty schoolchildren, Graham failing to keep his face straight, Melinda flushed with colour.

"Where have you two been hiding?" Stella asked acidly. "Mike and I have been going frantic wondering where you were."

"Would that be Mike the Invisible Man?" Graham asked. "Because I don't see him anywhere round here."

"He's gone to put a bet on. He'll be back in a minute."

"I wouldn't hold my breath if I were you, Stella," Melinda said. "My husband's very good at forgetting where he's supposed to be when there's a race on."

"And it appears *my* husband is very easily led astray by lonely women who should know better," Stella bit back.

"I didn't take any leading anywhere," Graham said. "I thought it would be a good idea for Melinda and I to go for a drink. After all, neither you nor Mike seemed to want us with you today." Graham smiled smugly. "Anyway, no harm done. We're both here now."

All three knew without anybody saying it that Stella and Mike could have called Graham and Melinda on their mobiles if they'd really been worried about them.

"Graham's been telling me about his new venture," Melinda said as they waited for Mike to re-join them. "You must be excited, Stella."

"I'm not particularly interested. It isn't as though he'll be going ahead with it."

Melinda threw Graham a puzzled look, and he shook his head, silently willing her to say no more. They hadn't got as far as discussing how Stella felt about his plans, but it could wait until later, once they'd got to know each other better.

Not for the first time since he'd met Melinda, Graham pulled himself up short. The fact she was easy to talk to and interested in his plans didn't mean their friendship could ever be more. They were both too old and too encumbered for a holiday romance, and after this week, they'd most likely never meet each other again.

***

It was a long time since Shona had had someone to talk to. She still kept in touch with some of her friends from university, but she was acutely aware of a slow growing away as their lives moved on whilst hers stagnated. As she and Carol sat in a coffee shop at lunchtime, she gradually opened up while Carol listened, nodded, sighed.

"I can't understand what went wrong," Carol said. "You don't have kids so they can look after you. You have them, you love them, and then you allow them to leave home, live their own lives, have families of their own. It isn't fair what your mother's doing to you."

Shona shrugged and stirred her coffee thoughtfully. "You say that, but I don't suppose any of us know what we'd actually do until we have kids of our own, do we?"

"I know what I'd do if I'd kept—if things had been different for me. I'd have given my child everything. Asked for nothing in return."

Shona was watching Carol, waiting for her to say more, and Carol realised she was at one of those crossroads. If she told Shona the truth, it might help to take her mind off what she was going through for a little while. But could she trust this girl to keep her secret for her? She already knew the answer to that. Of course she could. Shona wasn't a gossip.

"Look, this might come as a shock to you, but I had a child once. A long time ago."

"A baby? You?"

"Yes, me. It was a mess. I had an affair and ended up pregnant. The father was married with a child of his own by then. It wouldn't have been fair to ask him to leave his wife."

"What did you do? Have a termination?"

"God, no. That would never be an option for me. I was going to bring the baby up on my own. And I would have done. I'd have coped somehow."

"But you didn't, so what happened? Did you change your mind, have the baby adopted?"

"I wish I had. It would have been easier to live with. No. It was a lot worse than that. My baby went missing from the hospital."

"Missing? You mean it was stolen?"

"That's what the police said. Someone walked out of the hospital with her."

"That's awful!"

"They tried to find her, but there was no trace. They said if it had been a spur of the moment thing, there was a chance of finding her, but it looked like it had all been carefully planned. Whoever took her knew exactly what they were doing and how to cover their tracks."

That explained why Carol had no sympathy for Shona's mother. Carol would have made a brilliant mum; she'd have raised her child to be as independent as she was herself, and as Shona sat there, she wished, only for a brief moment, that Carol was actually her mother. Someone to go shopping with, talk to, share her dreams and ambitions with.

"Anyway," Carol said briskly, "if you've finished with that coffee you've been stirring for the past half hour, we might as well get a move on. I think some serious retail therapy is called for after all that angst, don't you?"

"Did the dad support you after she was stolen?" Shona asked, ignoring Carol's decision to leave.

"He never knew. I told you—he was married. The affair ended before I found out I was pregnant."

"That's a terrible burden to carry all on your own. I mean, did you have anybody to talk to about it?"

"Not really. My mother knew, of course, but she was a bit... unsympathetic, not the sort to show much affection. It toughened her up a lot when my father left."

"What about friends?"

"I'd lost most of them when I was having the affair. It happens." Carol shrugged philosophically. "You devote yourself to a man and then, when it's all over, you're suddenly on your own."

"Did you love him?"

"I thought I did at the time, but no. I think now it was just infatuation. I needed somebody's affection, and he was there. He was having a tough time at home—I know it sounds like the usual excuses, but his wife was desperate for a baby, and he was desperate for romance without it having to be a clinical event every time they made love."

"And once she was pregnant, he dumped you."

"Ouch! Harsh but, unfortunately, true." Carol sighed.

"I wish I could get my hands on him for you," Shona muttered.

Carol smiled a little ruefully and shook her head. "It would never have worked out between us. We were too different. Look, Shona, if I tell you who he is, can you promise me it won't go any further? Even the bit about the baby?"

"Of course! It isn't as though you're ever likely to see him again, is it?"

"Actually, that's not strictly true because you know him, see him every day like I do, but if you're going to bear a grudge against him, I can't tell you who he is."

Shona considered her colleague. Carol's eyes were clear again; the only real unhappiness she'd shown had been over the loss of her daughter, not her lover, and if she knew him, regarded him as a friend, then who was Shona to condemn him?

"I won't, I promise. You can trust me not to say anything to anybody—you know that, don't you?"

"'Course I do. Okay. I'll tell you who he is but only because if you know you won't slip up and mention any of this to anybody at work. It's Peter."

"What? Peter our boss? Peter…Tina's dad?"

"Yes. And before you ask, Tina was the child Valerie was so desperate to have. I'll bet she regrets that one now."

"But you all seem to be such good friends, and they gave you a job and—"

"I told you. I see him as a friend now, nothing else, but if Valerie ever knew about us, it would break her heart. She loves him so much."

"How long did it go on for? The affair, I mean."

"Almost a year."

"That's a long time to say that you can just be friends now. I mean, don't you feel anything at all for each other?"

"I don't, and I assume Peter doesn't. I rather think he may have forgotten all about it. It was a bad time for him—I was the comfort he needed, an escape from Valerie's attempts to have a baby. You understand why I said she must regret being so desperate for a child and ending up with Tina, don't you?" Carol asked, curious why Shona hadn't reacted to that.

"Well, she can be a bit difficult at times, but she is the boss's daughter, so I suppose she has the right to order us about."

"No, she doesn't. She's an idle little madam who keeps on trying to land you in trouble, or hadn't you noticed that?"

"Not really, no. I mean, I know I keep getting the orders mixed up and things."

"No, Shona, you don't. Think back to last night. Was there a problem with any of your orders?"

"No, but I didn't get the awkward customers, did I?"

"Right, I see. Well, let me tell you something. That couple Tina was serving last night—you know the ones who had to ask you for the wine list? The woman specifically asked for you as their waitress in future, said she wasn't prepared to eat in the hotel if

Tina was serving them again. Does that sound like you keep on making mistakes? I gave you your own tables for a good reason last night. I'm sick to death of Tina and her attitude, and so is her father. Even Valerie turned on her this morning when Peter brought her to help with the clearing up after breakfast, and you know how much effort it takes for her mother to say anything."

"Yes, and I can see why now, if she was so desperate to have her in the first place."

Carol smiled and shook her head as she stood up. "You know what, my love? You're too nice. Come on, shopping, before I say too much about the boss's daughter."

***

Carol had to be at the hotel by four o'clock to start prepping for the evening meals, and she gladly accepted Shona's offer of help. It also ensured the girl wouldn't go and see her mother. It was probably selfish that Carol was keeping her away. She was scared to death Mary would break down again and Shona would have no choice but to stay with her, leaving the fully booked hotel a waitress down.

Tina looked at them both suspiciously when they walked in together, but for once no snide comments were forthcoming. To Carol's surprise, Tina *actually smiled* at Shona and then asked them both if they'd like a drink before starting work.

"I was going to make myself a coffee anyway," Tina added.

"I'll not say no, seeing as you're offering." Carol shrugged, willing to meet the girl halfway.

Tina continued as she put the coffee on. "That awkward woman from last night's arrived back early from the races without her husband."

Carol groaned. "Oh, hell. I hope they haven't had a row or she'll be more difficult than ever. I'll tell you what, let's play safe and put her on one of Shona's tables tonight, shall we?"

Tina nodded. "Suits me. I'll probably throw her soup over her if she starts on me again."

Carol chuckled, puzzled but glad for Tina's good mood. "So apart from that, anything else going on?"

"Not really. Oh—Shona? Before I forget, your dad called round earlier looking for you. He said to tell you he's had a chat to your mum, and she'll be okay with the bills and things now, but give him a ring if you have any more problems."

Shona jumped as though she'd been shot, and Carol laid a hand on her arm, not surprised to see the scorn on Tina's face.

"He didn't say anything else, did he?" Shona asked.

"Not really, no. He wasn't here that long. Why?"

"Nothing. I just wondered, that's all."

So did Carol. Unless she was totally wrong, Tina knew a whole lot more than she was saying or else why was she being so nice to Shona? A leopard didn't change its spots so quickly.

Chapter Seven

It hadn't surprised Graham in the slightest when Stella suddenly decided to go back to the hotel and leave them at the races. She'd expect him to go with her, but after her comment to Melinda about 'stealing' him, he refused to give in to her silly ideas. There was nothing going on between him and Melinda, they both knew that, and if Stella chose to put her own interpretation on things, that was entirely up to her. It was high time she grew up and realised she didn't come first all the time. He also strongly suspected Melinda was increasingly anxious about Mike's whereabouts and he had no intention of leaving her there on her own. Instead, he offered to help her to look for him.

"I don't want him throwing too much money away," she mumbled.

"Look, I know it's none of my business but…do you think Mike's got a gambling problem?"

"Of course I do! I thought I'd made that obvious by now."

She had, but Graham had been trying not to pry. Now he wondered if he'd been trying too hard. "Yes, I suppose I did know you were worried. So what do you want to do? Go and look for him?"

"I don't know." She sighed. "Sometimes I wonder if I want to ever see him again. Oh, yes," she added, seeing the startled look on his face, "it has got that bad. The thing is, I had a miscarriage a while ago, and since then I don't even want to be with Mike anymore. It might be a reaction to losing the baby, I don't know— he certainly thinks it is. But either way, I don't know where this marriage is going. Sorry. I've said too much now, haven't I?"

"No. Of course you haven't. Truth to tell, I know exactly what you mean. I feel much the same about Stella and me at the moment. I guess I'm just tired of her attitude and everything. Like this new business venture of mine—she's got no interest in it at all, but at the end of the day, it's going to happen whether she likes it or not."

"Does she work herself?"

"No. Stella stopped working the day we got married. Apparently, it's my job to keep her in the style she wants to live. It doesn't matter if I don't like that lifestyle. I've got no choice but to go along with it."

"We're in a bit of a mess, aren't we, you and me." Melinda smiled.

"No. It's the pair we're married to who've got the problem, not us."

Aware they were revealing far more to each other than was emotionally safe, Graham suggested again they go and see if they could find Mike. Anything to keep away from the edge he was teetering on right then. He liked this woman—more than liked her—and it wasn't fair to either of them to get involved. They were both married and weren't going to walk away from those marriages, no matter what they said. And if Melinda and Mike were trying for a family, Graham had no right to come between them, however desperately he wanted to.

***

Stella's lips tightened when she saw Graham and Melinda walking back up the road to the hotel, laughing at some shared joke, Graham taking her arm when she stumbled slightly on the kerb. Anybody looking at them would have assumed they were a couple, even Stella, and she knew better. Or did she? Was it possible Graham had taken a shine to Melinda, felt sorry for her because her husband was so much older? Stella certainly wouldn't put it past him. He was probably suffering from some sort of mid-life crisis, what with his idea of starting his own business up and everything. Well, whatever was going on, she was going to put a stop to it before it could go any further. Stella had no intention of being left on her own with no husband and no income.

For all his bluster, the last thing Graham wanted was Stella having another go at Melinda, so when they couldn't find Mike, they'd come back to the hotel. Graham deliberately kept the conversation light, telling Melinda about past incidents with Darren, many of which had happened when they were at university.

"So you've known each other for years?"

"Oh, yes. He was best man at our wedding, but Stella isn't fond of him. I think he's a bit too rough and ready for her liking."

"And he's married too?"

"Yes. Married with a couple of kids, and his wife supports him in everything he does. She's got a job and she's bringing up the kids. She hasn't got time to put on all the airs and graces Stella does."

"Maybe Stella would change if you had a family," Melinda suggested.

"Oh, believe me, the one thing Stella would never do is have a baby. She couldn't cope with having to put someone else first. Speak of the devil…"

Melinda couldn't hide her amusement as Stella came out of the hotel to meet them, making a great show of linking her arm through Graham's, glaring at Melinda.

"I thought you'd both eloped or something," she declared with a tinkling little laugh. "Where on earth have you been?"

"We were looking for Mike."

"Not that we found him," Melinda said. "But that's my husband for you."

***

Tina grinned as she watched the three people standing outside. "Now there's trouble brewing—you can tell a mile off that those two will be having an affair before the end of the week."

"Don't be daft," Shona said, joining her at the window. "His wife's hanging onto him like a limpet."

"Exactly. Wives of that age don't do that unless there's a damn good reason."

Shona was enjoying Tina's more friendly attitude of late. It meant Shona wasn't constantly ready for trouble and could greet her civilly, confident she wouldn't get her head bitten off. Not that she thought they could ever be friends—they didn't have enough in common for that—but at least it had relieved some of the tension in the kitchen.

Carol, though, wasn't as convinced by the new Tina. She could be as nice as she wanted on the surface, but Carol knew what lay beneath. The girl could revert to type at any moment, and Carol wasn't risking anything as far as the dining room was concerned.

***

In the office, Peter sighed as he laid down his pen and looked at Valerie across the desk. He was still upset about the complaint they'd had from Stella and was unsure about what to do about it. All right, they'd made a joint effort with Tina that morning, but it wouldn't last. Valerie would soon back down, unless he could strike now, persuade her it wasn't working, employing their daughter in the hotel, while Valerie was still annoyed with Tina. Cautiously, he cleared his throat, and she looked up.

"What?" she asked.

"I was just thinking about Tina. It's not a good idea having her working here, is it?"

"She seemed all right earlier. I heard Shona and her talking to each other."

"You mean she was trying to cause more trouble?" Peter scoffed.

"It didn't sound like that to me. They were on about those two couples—you know the one who complained last night and the one who's got the young wife."

As descriptions went, it was accurate enough for Peter to know exactly who she meant.

"Which reminds me—I don't want Tina serving her again. Can we move them to another table, one where Shona will serve them?"

"No problem. I've already had a word with Carol. It's already sorted out."

"Right, that's good. But I still think Tina should be looking for a job somewhere else—a career."

"She's happy here," Valerie protested.

"No, she isn't, love. She thinks it's a cushy number, and I won't have that. She's not pulling her weight, and if she wasn't our daughter, she'd have been out weeks ago. I'm going to suggest to her she goes down to the Job Centre on Monday, see what else is available to her."

"There'll be nothing if she's got no qualifications."

"Do you think I don't know that? I want her to come to her senses, get herself back into education before it's too late."

"And you think she'll go along with that?"

"I think she won't have any choice," he replied firmly. "And while I'm on the subject, I don't want you giving in if she comes to you whingeing about it. Okay?"

Valerie sighed and nodded her agreement. He was right; they had to do this for Tina's own sake. She couldn't carry on as she was now. She needed to break away from them, to face up to reality. They were only allowing her to destroy herself by letting her work in the hotel. She needed some pride in herself and she wasn't getting it here.

"I'll back you up," she promised with no premonition of how much she'd regret that promise later.

***

Tina honestly believed she was making a real effort with Shona that evening, and she was stunned when her father confronted her as they were finishing the tables off for the evening meals.

"Can I have a word with you, love?"

"What, now?"

"Good a time as any."

She could have said she was busy, but her father was the boss. If he delayed her, it wasn't her fault. Given the opportunity to get out of work, her inherent laziness came to the fore, despite all her earlier resolutions, and she followed him into the office.

"Look, love, this isn't easy for me," he began, "but your mother and I have decided it isn't right for you to be working in the hotel. You should be starting your own career—finding a different job, I mean. Don't get me wrong, we'll always be glad of a hand here if you want to help out, but you don't want to be a waitress all your life, do you?"

Tina stared at him for a moment, not realising at first what he was saying, and then, as the penny dropped, her temper flared.

"You've got to be joking! After I've spent all day bending over backwards to be nice to Shona, you turn round and sack me?"

"I'm not sacking you."

"Then what do you call it? 'Go out and get yourself a job but you're more than welcome to work here for free when we want you to'."

"Now you're overreacting, Tina. We're doing this for your sake. You need more than this—you're throwing your life away working here. Let's be honest, you're not exactly happy, are you?"

"But it's a family business. Why would I want to do anything else? I thought you and Mum took it on so I'd have something for my future."

"Oh, so you think this is your inheritance, do you? That once we're dead and gone, you'll suddenly be able to take over? You have no experience of running your own business, no qualifications for it. No, Tina, we're not running this place for your benefit—for all you know, we may decide to sell it and retire on the proceeds at some stage. I certainly have no desire for us to be thrown on the scrap heap when you decide we're too old to run it."

Another person would have realised they'd gone too far already, but Tina wasn't known for her caution or tact, so it was no surprise the discussion ended up as a slanging match between father and daughter, which could be overheard by anybody who was in the vicinity of the office.

***

Carol shook her head at Valerie as she came downstairs and made to go towards the scene of the battle.

"I wouldn't go in there if I were you. It sounds like World War Three's going on."

"Between?"

"Peter took Tina in there a while ago. I don't know what he's saying to her, but it's obviously upsetting her, whatever it is."

"I know what it is. He's telling her to find a different job, get herself a career away from the hotel."

"I wish he'd chosen a better time." Carol sighed. "I mean, couldn't he have waited for next weekend when we're not so busy? She'll rebel now, and I can't do with that. For God's sake, Val, she's even gone out of her way to be nice to Shona. I thought I was making progress with her, and then he goes and does this."

"He wasn't to know that, was he?" Valerie snapped, not mentioning that she'd said much the same thing to him when he told her what he was going to do. How could she back down now when she'd promised to support him against Tina?

"Well, I'm telling you right now. If there's any trouble tonight, I'm holding Peter fully responsible, and I, for one, won't be working here tomorrow, never mind Tina." Carol slammed back into the kitchen, leaving Valerie gasping.

They could cope without Tina; she could do the waitressing herself, but without a chef, they were completely sunk. There was no chance of them getting a temp in when the races were on, and most of their guests were eating in the hotel that evening. She knew Carol—it hadn't been an idle threat; she meant every word of it—but she also knew her daughter. It would be a miracle if she didn't kick up over this tonight. And what if Shona walked out as well? What would they do then? Neither she nor Peter could do the cooking. Breakfasts, yes, but certainly not evening meals. This could be the end of the whole business.

Chapter Eight

Melinda frowned at the sound of Mike whistling as he walked up the stairs to their room. There could only be one reason why he was in a good mood: he must have won some money for once rather than losing it. While it was a relief, she couldn't seem to raise any enthusiasm herself when he burst through the door and waltzed her around the room.

"Tonight, my darling wife, we celebrate. I've had the best day ever. It'll be champagne and caviar all round."

"Somehow I don't think they'll have caviar on the menu here," she remarked, freeing herself from his arms. "So how much is this enormous win you've had?"

"Just over a grand."

"A thousand pounds! How?"

"By some very careful betting, my love. All it takes is a good knowledge of what you're doing."

"You mean all it takes is good luck instead of your usual bad luck," she corrected him.

He frowned and shook his head. "Come on, what's wrong with you now? It's a spectacular result, and all you can do is be negative about it. At least give me some credit for it."

"I'm sorry. I'm just tired, and I was worried when I couldn't find you. And then Stella had a go at me and…to be honest, I've had enough today."

"Well, we'll show her, won't we? Come on, get your glad rags on. I thought we'd eat here tonight—we could ask Stella and Graham to join us. I'll soon shut her up when she knows how much I've won."

He hadn't listened to a single word Melinda had said, but that was nothing new. After all this time she should know better than to expect him to pay attention.

***

Graham's eyebrows rose when Mike and Melinda joined them in the bar half an hour later. Even Mike had made some effort to get dressed up, his usual jeans and T-shirt replaced by trousers and a smart shirt. As for Melinda—he wouldn't have dared comment on how stunning she looked, not with Stella sitting at his side. His wife would instantly guess how he felt about Melinda if he did.

"You look as though you're off out on the town tonight," Stella drawled lazily.

"No. We're eating here. In fact—" Mike smiled "—how would you and Graham like to join us? We've got some celebrating to do."

Graham's heart sank like a stone at those words. *She's pregnant. She's never going to be free of him.* He couldn't possibly split them up if she was expecting Mike's baby.

"So what exactly are we celebrating?" Stella asked.

"A win. A very big win." Mike grinned, and Graham let his breath out in a long sigh of relief even as he wondered why he'd been so worried. He caught Melinda's eye, and she shrugged and smiled ruefully. This must have been the way she lived her life—one moment despair at how much he'd lost, the next relieved at how much he'd won. It was no sort of life for anybody to have to endure. Melinda was like Graham; she liked everything nice and straightforward, not this continual roller coaster of emotions.

Mike continued over to the bar. "Hi. Do you have any champagne?"

Peter looked at him with raised eyebrows, then nodded. "I'm sure we can lay our hands on some for you. Shall I put it on ice?"

"That'd be fine and, in the meantime, can I offer yourself and your good lady a drink?"

"That's very generous, although I'm afraid Val's tied up in the kitchen at the moment. Maybe later?"

Stella made no effort to hide her disdain of Mike's expansive behaviour. If one had some good luck, one kept quiet about it, used the money for one's own benefit and certainly didn't throw it away willy-nilly on all and sundry. So common.

***

Carol gave Peter a sour look when he walked into the kitchen in search of an ice bucket for the champagne.

"I've got a bone to pick with you," she muttered.

"If it's about Tina, I already know. Val's told me how upset you are with me. I'm sorry. I know I could have timed it better, but I thought I was doing the right thing."

"And did Val tell you what my response was?" Carol asked.

"That you might walk out? Yes, she did. But come on, Carol. You're not going to do that…are you? We go back a long way, you and me. You can't throw our friendship, everything we've been through, away over this."

"Shush!" Carol hissed. "Keep your voice down. Val's only out in the dining room."

"Sorry. I didn't think."

"Well, I did, and we've kept it quiet for nineteen years. I don't want her finding out now."

***

Tina frowned as she moved away from the kitchen door as quietly as she'd arrived. Just what were Carol and her father talking about? What was it that had gone on in the past that they had to keep from her mother? Suddenly, and unusually for her, Tina felt weighed down by all the information she'd gleaned today, any ideas about causing problems in the restaurant forgotten as she mulled over what she'd overheard.

***

Noticing how preoccupied Tina was, Shona left her alone, quietly doing her own jobs. The other girl may have been acting more friendly, but Shona wasn't risking getting her head bitten off just for the sake of it.

Carol, too, found it odd Tina hadn't said anything out of place yet. The trouble she'd been expecting didn't look as though it was going to materialise after all, and she breathed a sigh of relief. She could cope with Tina being quiet; even if she was a little surly to the customers, it was better than her continual sniping at Shona.

It was only later, as the first diners were served their first courses, that Carol started to wonder just what was on Tina's mind. Was it to do with what Shona's father had said to her? Or was it something else that had got her thinking? Carol reeled slightly as she recalled the conversation with Peter in the kitchen. There had been a moment when she'd thought she'd heard somebody outside the door, and it hadn't been Valerie. She'd been at the other end of the dining room, which left either Shona or Tina. Her heart pounded with near panic as she saw Tina's barely disguised sneer that confirmed she was the eavesdropper. Tina knew Carol and Peter shared a secret and would now have a hold over her father even if she didn't know what that secret was. But she could find out. That was Tina's way: dig and dig until she found what she was looking for, and heaven help them all then.

Common sense told Carol she should warn Peter, but she was reluctant to do it. Wouldn't it be better to establish what Tina had heard first? It would be just like Peter to say something to Tina, which would be stupid…if Carol was wrong.

***

Any awkwardness between the two couples was soon dispelled when Mike launched into an account of his win, ensuring nobody else needed to carry the conversation until they'd eaten their first course. He'd already ordered wine to go with their meal, asking for the champagne to be kept on ice.

"No need to rush the evening, is there?"

"There's no need for us to have a late night either," Melinda retorted sharply.

"Come on, where's your sense of occasion gone? You know me—I love sharing my good fortune with my friends."

Melinda hardly looked on Stella as a friend, but she held her tongue.

"So I take it you win more than you lose, as a rule?" Graham asked. Mike shook his head as he drained his glass again, calling Shona over and ordering a second bottle of wine.

"Not at all. I don't do too badly, but you can't win all the time, can you? I mean, take yesterday, for instance—one bad bet and I'd lost a couple of hundred, but—"

"You lost *what*?!" Melinda gasped and, too late, Mike realised his mistake. "Is that why you wanted to come here? To try and win it back again? For God's sake, Mike, what if you hadn't won? We can't afford to lose that much money."

"And we shouldn't be talking about this now," he murmured warningly. "We're in company, Melinda, keep your mouth shut for once, will you?"

"No, I damn well won't! I'm sick of it, Mike. You've gone out today and deliberately gambled with money we haven't got—"

Graham half-rose to intervene as Mike leapt to his feet, grabbed his wife's arm, dragged her out of the dining room and out of the hotel. As he was facing the window, Graham could see the argument going on outside, and he wanted to go to Melinda's defence but was equally aware of the expression on his own wife's face.

"I don't understand it." Stella wafted a dismissive hand in the direction of the arguing couple. "Surely the woman could have waited until they were behind closed doors to create that little scene. I do hope people realise we aren't good friends with them."

"If we were, we'd be going out there to break the argument up," Graham said.

"We most certainly would not! Next thing you'll be telling me you've decided to go into marriage guidance as your new business. Now, where is that waitress? We may as well have our main course while we're waiting for them."

"No, we won't. We'll do the right thing and wait for them to come back and join us," Graham replied firmly, and for once Stella didn't argue with him.

***

"What's going on out there?" Carol asked, instantly suspicious when Shona asked her to hold back the two couples' main courses for a while.

"I'm not sure, but one chap fair dragged his wife out of the dining room. It sounded like an argument over the races to me."

"I must admit, I wondered if the older one was a gambler when they arrived yesterday. They have a certain look about them."

"What sort of look?"

"Oh, I don't know. Desperate, I suppose, as though they can't wait for their next win."

"Well, from the sound of it, he'd lost quite a bit of money yesterday, and she got upset he'd gone to the races and started betting again."

"And I don't suppose he told her how much he lost," Carol guessed. "If he even bothered to tell her at all. Probably thought he could get away with it, and now he's let it slip after all."

"That's the trouble with people," Tina added slyly. "Everybody likes to have secrets, don't they, Carol?"

"I don't." Shona shrugged. "My life's in enough of a mess already without me finding out people are keeping secrets."

"Then it's as well you don't know what your parents are keeping from you, isn't it?" Tina sniped as she collected her next tray of food.

"What—?"

"No, leave it," Carol warned quietly, though it was fortunate Shona had spoken up before Tina could take it any further. "She's only trying to cause trouble again."

***

Mike had never been particularly good at coping with emotions, but he could certainly cope with his wife's anger. Thick-skinned as he was, he knew what Stella thought of him, and he wasn't prepared to have Melinda throwing a tantrum in front of these people and showing him up. He expected Melinda to make her point quietly and, more importantly, privately, not in a hotel dining room, surrounded by people they didn't know. What he couldn't cope with was her determination to fight back this time. He'd already had one volatile wife, and he had no intention of going back to that situation again.

It was only when they'd been outside for ten minutes that he fully grasped what Melinda was saying to him, and the words were like a cold shower.

"I've warned you before, Mike, but now it's not just a warning. If you don't stop gambling, I'm leaving you. There's no reason for us to stay together, not since I lost the baby."

He stood in stunned silence as she turned on her heel and walked back into the hotel, joining Graham and Stella with a bright, if forced, smile.

What did she mean—no reason for them to stay together? Didn't she love him anymore? Had she only been with him so she could have a child? He'd given her a good life, an easy life. What more did she want? He was entitled to have a bet now and again;

any man was. It was his way of relaxing. What did she want him to do? Spend all his time in the pub getting drunk and coming home to beat her up? The woman was being totally unreasonable.

***

"Everything all right now?" Stella asked brightly as Melinda sat down.

"Yes, fine. I'm sorry about that. It just came as a bit of a surprise to find out Mike had lost so much money."

"Where is he?" Graham asked.

"He'll be here in a minute. It isn't just me who's had a shock."

He longed to ask her—needed to know—if she was staying with Mike, but he couldn't do that in front of Stella, especially with her watching his every move.

***

Mike chewed anxiously on a hangnail as he mulled over what Melinda had said. She couldn't possibly mean it. She'd made these threats before and not carried them through. If only she hadn't lost the baby, everything would be different. She'd be too engrossed in her pregnancy to bother with what he was doing.

Of course! That was the answer. It came to him in a flash of inspiration. He'd hide his gambling from her until she was pregnant again, and then it wouldn't be a problem any longer.

Chapter Nine

CAROL LAY AWAKE for a long time that night. She should have fallen asleep as soon as her head hit the pillow, tired as she was from the busy evening they'd had, but she couldn't settle. Since telling Shona about her baby, she'd been restless, all the old wounds from the abduction which she'd so carefully compartmentalised deep at the back of her mind suddenly back with her, wide open and hurting. It should have been her daughter she was out shopping with that afternoon; her daughter should be asleep in the room next to hers, giving her a purpose in life, a reason to be on this planet at all. Should she have tried harder to find her and not given up when the police did? Other parents appealed, searched for years for their missing children, but she'd sat back and let her daughter go. She hadn't even told Peter he had another child somewhere.

The boundaries she'd set for herself had suddenly become hazy, blurred by her own sense of loss. Tears rolled down her cheeks as she lay in her suddenly lonely, empty house. And it was just a house; she couldn't call it a home, not without her daughter in it as well as her. She was destined to die lonely, unloved, unknown to her child and grandchildren if there ever were any—if her daughter was still alive.

Through that long, lonely, sleepless night Carol acknowledged she had never got over the abduction. Somewhere a child may know she didn't belong to her parents and might be wondering who her birth mother was—why she'd never come looking for her. Carol owed it to her daughter to try again find her, but first, she had to tell Peter. She needed him to know so he was ready for the inevitable publicity there would be. As soon as people knew the child's date of birth, he'd put two and two together anyway, and she wouldn't risk Valerie seeing his reaction to that.

***

Whilst Peter had never forgotten about his long-ago affair with Carol, he, like her, saw their relationship only as that of good friends now. They'd both been in a difficult place and had each been able to comfort the other, but they'd never really loved each other. If Valerie hadn't been quite so desperate for a baby, it would never have happened in the first place, but she'd become so technical about their love-making it had taken all the gloss off the marriage—for him at least. He couldn't cope with the charts and the thermometers and the right and wrong times to make love. In fact, he sometimes wondered how she'd eventually become pregnant because his heart definitely hadn't been in it at that time.

After the discussion with Carol last night, when he'd practically blackmailed her into staying on as their chef, he found himself thinking back to that summer so long ago. It was strange how little things could trigger old memories. However, he was far more concerned by the snide comments his daughter had suddenly started making.

"What's wrong with her?" Valerie demanded impatiently after Tina had made a particularly vicious comment about her father not being the upstanding citizen they all thought he was.

"She's annoyed with me for having a go at her." He tried to shrug it off.

"I'm not standing for it. She's got to pull herself together, show us the respect we deserve as her parents."

He grinned and hugged her, dropping a kiss on her forehead. "You mean you're going to go all Victorian on her? Force her to do what you want her to do? I can't wait to see this."

"Don't be silly. No, I want her to stop this continual sniping."

"Well, I suppose it's better if she directs it at me rather than poor Shona if this is what the poor girl's had to put up with since she came to work here." He sighed. "The trouble is, Val, Tina has a chip on her shoulder that nothing's going to shift until she gets away from us—from the hotel—and has a career of her own to focus on."

"She could always do a business course," Valerie said. "Maybe that would make her feel better—if we suggested we just wanted her to learn more about running this place."

"I've got no intention of handing it over to her. This is our business, Val, not hers. If she'd been more amenable all along, it would be different, but she's fought us every step of the way. I can't risk her wanting to take over completely. She's the sort who'd shove us in an old folks' home and forget all about us."

Valerie laughed. "Don't exaggerate! She's our daughter! Of course she won't do that. You make her sound like a monster."

Peter could have told her that sometimes Tina *was* a monster as far as he was concerned, but he held his tongue.

Was it because she'd been conceived through IVF? Maybe if it hadn't all been so clinical, it would have been different. But then he shook himself. Of course it wasn't because of that. It was the way Tina was. Idly, he wondered what things would have been like if they'd had another child. Would that one have turned out differently? Would it have done Tina good if she'd had a brother or sister, not been as spoiled by her mother? They would both have liked more children, but it wasn't to be. Despite the doctors assuring them that once Valerie had had one baby there was no reason why she shouldn't conceive again, she never did. Truth to tell, it hadn't seemed to worry her as much as him. She was content to nurture the one child she'd been given. It was just unfortunate that nurturing had turned into a desire to give Tina whatever she wanted, whenever she wanted it. It wasn't healthy for either Val or their daughter.

***

Shona stared in disbelief at her mother, who was sitting in the chair right in front of the fire, which really didn't need to be switched on in the middle of summer. The room was stiflingly hot, and Shona longed to open the window, knowing full well the fire was only on because her dad had agreed to pay the bills. If her mother had known how to switch the central heating on, she'd have done that too; she was determined to waste as much of his money as she could.

"Do you feel better now that you've seen Dad?" Shona asked, sick of the silence.

"I don't see why I should. It's not as though he's stayed, is it?"

"What did he mean when he said there were things you should have told me?"

"I didn't hear him say that," Mary retorted, refusing to meet Shona's gaze.

"Don't play that card again, Mum. There's nothing wrong with your memory, so I'll not have you say you can't remember things. Whatever it was, I want to know."

"If it's so important to you, ask your father." Her mother shut her down.

Shona had no choice; she was going to have to meet up with her father again and demand he tell her what he'd meant.

***

Carol caused a few raised eyebrows when she didn't leave the hotel after the breakfast shift and instead took a cup of coffee through to the bar, not surprised when Peter and Valerie joined her immediately afterwards.

"Not working overtime, are you?" Peter asked with his usual humour.

"No. I just wanted a chat before I went home."

"About anything in particular?" Valerie asked cagily.

"No, not really," Carol said. "I'm not about to leave if that's what you're worried about." It amused her the way they both relaxed at her words. If only they knew what she really wanted to say... "Actually, Peter, it was you I was hoping to get some advice from."

Valerie smiled and stood up, proving she'd only been there to support her husband. "That's good. I was going to go for a long walk this morning anyway, clear my head a bit, so I'll leave you to it."

After Valerie had left, Peter watched Carol, trying to figure out what she was about to say. Something told him he wasn't going to like it. He didn't usually work on his instincts, but there was a feeling of sick dread inside him that he couldn't ignore.

"Is there anybody around who might hear us?" she asked.

"Not once Valerie's gone. Tina went out as soon as we finished serving. Why?"

"I wanted to be sure we were alone, that's all."

"Come on, Carol, spit it out. I already know I'm not going to like this."

Now the opportunity was here, she didn't know quite how to begin. How did you tell a man he had another child somewhere, especially when you didn't know where that child was yourself? It didn't matter their daughter had been stolen; Carol had done nothing to find her and had merely protected herself and Peter. The longer she remained silent, though, the more anxious he became until, finally, he stood up and paced across the room, making sure Valerie had actually left.

"Right, the coast's clear. Now will you tell me what this is about?" he begged.

"You aren't going to like it."

"I don't like it already and you haven't said anything yet."

"Sorry. I'm making a mess of this. You remember when we were—were together, don't you?"

"Yes."

"Well, after we ended the...the affair, I found out I was pregnant..."

"Bloody hell. I wasn't expecting that one!" He sat down abruptly.

"Oh, believe me, it gets worse. I had the baby—a daughter. I was going to raise her on my own, but…but I lost her."

Immediately he was beside her, his arm around her shoulders.

"Oh, hell, Carol, I'm sorry. I should have been there for you. I would have been if I'd known."

"No, you wouldn't, Peter. You had Valerie and your daughter by then. It wouldn't have been fair to make you choose between us, not when we didn't love each other. I don't know about you, but I've never regretted it being over when it was."

"Thanks for that." He grimaced.

"Sorry, I didn't mean to sound harsh, but you know as well as I do that it's the truth."

"So your baby died?"

"I said I *lost her*, not that she died."

"You had her adopted?"

"No. Someone stole her. Just walked out of the hospital with her, and they never caught them. The police never found them."

Slowly he moved his arm away and looked at her, waiting for her to say more, as he knew she would.

Already, she could sense a coldness, an incredulity in him. "The thing is, I accepted what the police said—there was no point in carrying on looking for her—so I sort of pushed it all to the back of my mind and tried to move on."

"Why are you bringing this up now? Why decide to say something after all this time?"

"Because now I accept I was wrong to do that. I know it's nineteen years on… I want to try and trace her, Peter, but I'm scared I won't be able to keep your name out of it."

Peter sighed. Sat back in his seat. Frowned. Carol wasn't the only one who was scared. What if Valerie found out? It didn't matter it had all happened so long ago. She'd still be hurt and betrayed. And what about Tina? How would she feel knowing he'd fathered another child? He couldn't let Carol do it to them. If she wanted to find her daughter, that was up to her, but he couldn't allow her to release his name as the father.

"Look, I can see why you want to find her, but I can't let you say who I am. You'll have to try and find her without bringing my name into it."

"I've got to say something. Valerie, at least, will start asking questions when she knows what I'm doing."

"It was almost twenty years ago—she didn't know you then. Just tell her it was some lad who dumped you when he knew you were pregnant. Anything. I'm begging you, Carol, don't involve me in it, don't tell Val what went on between us."

"I can't do it on my own," she whispered.

"I'm not asking you to. We'll help you, both Val and me, but I can't if you tell her it's my child. It'll kill your friendship, our marriage—everything."

Carol nodded. It wasn't ideal, but maybe it would be better if they both helped her, supported her when the press inevitably got involved. Sometimes good friends could be more useful than lovers, especially when that love was long dead.

***

It didn't strike Peter until after Carol had gone that he might have been a bit tough with her. It must have been hell for her to know she had a child somewhere out there all these years and not be able to tell anybody about it. And to be fair, she had warned him before she'd done anything about finding her. He'd been too worried about protecting himself to think what it must have taken for her to finally tell him about the child. She could have gone straight to whoever she thought could help her, but instead, she'd done the decent thing and told him about it first. He'd had no right to turn on her like that.

***

Shona looked at Peter quizzically when she found him sitting outside as she walked down the road.

"Don't say you've come to drop a bombshell on me as well," he grumbled, and she shook her head and smiled.

"No, I'm going into town for a while. Why, is there something wrong?"

"Oh, you know. Life, the universe, everything. You name it this morning, and it's wrong." He sighed.

Uninvited, Shona sat beside him on the garden seat. She watched him as if she expected him to explain himself.

"Oh, Shona love, promise me you'll be careful what you do with your life. It's so bloody easy for something to come back and bite you years later when you think everything's running along smoothly."

"That sounds serious. You've had a shock, haven't you?"

"The biggest shock of my flaming life, but…well, it's not my place to say anything about it. I just wish I'd handled it better when I found out about it."

Shona had a strong suspicion Carol had told him about their baby, but she didn't dare say anything in case she was wrong.

"Look, I'm sorry. I've said too much already. You get yourself off and leave me to wallow in my self-pity," he said with a weak attempt at a smile.

"It's strange," Shona tried carefully. "Carol was feeling a bit down yesterday as well. It did her good to have someone to talk to."

"It wouldn't be something in her past she was talking about, would it?" Peter asked. He tried to sound casual but failed miserably.

"Yes, she was telling me about her baby being stolen." With those words, Shona saw the anxiety drain out of Peter.

"The thing is," he said, "I can understand why she wants to trace her daughter. It's just…I can't understand why she kept quiet about it for so long."

"I think she's kept quiet because she didn't know how to tell—" Shona checked herself "—how to tell the father."

Peter closed his eyes. "You know the whole story, don't you?"

"It's okay. I'd never say anything to anybody about it."

He nodded in gratitude. "You know what, Shona? Of all the people Carol could have talked to about this, I'm glad it was you."

Shona blinked back sudden tears. She wasn't used to people being nice to her and couldn't bring herself to say anything in response.

Peter patted her hand. "I'm sorry, I didn't mean to upset you. I'm scared to death Tina or Val will find out."

"Carol won't say anything about you if you've asked her not to. She doesn't want to cause trouble for anybody else—certainly not you or your family," Shona assured him. "I think she just wants to find her daughter. Anyway, I'd better get going. See you later."

***

Peter watched her walk away. Where was the justice in the world when Shona, who had far more reason to be resentful, got on with her life without a backward glance and Tina, who'd brought everything on herself, had that huge chip on her shoulder?

***

Unseen by her father and Shona, Tina quietly shut the window to Room One and walked away.

Chapter Ten

MIKE KNEW HE was in trouble. No matter how he tried to convince himself otherwise, Melinda was avoiding him, or as much as was possible in the current circumstances. Sunday was horrendous. He fulfilled his promise of taking her to Wales, and they ate lunch in a pub near Llanberis, but she showed little enthusiasm and left him to do all the talking. He asked her straight up if she was committed to their marriage and even suggested they try for another baby. Nothing broke through the cold shell she'd retreated into...until they got back to the hotel, where she laughed and chatted the evening away with Stella and Graham as though she hadn't a care in the world.

By Monday morning, Mike's only hope was that Melinda's attitude would thaw once they moved out of the closet that was Room One into a better room. Alas, it was not to be. The larger, en-suite room meant she could to get even further away from him...or avoid him completely by taking a long bath so she didn't have to speak to him. On the way down to breakfast, Mike came up with some ideas for the day ahead, but before he could open his mouth, Melinda agreed to go for a walk into Chester with Graham and Stella.

So that was how he spent the morning: trailing miserably behind his wife and her newfound friends, feeling like an unwanted guest in his own marriage, although he cheered up slightly when he spotted the bookie's on the High Street. They wouldn't miss him if he slipped away—he doubted Melinda would even notice.

***

Stella, however, had seen Mike heading towards the shop and had no compunction about telling Melinda. The man deserved all he got with his gambling habit, and Stella deserved some time away from the pair of them. She was here with her husband not as a babysitter for a stupid woman who didn't have the courage to get rid of her ancient, good-for-nothing husband.

"Right, that's got rid of those two," Stella declared brightly as Melinda stormed off across the street after her errant husband. "Now, I think we'll go to Browns." She linked arms with Graham, who was shaking his head in disdain. "We can have a cup of coffee—they won't think to look for us in there. Not their scene at all."

"We'll do nothing of the sort." Graham tugged his arm free and strode away, calling back, "I'm going to make sure Melinda's all right. If she causes a scene in there, she could be in trouble."

Stella almost shrieked in outrage. *How dare he go after that woman and leave me—his own wife!—standing in the middle of the street with all these people walking past, staring and laughing at me? He's a fool! This mid-life crisis of his is worsening by the day! Well, if he wants to go after that woman, I'll do exactly what I want too!* She set off for Browns, where he could find her later, when he came to his senses.

***

Melinda stood silently behind Mike while he filled in his betting slip. He turned and jumped guiltily when he saw her.

"I was just—"

"I can see what you were 'just' doing. You were 'just' making it clear where your real affection lies, and it certainly isn't with me."

"Come on, you've spent two days ignoring me. Do you blame me for trying to get a bit of pleasure out of my day? It's my holiday as well as yours!" he blustered then groaned as Graham joined them. "Oh, for God's sake, you're not all here, are you? Just go and do what you want to do and leave me alone!"

Graham nodded. "Sounds like a good idea to me. Melinda, what do you want to do?"

"I want him to tear up that betting slip," she spat. "But he's not going to do it, so you know what, Graham? I think I'll head back to the hotel, pack up and go home because I can't see the point in my being here."

"Or better still…" Graham began, trying to ignore the inner voice that mocked his desperation to keep her near him, "you can spend the day with me and Stella, cool off a bit, and maybe talk this through later. Doesn't that sound more reasonable?"

If she went home, he'd never see her again, and he couldn't face that prospect, although God alone knew how Stella was going to react to her spending the day with them. But it was more than that. Melinda was the woman he'd expected to get when he'd married Stella. In the space of three days, he'd fallen in love with her, and he was going to do all he could to make sure he didn't lose her. Mike didn't deserve her loyalty. She'd asked him to stop gambling, and he wasn't even prepared to tear up a betting slip let alone seek help with his problem.

Melinda deserved better than a man who didn't value her opinions and feelings. As for Graham's own marriage: he'd known before they came away that they'd reached the end of the road. Stella refused to support his new venture, and he couldn't give up on his dream. Not now. If he didn't do this, he wouldn't get a second chance to make his mark—to get his life back on track—and for that, he wanted Melinda at his side.

***

Graham and Melinda walked through the park, watched the children in the playground, fed the squirrels, found a pub near the river where they ate lunch, walked along the city walls…and they talked. For the first time in a long time, Melinda could open up, talk about anything, knowing Graham wouldn't laugh at her or belittle her opinions. He asked her advice about his new business and listened to her answers, making her feel as though there was a purpose to her being with him. It seemed the most natural thing in the world for him to take her hand in his, and it was only when they set off back to the hotel Melinda realised the enormity of what was happening to her and the guilt of betraying Mike and Stella.

They couldn't do this. Not while they were both still married. It wasn't right. She'd made solemn vows to Mike and couldn't renege on them just because another man paid her attention, treated her as an equal. She'd known what Mike was like from the start—well, apart from his gambling—and she couldn't walk away, not least because Graham was also married, if not happily then securely. For all she knew, he was flirting with her and had no intention of taking this 'romance' any further.

Graham sensed her moving away from him emotionally and was tempted to plead his case then and there, but he didn't. Common sense told him he had to be patient and not rush her into anything. And he could wait. He had the rest of the week. She wouldn't go home now; she would be feeling too guilty about them spending the day together and leaving Mike in the lurch. It was all Graham needed for the time being.

***

Stella wasn't the type of woman who took humiliation lightly and that was exactly how she felt: humiliated. She'd sat for over an hour in Browns' coffee shop, but in the end, it wasn't Graham who'd joined; it was Mike. Not content with showing her up in Browns of all places, he'd had the effrontery to offer to escort her for the rest of the day. As if she'd have been seen dead with a man like him! Thus, when Graham finally arrived back at the hotel, Stella made sure he knew how furious she was.

As Graham listened to the litany of his misdeeds, any love he'd had left for his wife slowly withered away. It wasn't her attack so much as her attitude which annoyed him. All right, Mike was a different sort of person to their usual friends, but Stella was a snob. If she couldn't accept Mike for who he was, there was no way she was ever going to accept Darren as Graham's business partner. Darren hadn't been 'moulded' into a businessman; his wife was happy to let him remain a free spirit. On the few rare occasions the two couples had come together, Stella had looked down her nose at Darren and his wife, and today had proved she was never going to change.

"Why aren't you answering me?" she demanded, bringing his attention back to the present. "I asked you a question and you're totally ignoring me!"

"Did you? Sorry. I stopped listening about half an hour ago." He'd yet to sit down, but rather than do so, he moved away to the window that looked down onto the garden, where Melinda and Mike appeared to be having a similar, if not quite as one-sided, conversation.

"For God's sake, Graham, what is wrong with you? Do you need to see a doctor? Maybe you're having some sort of a breakdown, and I will not stand for that. I mean, what would our friends think if you ended up in some sort of psychiatric hospital? I'd never live it down."

Graham snorted his amusement at that. *Breakdown? No.* The only thing happening to him was he was finally coming to his senses, could see his wife for what she was, and it meant he was finally content to walk away from her once and for all.

***

Unlike Stella, Mike was trying a different approach with Melinda. Yes, he was angry, but he had enough about him to know saying the wrong thing would make matters so much worse. He had to convince her he was going to stop gambling, but there had to be some give and take. He couldn't do this on his own. He needed to be sure she'd stay if he gave up the habit or else he'd be left with nothing at all.

This was the first time she'd really scared him—had made him wake up to what he was in danger of losing. He'd gone into the bookie's on a whim, fed up because he'd felt left out. All it had done was prove to Melinda he couldn't resist the lure of the betting shop.

They sat on the seat where Shona and Peter had been the day before, Melinda shivering as the air began to cool around them, Mike twisting his hands nervously between his knees.

"I didn't believe you, you know," Mike admitted. "I thought it was another empty threat, but now... Well, I guess I know exactly how you feel, and the truth is, Mel, I can't face life without you."

"Like you can't face life without gambling?" she retorted.

"No, I promise you. I'll get help—anything you want. Just please don't leave me. Not now, not until I've made an effort to stop."

Melinda didn't answer. How could she when she'd already decided she was leaving him? She couldn't—wouldn't—lie to him, but would it be a lie? Only an hour ago, she'd told herself falling for Graham was wrong and that she had to honour her wedding vows.

"Mel? What do you think? Are you going to give me a chance?"

She sighed. "I can't say no, can I?"

"We could go home tomorrow if you want. Make a fresh start."

"No," she said quickly. "Let's stay for the rest of the week. They've given us a better room now. It wouldn't be fair to leave early." And she couldn't face the prospect of leaving Graham behind.

But she could promise that much: help Mike deal with his gambling addiction and do this properly. She didn't have to make any promises about what would happen to their marriage in the future. There was a long way to go before they got 'back on track', as Mike put it. She didn't even know if she still loved him—if she'd ever loved him.

***

One look at her face when they all met up in the bar was enough to tell Graham that Melinda was torn between him and Mike. The latter kept a firm grip on his wife's hand as they sat down with their drinks, glaring at Graham, not at all bothered about being polite to him.

"So are we all eating together again?" Graham asked brightly.

Mike shrugged. "I thought Mel and I might go into Chester—"

"If you don't mind," Melinda interrupted, "I'd rather eat here, so yes, Graham, we'd love to join you."

Mike's usual bluster deserted him in the face of her defiance. "If that's what you want," he muttered. "Doesn't matter to me either way."

Stella looked from one man to the other with a smug little smile. However Graham and Melinda felt about each other, Mike wasn't letting his wife go easily, and Stella was going to make sure Graham forgot any ideas he had about this other woman.

Chapter Eleven

Tina was still reeling from her abortive visit to the Job Centre that morning. She'd gone in expecting to be offered all sorts of opportunities only to discover the best they could had was shop work for a mere pittance of a wage. Stunned, she'd explained to the woman interviewing her that her parents owned their own business and that she already worked as a waitress for them.

"So why are you looking for something else?" came the curt response. "We've got so many people on the books who genuinely need work, it seems silly leaving a family business to do something that won't pay you as much."

What could Tina say? She wasn't going to admit her father had practically sacked her, so she'd mumbled something about wanting a career of her own.

"Well, then might I suggest some further education? It's the only way to get something decent, and you don't seem to have any qualifications at the moment…"

The woman must've been on familiar territory as she reeled off a list of 'suitable courses'—in the advisor's opinion—the worst of which—in Tina's opinion—seemed to be bookkeeping. The IT ones she might have considered, but not, *ever*, something as boring as bookkeeping.

She'd come away thoroughly disgruntled, annoyed with her father for making her go through that meeting and determined to make him pay for humiliating her. And, thanks to the conversation she'd overheard between Shona and Peter, she could make him pay in spades. There'd certainly be no more talk of her leaving the hotel.

***

Taking the new friendship between Shona and Tina at face value, Carol let them go back to sharing the work on Monday evening. The restaurant wasn't as full as it had been at the weekend; three couples had left already, but she was all too aware Stella was eating in the hotel again.

"The only thing I'll say," she warned them both, "is keep an eye on table three. It's that woman who complains all the time, so you, Tina, try to keep calm with her, please."

"I'll do my very best to keep out of her way," Tina promised earnestly.

Carol threw her a suspicious look. She didn't like the girl's sickly sweet response. It smacked of thinly veiled insolence. "Did you get to the Job Centre today?" she asked.

"Of course. I didn't have a choice, did I? And no, before you ask, I didn't find anything I wanted to do, so it looks as though you're stuck with me for a bit longer yet."

She was out of the door before Carol could say any more, off to show Stella to her table, deliberately ignoring Carol's warning.

***

Stella saw the bolshy waitress approaching them in the bar and prepared herself for a row. She'd made it patently clear she wouldn't be served by this girl again.

"I'll show you through to your table if you're ready," Tina offered, barely politely.

"That's fine, thanks," Graham answered before Stella could get a word in. "Can we bring our drinks with us?"

"Of course."

"And are you going to let us have a wine list this evening?" Stella asked.

"I'll take it through with us."

Mike looked from the waitress to Stella with a frown. He hadn't seen what had happened on the first evening and couldn't understand why Stella was being so objectionable. If anything, the girl was almost too polite—in her shoes, he wouldn't have tolerated the sharpness of Stella's request for a wine list. Nobody had a right to treat someone like that, and he made sure he thanked the waitress wholeheartedly when she seated them at their table.

Of course, his over-effusive thanks when Tina seated them made Stella's lip curl. Yet another example of his working-class background, and as soon as Tina had left them, Stella turned her attention on him.

"I'm not happy about that girl serving us again. She was extremely rude the first night we were here."

"She seems okay to me. Are you sure it wasn't you who was a bit too demanding?" Mike asked with a grin.

"In the circles Graham and I move in, we expect good service. We certainly don't expect to be treated like second-class citizens."

"And, by the same token, I don't like to see waitresses treated as second-class citizens."

Stella glowered at him.

Graham sighed. "Are you going to be in a temper all night, Stella, or can we expect you to calm down a bit?"

"I'd have thought that was up to you, dear, not me," she snapped.

"Look," Mike interrupted them, "we've all had a bit of a traumatic day. Let's put it behind us and make the most of the rest of this week, shall we? After all, holidays are all about relaxing and enjoying yourself."

Melinda and Graham didn't look at each other, but Stella picked up on the frisson of emotion that passed between them. Surely it wasn't too late for her to pull her husband back into line?

Mike wasn't going to give his wife up without a fight—or was he too obtuse to see what was happening right under his nose?

***

The tension in the dining room was shared in the kitchen. At no time did Tina put a foot wrong, but Carol was aware of the simmering resentment bubbling beneath the surface and that, for some reason, it was being directed at her rather than Shona. She wondered what she'd done to upset Tina, not that it took much. All right, Carol had been as quick as Peter to scold her, but she'd made a point of trusting her not to undermine Shona this evening and Peter and Val were leaving her alone too. Which was another odd thing. Usually, he'd be in and out of the kitchen, but so far there'd been no sign of him, and she was a bit hurt he'd taken the news about his child so badly. Did he know how harsh he'd been with her? She'd done nothing wrong and had promised not to reveal his identity—what more could she do? She blinked back sudden tears.

"Are you okay?" Shona laid a hand on Carol's arm.

"I'm fine. Just ignore me, love. I'm having a bad day, that's all."

"Has Peter said anything to you?"

"No. Not a word. And keep your voice down, I don't want Tina hearing us."

Shona squeezed her arm and nodded, and Carol relaxed again. She'd had a good friend in Shona, someone she could talk to any time she needed. She wasn't totally alone in this.

***

Terry scowled at his wife as she sat in front of the television, deliberately ignoring him. He'd come here to talk to her, try to reason with her, but if she wouldn't even acknowledge him, there was little point.

"You know you're going to have to tell Shona the truth sooner or later, don't you?" he said for the second time since he'd arrived.

Silence.

"Okay. So if you aren't going to tell her yourself, how do you think she'll feel if she finds out from someone else?"

That got a reaction.

She swung her gaze to him and frowned. "How would she find out from anyone? There's only us who know the truth, and you've got as much to lose as me if you tell her."

"But it isn't just us. Not anymore. Somebody else knows now. Her friend who works at the hotel."

"What friend? The only person she talks to there is the chef, Carol."

"Not her. Young Tina—"

"Tina? That girl who's always getting her into trouble?"

Terry frowned. What did she mean? Tina had told him Shona was her friend, that they talked about all sorts of things. He groaned when he realised what he'd done.

"You always were a bloody fool, weren't you?" Mary spat. "Now we'll have to tell Shona and it's all your fault."

"No. *We* won't. *You* will. I'm sorry, Mary, but this was all your doing. I'm not going to be the one to tell her."

"You won't need to. That girl's probably already done it for you."

Terry gnawed on his lip anxiously as his wife turned her attention back to the television screen even though she wasn't actually watching it. What did he do now? It was bad enough Shona was about to find out the life she thought had been secure shouldn't have been spent with him and Mary, but if she found out from someone other than them… He'd told Tina he was worried about Shona's reaction; now he was terrified she might already know.

"What time does she finish work?" he asked.

"I don't know."

"Well, what time does she usually arrive home?"

"Whenever it suits her."

He didn't have time to think about whether Mary was being deliberately vague to annoy him or whether she really didn't know.

"I'm going to go and meet her when she finishes."

She looked around with a frown. "Why?"

"Because I've created this mess. I gave you time to tell her yourself and you haven't, so it looks like it's up to me after all. I just hope that girl hasn't said anything."

His thoughts were in turmoil as he walked along the road. How the hell could he have been so gullible, to fall for such blatant scheming? He'd needed somebody to talk to, and Tina had been there—sympathetic, willing to listen, claiming to be Shona's best friend. And he'd fallen for it.

He stopped walking and pulled his mobile out of his pocket, bringing up the text he'd received from Shona that morning. It was normal, chatty, giving no indication she knew anything she shouldn't. If Tina was going to say anything she'd have already done it, wouldn't she? She wouldn't have waited all this time. Maybe Mary was wrong; maybe the two girls *were* friends. In fact, how would Mary know whether they were or not when she didn't take any interest in her daughter's life beyond conning her into giving up university to come home and look after her mother instead of pursuing her education?

In one way, it was a relief, but it made his dilemma even greater. He couldn't afford to wait and risk Tina telling Shona, but Mary should be there when he told her. With a determined little nod, he turned on his heel and headed back to the house.

They'd wait until Shona arrived home, and then one of them, be it him or Mary, would tell her the truth.

Chapter Twelve

Faced with what she was going to have to do, Mary turned off the television and made a pot of tea, nodding and smiling at Terry as she sat down again.

"You're quite right, of course. We have to tell her now. It won't matter—lots of people don't find out for years they've been adopted."

"What do you mean, *adopted*?" he asked incredulously.

"I gave her a loving home. She wouldn't have had that if she'd stayed in that hospital, would she?"

"How the hell do you know that?"

"Because the girl wasn't married. We tried to reason with her, but she wouldn't even entertain the idea, like she didn't want to give the baby a good start in life. As if she could have raised her herself with no help from anybody."

"Look, Mary, you can't tell the story how you think it was. Shona's birth certificate has our names on it. If she was adopted officially, it'd say so. It's going to be obvious as soon as she starts asking questions about what really happened."

"No, it isn't. She won't think of anything like that unless—" Mary narrowed her eyes. "How much did you tell that girl at the hotel?"

"Don't worry. I only said Shona wasn't our biological daughter. As far as Tina's concerned, Shona was adopted but doesn't know."

"Well, that's all right then, isn't it? There's no problem at all. We tell her she was adopted and there's an end to it."

Terry knew his daughter even if Mary didn't. Shona wasn't going to just accept this and not want to know who her birth parents were. And that was when the trouble would really start because there was no way they could ever tell her.

***

Shona stopped in her tracks when she saw Terry's car parked outside the house. When he'd replied to her text that morning, he hadn't said anything about coming over to see them. In fact, it had been one of the most normal messages she'd received from him since the day he'd walked out on them. Slowly, listening out for an argument, she opened the front door and walked into the lounge. Her parents were sitting in the chairs furthest away from each other, which confirmed there wasn't a reconciliation about to take place.

"We've got something to tell you, love," her father said.

Shona frowned. Was this the point where they decided to go for a divorce, end things for good? She took off her jacket and sat on the sofa waiting for one of them to speak, surprised when it was her mother rather than her father.

"There's something we should have told you a while ago, but we never got round to it. It's one of those things which gets put to the back of your mind, you know?"

"Go on then." Shona folded her arms defensively. "What is it?"

"You…well…you're not our biological daughter."

For a fleeting moment, Terry thought Mary was going to tell her the truth, but then Shona herself pre-empted that.

"You mean I'm adopted?"

"It doesn't mean you aren't our daughter. You know you are, but—"

"Why didn't you ever tell me? It's not as though it's a big thing, is it?"

"I was worried you'd want to know who your birth parents are. You know, try to find them."

Terry groaned aloud. So much for hoping Shona wouldn't ask questions; that last comment had guaranteed she would.

Shona was trying to assimilate the news. "Why exactly are you telling me now? I mean, it seems a bit odd telling me at what—ten-thirty on a Monday evening? It's not the sort of thing you do at this time if you haven't said anything for nineteen years, is it?"

"I had a chat with Tina the other morning," her father said cagily. "I let slip that we were a bit worried about telling you."

Shona couldn't believe what she was hearing. "Excuse me? You told a total stranger I was adopted before you told me?"

Terry had told Tina far more than that, but he wasn't in a position to elaborate. He just wished he could remember exactly what he had said.

"I needed to talk to someone," he blustered. "You know? Not just leave things as they were…"

"But Tina? Why couldn't you have just asked her to tell me to ring you or something, Dad? At least I know why she's been so nice to me, but it doesn't make it any better that she knew I was adopted before you even thought to tell me. What if she'd decided to tell me herself? Did you think of that?"

"You know your father, Shona," her mother said with a malicious little smile. "He never does think before he actually does things, or else he wouldn't have walked out and forced you to give up your education, would he?"

"It wasn't Dad who made me give it up, though, was it, Mum?" Shona retorted, unwilling to go down that route again at the moment. "So what can you tell me about my real parents?"

"Oh, the adoption agency didn't share any information with us."

"Well, I suppose I can always contact them myself if I want to."

Mary opened her mouth to speak, and Terry shook his head at her. Shona's comment had sounded vague enough for them to not have to worry about it yet. Maybe if they kept quiet, she wouldn't try to trace her parents after all. It was a vain hope, but it was all they had.

***

Stella couldn't sleep that night. She lay staring into the darkness as Graham snored gently beside her. There had to be some way of keeping her husband, something she was missing somehow. If they had children, he wouldn't even be thinking about making such a drastic change to his life—career- or relationship-wise. If they had children…

She sat up suddenly, got out of bed, walked over to the window. That was it, the answer. Why hadn't she thought of it before? She'd actually said as much to him when he'd first told her his plans, and he'd laughed at her, said she'd never want a child. Well, maybe she wouldn't, but there was nothing to stop her letting him think she was pregnant. At least it would buy her some time to get things back on track, back to how they should be. With a satisfied smile, she slipped back into bed and almost immediately fell asleep, her worries gone.

***

Graham looked at Stella in surprise when she declared she couldn't face breakfast the following morning.

"Not got a hangover, have you?"

"No. I just feel a bit queasy. Can't think what's wrong with me."

"At least see if you can manage some toast or something."

She nodded lethargically and followed him downstairs, smiling wanly at Valerie when she came to take their orders.

"Just toast for me please," she murmured.

"Are you all right?"

"A little nauseous."

"Oh, I can remember what I was like when I was having Tina. I was plagued with morning sickness." The other woman nodded with a knowing smile, and Graham stared at his wife in disbelief.

"Stella?"

"What?"

"What she said. You don't think…I mean, you can't be…"

"Oh my God," she gasped. "You don't think? No, I couldn't possibly be pregnant. Not me."

"It's not beyond the realms of possibility."

But Stella, a mother? He looked at her again as she sat back in her seat, giving every appearance of a woman in shock. It was nothing compared to the shock Graham was feeling. Only a couple of days or so ago, he'd told her she'd never want a child, and he still stood by that. Suddenly all the plans, all the ideas he'd had, were flying out of the window. He couldn't leave Stella in the lurch if she was pregnant, couldn't even risk going into a new venture with Darren. He was going to have to stay with the firm he was with now, hope he could ride out the redundancies, keep things as they always had been. And let Melinda go.

With a jolt, he realised the thing which hurt most was having to watch Melinda walk out of his life. That the future he'd been planning for them had gone before it had a chance to begin. It didn't occur to him to suggest Stella had a pregnancy test; if the hotel's manageress could see it just by looking at her, what would be the point?

"So how do you feel about this?" Stella asked him.

"Well, thrilled of course," he replied, struggling to sound enthusiastic. A few months ago he'd have been over the moon, but now? Now he'd met Melinda, been given a chance to realise his ambitions with Darren. Now it was a little bit too late.

"You don't seem thrilled to me," she accused.

"It's come as a bit of a shock, that's all. You know, with the plans I was making with Darren and…things."

"Oh, yes, of course, your new business. Well, that's all in the past now. There's going to be a child to support. You'll have to rethink your plans."

"I know. Still, we can talk about the future and everything once we go home, can't we?"

Because the last thing he wanted to do was think about it now, when Melinda was close by and he was trying to come to terms with the idea of being a father, and with Stella as the mother of his child. It didn't feel right.

***

Carol stared at Valerie in astonishment when she reported that Stella only wanted toast for breakfast.

"That's barmy. She goes out of her way to put in difficult requests—she's not building up to food poisoning from last night, is she?"

"No. If you ask me she's pregnant."

Tina snorted. "Pregnant? Her? You've got to be joking. She's that bloody difficult I doubt if her husband gets anywhere near her."

"Don't you be judging people, young lady," Carol ticked her off. "These things happen whether we want them to or not."

"Anyway," Valerie said, "if she is pregnant, it might explain why she's been so difficult while she's been here. I know my hormones were in absolute chaos when I was having Tina."

"It's going to be a shock to the husband. I got the impression the marriage was breaking down," Carol mused.

Tina nodded. "That's right. And that other couple they've palled up with are always arguing as well. The other day, her husband came back with the old bloke's wife. Makes you wonder what's really going on."

"It makes me wonder if she's really pregnant," Carol said.

Valerie frowned. "It's a hell of a big thing to tell someone you're pregnant if you aren't."

"It's not unheard of though, is it?" Tina said. "Telling people about pregnancies, I mean." She gave Carol a sideways look. Carol flushed and turned away.

"Let's get these breakfasts done, shall we, instead of playing guessing games about the guests?" To her relief, Tina fell silent, and it was left to Valerie to carry on musing about Stella and Graham with Carol willing her to shut up. She was nervous enough already without Valerie giving Tina food for thought about her past.

There again, was this the ideal moment to mention her own baby to them both? She certainly wasn't going to get a better one.

"I'm sorry," she began, "but I'm struggling to talk about this. You see, I had a baby that was stolen from the hospital years ago, and…well, it still gets to me when I see people like that woman who are pregnant and obviously don't want to be mothers."

The resulting silence in the kitchen could have been cut with a knife.

"Why haven't you said anything before?" Valerie the first to speak, while Tina was moving towards the door as though she was about to run away.

"It's not the sort of thing you just drop into a conversation, is it?"

"You've just done it," Tina muttered.

"I wanted you to know why I was a bit off. And, also, you'll know soon enough anyway. I've decided to have another go at tracing her."

"How long ago was it?" Valerie asked sympathetically.

"Nineteen years. Yes, I know it's a long time, but she must be out there somewhere, and I want to know she's happy, loved."

"So you think whoever stole her brought her up, do you?" Tina asked. "I mean, for all you know, they might have killed her or—"

"Tina, that's enough!" Valerie interrupted sharply. "Of course they wouldn't have murdered her or else why take her in the first place? No, I'm sure it was some woman who was desperate for a child and took the chance to get one when she saw it."

"So wherever this kid is, she's not going to have the foggiest idea that she's with the wrong mother," Tina reasoned. "I mean, it's not the sort of thing they're ever going to tell her, is it?"

"But maybe if she's ever needed to know her blood group…" Valerie suggested.

"I don't know," Carol said. "I haven't really thought it through. I just know I want to have a shot at finding her."

"So where will you start?"

"At the hospital where she was born, I suppose. Maybe some of the staff there will remember something."

"After nineteen years? You've got no chance." Tina scoffed. "How many people stay in the same job for nineteen years?"

"People like you, maybe, who can't be bothered to move on," her mother snapped, and at last the girl beat a hasty retreat before the attention was turned on her.

It wasn't until they'd finished with the breakfasts that Valerie and Carol had a chance to sit down and talk properly. Carol knew there were going to be questions she didn't want to answer, especially as she'd have to lie about the baby's father.

Sure enough, now her initial shock had worn off, Valerie wanted to know all the details, and Carol gave her the carefully edited version she'd prepared in her head after Peter had pleaded with her to keep his name out of it.

"So you never knew what happened to her father?" Valerie asked when she'd finished.

"No. We hadn't been together long when I got pregnant, and he ran a mile when I told him. To be honest, I wasn't going to contact him again anyway."

"So his name won't be on her birth certificate?"

"She didn't have one. She was only a day old when she was snatched. Does that sound better than stolen?"

"Not really. It's the same thing whichever way you say it. Someone decided they wanted your baby and they just took her."

Valerie's words eased a little of Carol's guilt. "It's strange," she said. "I remember one of the nurses going on and on at me to have her adopted—more so than anybody else did."

"Then that's your starting point. The nurses. Maybe they'll be able to remember something, especially that particular one."

It wasn't much, but it was certainly better than nothing. And, like Valerie said, it was a starting point.

Chapter Thirteen

MELINDA LOOKED AT Graham hopefully when Mike suggested another trip into Wales.

"You're more than welcome to join us unless you've got other plans," Mike said.

"Oh, I rather thought Graham and I would spend the day alone," Stella replied smoothly.

Graham, who would usually have jumped at the opportunity of spending a day with Melinda, nodded and sighed. "Stella and I have a lot to think about at the moment. We wouldn't be very good company."

"Now don't be coy, darling," Stella teased. "What my husband is trying to say is we've just found out I'm pregnant. Haven't we, darling?"

"We think you could be," Graham corrected, but he'd already seen how Melinda paled and knew it was too late to say the pregnancy wasn't definite yet. Stella had staked her claim, and there was no way back for him now.

"Congratulations!" Mike said. "So there'll be no more late-night drinking sessions for you, will there, Stella?" He chuckled.

Stella merely shrugged. Giving up drinking was a small price to pay to retain her husband. She watched Melinda, waiting for her to say something, but she said nothing and turned to stare out of the window while Mike held the floor and Graham stood in miserable silence.

"Still, there's nothing to stop us celebrating the news in style tonight, is there?" Mike suggested. "What do you say—dinner here again this evening? That suit you, Graham?"

"What? Oh, yes, of course. We'll see you about seven then, shall we?" He took Stella's arm and guided her out of the lounge before anybody could say anything else.

"Did you have to tell them?" he muttered once they were outside.

"Why wouldn't I? I can't help it if I'm excited about this."

"Excited? Stella, you told me you never wanted children, that they'd interfere with your social life."

"Well, yes, but that was years ago. No, I think this is the right time for us. It couldn't be more perfect."

"Perfect? For God's sake, I'm looking at possible redundancy—I was about to start a new career. What's perfect about that?"

"Now don't be silly, darling. You said yourself—you were only *thinking about* taking up the redundancy offer. There'll be plenty of other people wanting to go, and that leaves the way open for you to climb higher through the company ranks."

He groaned at the thought of staying with that company for the rest of his working life…felt his heart break at the thought of letting Melinda walk away from him. What did it matter who Stella told? His life was over now anyway.

***

Shona had expected her task to be difficult, but she got through to the adoption agency at her first attempt, the woman on the other end of the telephone instantly helpful.

"The thing is, a lot of young people decide to do this at some point, and we do our best to help them, but we can't promise that your parents will actually want to meet you. All we can do is act as a go-between for you in the early stages."

"Oh, that would be fine. I wouldn't know what to say to them if I was contacting them cold."

"Okay, then I'll take some details off you, and we'll see what we can do."

Half an hour later Shona put the 'phone down, happy that the wheels were in motion to trace her birth mother, jumping slightly when Mary walked into the room.

"I suppose that was the adoption people, was it?" she asked sourly.

"Yes. They've taken all the details, so I just have to wait for them to get in touch with me now."

"Don't hold your breath. I doubt your birth mother will want to meet you. I mean, why have you adopted in the first place if she cared about you?"

Shona shook her head and forced out a smile, refusing to be undermined. "If you really believed that, you'd have told me years ago. You're the one who brought me up, but it doesn't mean I don't want to know where I came from—who I am. Why she gave me up. You'd be the same, wouldn't you, Mum?"

"No, I wouldn't. I'm not one to brood on the past like you seem to be."

Shona chuckled and hugged her. "Of course you're not, Mum. That's why you've sat here for months wanting Dad to come back home, isn't it?"

"That's different, and well you know it," Mary snapped, disentangling herself from her daughter's embrace.

Shona couldn't see how it was different, but she didn't argue. If her mother chose not to understand, it was up to her, but Shona was going to find her birth parents whether Mary liked it or not.

It didn't take long for the adoption agency to ring back, however, Shona's initial delight changed to puzzlement as she listened to what the woman had to say.

"But there must be a record of the adoption," she protested. "I mean, have you ever lost one before?"

"We haven't lost it. There's no trace of it. Now, sometimes these things are done...privately. All I can suggest is you talk to your parents, ask them what actually happened when they took you on."

"But they said—"

"I'm sorry. We can't help you, but I'm sure your parents will be able to."

As the line went dead, Shona noticed her mother look away. What was she keeping from her? She'd been adamant last night that the adoption people hadn't told them anything about her real parents, yet now it looked as though they'd actually known them. They must have if there was no official record of her adoption.

***

The thoughts, doubts and worries tumbled around in Shona's head as she walked to work. The more she thought about it all, the more suspicious she became. Why had her parents waited so long to tell her she was adopted? Why had her father been so worried about her reaction that he'd ended up talking to Tina—a stranger—about it? Something wasn't adding up.

"You going anywhere in particular?"

At the sound of Carol's voice, Shona turned and smiled, pleased to see her friend.

"Not really, no. I was going for a walk before work, trying to sort things out in my mind."

"You can tag along with me if you like. I could do with a bit of moral support."

"Why? Where are you going?"

"To the hospital where my baby was born. Thought I'd start trying to find her."

"Okay. At least it'll give me something else to focus on." Shona got into the car beside her.

Ordinarily, Carol would have picked up on that comment, but today, she was preoccupied with her own mission, to Shona's relief. Unlike her father, she wasn't ready to talk to anybody about this yet; not even Carol.

***

They were met with an incredulous stare when they arrived at the hospital. The receptionist had never had a request like theirs before.

"I'm sorry, but after so many years, I doubt we'd be able to help you. All I can suggest is you go down to the maternity unit and see if they've got any records from back then."

Carol's heart sank like a stone.

She should have guessed. Of course they weren't going to have any records up here—probably wouldn't have any in maternity either—but she was here now, and Shona was looking at her expectantly.

"Come on then." Carol sighed. "Let's see if we can find anything out."

Compared to the rest of the hospital, the maternity unit was reasonably quiet, and the woman on the reception desk was more than happy to talk to them, although she, too, looked doubtful when she heard Carol's request.

"I don't know who the staff were back then, and I've worked on here for ten years. Although...Amy?" she called to a homely looking middle-aged woman in a blue uniform. "Can you spare us a minute?"

The woman joined them with a smile and an enquiring look.

"You've worked here a long time, haven't you?"

"Almost thirty years—came here when I first qualified. Why?"

"I wonder if you can help this lady at all? I'll let her tell you what the problem is."

Amy led Carol and Shona into the relatives' room, watching them curiously as they took a seat. As soon as Carol began to speak, Amy nodded.

"Yes—I remember that. Someone upped and offed with the baby, and the poor mother—oh, of course, it must be you."

"It is. The thing is, I wondered whether you remembered anything at all from back then."

"It's not something you forget. They didn't half tighten up on security afterward, not that it was any use to you."

"I don't suppose you recall that nurse who kept going on at me to have the baby adopted, do you? She got really aggressive with me at one point."

Amy thought for a moment and then she chuckled. "You know, I'll just bet it was Mary. My God, she was a little tartar. The trouble was, she desperately wanted a baby of her own, and she couldn't seem to carry to full term, so any girl who arrived in here without a husband—well, the child was fair game to Mary."

"But couldn't she have adopted?" Carol asked.

"She may well have done. She left after your baby was stolen. Personally, I think it was all too much for her. She wasn't the right type of person to be working on a maternity unit anyway."

"What was her surname?" Carol asked, and Amy shrugged.

"I only ever knew her as Mary. Why? You don't think she took your baby?"

"No, I don't suppose she did, but it's odd she left so suddenly."

"To be fair, we were all shocked by it. I don't imagine she was the only one who left after that."

"You say she was here after my baby was stolen?"

"I couldn't say for sure. I was on leave, and she'd gone by the time I arrived back. Oh God, if it was her…"

"The police would've interviewed you all, wouldn't they?" Shona pointed out hastily.

"Oh, yes, the place was swarming with them for days afterwards—well, you know that yourself."

Carol nodded, although her memories of that nightmare time were jumbled now. She could remember the shock of being told her baby was gone. After that, it was all a blur. She did recall the police hadn't had many questions for her; they'd wanted to know if any of her own family could have taken the baby and if the father knew about her, but that was all. She'd had an occasional visit from a woman police officer to update her on what was happening, but once she was discharged from the hospital, there was nothing. No contact, no news. The police had done all they could and drawn a blank. There was nothing else they could do.

That had been the worst moment of all, when she had to accept her baby was gone from her forever. There was no chance of her ever seeing her again, holding her in her arms. She'd been a mother for just a day and then it was all taken away from her quicker than if she'd agreed to have the baby adopted like that nurse had wanted.

***

They were both quiet for a while when they got back in the car. The only other stop they'd made on their way out of the hospital was at the main reception to ask if there were any personnel records on the nurse who'd left, but it was too long ago for the woman to help.

Carol drummed her fingers on the steering wheel, deep in thought, not noticing how quiet Shona was.

"Should I contact the press?"

"I thought you already had," Shona said.

"Not yet. Valerie thought it might be a good idea to come here, see if they could tell me anything first."

"In that case, yes, I think you need to put something in the local paper. I'm sure Peter would have suggested the newspapers rather than the hospital if you'd asked him."

"Whoever took her isn't going to come forward, are they? And my daughter probably doesn't know."

"No, but if someone's neighbour suddenly arrived home with a baby, they'd be curious, wouldn't they?"

"Unless they've moved house."

"Oh, come on, Carol, you've got to try at least."

"Sorry. It's getting a bit much to deal with." Carol suddenly remembered what Shona had said when she picked her up. "So what was it you were worrying about earlier?"

"What? Oh! It was nothing really." Shona shrugged.

"Are you sure? The least I can do is listen after you came with me."

"No. It's something I need to sort out in my own head first."

And that was no exaggeration. There was a lot she needed to get straight. On top of there being no official adoption records for her was the knowledge that the nurse had the same name as her mother. She didn't dare mention any of that to Carol even though Shona didn't believe her parents would have done something so cruel to another human being. And anyway, it wasn't as though her mother had ever been a nurse or ever worked in a hospital. Of course it wasn't her!

***

Peter watched his daughter suspiciously. Tina was humming to herself as she browsed through a magazine in the office.

"You okay?" he asked, and she looked up with a vague smile.

"I'm fine. Why?"

His daughter in a good mood was a rare occurrence, and after the row they'd had at the weekend, it didn't make sense. "How's the job hunting going?"

"I don't think I need to bother. It's not as though I'll actually be going anywhere."

"Well, you certainly won't be working here, and I'm not prepared to keep you here rent-free so, yes, you will be going somewhere."

She calmly laid her magazine aside. "Did you know Carol's going to be looking for her daughter?" she asked.

"What? What daughter?" he replied, carefully vague.

"The one she had nineteen years ago. It came as a right shock to Mum when she told us about it."

"Yes, well, I can't say I know anything about it either."

"Don't you, Dad? That's strange. I could have sworn I heard you talking to Shona about it the other day."

"Why would I be talking to Shona about something like that?"

"Come on, Dad. Cut the crap. I know Carol had a baby, and I'm pretty damn certain you were the father. So, what were you saying about me leaving here?"

Peter paled. He wondered briefly if he could bluff his way out but knew in his heart he couldn't. Knew he had to rely on his daughter to keep his secret for him. It wasn't a pleasant prospect.

Chapter Fourteen

Peter's nerves were becoming more shredded by the hour. Tina was walking round like the cat who'd had all the cream, and he couldn't do a thing about it. He was excruciatingly aware of Valerie watching him and knew it was only a matter of time before she asked him what was going in.

Eventually, cornered him in the bar "What's wrong with you?" she demanded. "You're walking round like you've got the weight of the world on your shoulders."

"Nothing in particular, although I was thinking...maybe I've been a bit too tough on Tina, telling her to get another job. Like you said, she'd be better off doing some sort of a management course."

"I never said anything about a management course. Business course, yes, but not management."

"Well, no. Of course I meant business. But, you know, I think I've probably shocked her enough now to make her pull her weight."

Valerie shook her head but didn't argue with him, and he breathed a sigh of relief that she seemed to be accepting his decision. He wouldn't have rested quite so easily if he'd known she'd only let it go because she was distracted by planning the next move in the search for Carol's daughter. His daughter.

***

As soon as Carol arrived at work, Valerie followed her into the kitchen, eager to know what she'd found out and as disappointed as Carol that the hospital hadn't been able to help. But once

Carol told her she was going to contact the press, Valerie jumped at the idea.

"Have you thought of offering a reward for any information?"

"Oh, no. I'd just end up with a load of cranks, wouldn't I? Anyway, I couldn't afford to pay a reward."

"Don't worry about that. Let me think about some fundraising," Valerie said. "You get in touch with the paper and get them to come and interview us."

"Us?" Carol asked in alarm.

"Of course! Peter and I will be right behind you on this, you know that, don't you?"

Carol bit back her panic. She mustn't give herself away, must appear to be grateful to Valerie for the help she was offering. She'd promised to keep Peter's name out of it, and now his wife was intent on involving him. Carol couldn't even warn him about Valerie's plans without it being obvious she was looking for him for some reason other than work. This whole thing was suddenly getting out of hand.

***

Tina had no intention at all of telling her mother about her father and Carol's affair. Her life was much too comfortable for her to risk her parents splitting up, but that didn't mean she was going to let him off the hook. Not yet. As long as she could hold this over him, it meant her job was safe and she could forget about having to face that woman at the Job Centre again. Strangely enough, she wasn't averse to the idea of going to college. Her friends were there; if she could find a course which was on at the same time as theirs, she'd be able to hang out with them, and it would save her from having to do any work at the hotel. Now it was a matter of making sure she got herself on the right course—one which didn't involve bookkeeping!

Tina found herself wondering why Carol and Peter had had the affair and, more importantly, how they could work together now without giving their secret away. They certainly couldn't have cared much about each other if they could move on like this. There again, they were fairly old now. Tina couldn't imagine her father having a mad, passionate affair with anybody, least of all their chef. She supposed she should feel sorry for Carol, losing her daughter like that, but it must have been better for the child to be brought up by a couple than living hand-to-mouth like she'd have had to do with Carol. Tina certainly didn't think there was any hope at all of the girl being found now. If it had been her, she wouldn't want to know, although it wasn't as if her parents would have told her the truth anyway. Still, if it was keeping them off her case, she wasn't going to argue about it. Her mother liked a challenge, and it was much better if it was coming from Carol instead of her.

With her mother and Carol occupied with their plans for contacting the press, Tina worked side by side with Shona all evening without a cross word. In fact, she was beginning to wonder why she'd been so against Shona in the first place. Now they were talking to each other, she was finding it much easier to accept her presence, not to mention that Shona was more than willing to do the majority of the work, which suited Tina just fine. Shona was even prepared to take on Stella's table, leaving Tina to deal with the quieter customers.

And quieter was the operative word: Mike was in good form, laughing and joking as he relaxed in the knowledge he'd kept his wife. It couldn't have been better news for him that Stella was pregnant. There'd been a nagging fear at the back of his mind that Graham was showing a bit too much interest in his wife, an interest which Melinda seemed to revel in. With that attention no longer available, it meant she'd be concentrating on him again, on keeping their marriage alive.

***

As the evening wore on and Mike became louder and louder, Graham watched Melinda anxiously. Was this normal behaviour? It wasn't as though Mike had drunk any more than on previous evenings, so he had to be wound up about something else. Was it that he thought he was safe now as far as Melinda leaving him was concerned? Did he think he could carry on as normal—gambling, being the life and soul of the party? Or had he picked up on a vibe from Melinda that she was interested in another man? If he had, it meant she felt the same way—

Stella laid a hand on Graham's arm, pulling his attention back to the conversation and putting paid to that brief flash of hope. It didn't matter how Melinda felt about him; he was never going to be free of her now.

Watching Stella, Melinda frowned. There was something about this that didn't add up. For one thing, slim as Stella was, there was absolutely no sign that she was pregnant at all, not even the smallest of bumps. Surely she wouldn't be telling people and especially not relative strangers, if she was in the very early stages? Most people waited until at least twelve weeks before they said anything. And why would she have decided to tell Graham now, when they were on holiday and she couldn't see a doctor? It wasn't exactly the right environment for doing a pregnancy test. Melinda certainly wouldn't have bothered with one if she was on holiday. So what if Stella wasn't actually pregnant at all? Could this be the desperation of a woman who thought she was about to lose her husband? Did she see Melinda as that much of a threat?

Even if Stella was bluffing, it wasn't Melinda's place to accuse her of lying. It was up to Graham to see for himself what she was playing at.

It became even more apparent when they took their coffees into the lounge and Mike made a comment about Graham starting on a new life, what with his baby and a change in career.

"Oh, the career change won't be happening now, will it, darling?" Stella remarked.

Melinda looked at Graham in alarm when he merely shrugged and shook his head.

"It's too risky now Stella's pregnant."

"That's ridiculous!" Melinda said, aware she should be keeping out of this but not really caring. "Surely it's far more risky to stay with a firm who are in difficulty? The next redundancy round may not be as good—you could find yourself in a position where the place closes down and there's no compensation at all, couldn't you?"

"Hey, steady on, Mel," Mike appealed. "What do you know about business? You haven't worked in that sort of environment, have you?" He smiled amicably. "I'm sure Graham and Stella have discussed this and know exactly what they're doing."

"We don't discuss anything," Graham replied dully. "Stella decides and I go along with her."

Melinda's heart went out to him. He looked like a boxer who'd been knocked down one too many times, and she couldn't bear it. He didn't deserve this. He was a decent man who cared about people, unlike his wife, who blatantly cared about nobody but herself.

"So when's the baby due?" Melinda asked brightly, and Stella blinked at her in surprise.

"Err, I'm not sure, not certain. I suppose it'll be early next year."

"You must know how far on you are!"

"Stella hasn't seen a doctor yet," Graham said, gallantly coming to her rescue. "I suppose we'll get to know the dates and things then."

"I knew when my baby was due before I saw the doctor," Melinda argued. "It's not that difficult to work out."

"All right then. If you're so desperate to know, I'll work it out for you," Stella snapped.

"Don't worry about it, Stella," Mike soothed hastily. "Melinda's just trying to make conversation."

Graham was frowning, and with a little surge of triumph, Melinda realised she'd made him think, wonder why Stella was so vague about her dates. Hopefully, it would be enough for him to question the pregnancy and the suddenness of the announcement. Not that Melinda cared, of course; she was just looking out for him, or at least, that was what she tried to tell herself whilst ignoring the little voice that said *of course you care!* Whether she listened to it or not, she had no right to involve herself in his life.

Once Melinda had sown the seeds of doubt in Graham's mind, they continued to grow, and by the time they'd finished their coffees and Stella had taken herself off to 'freshen up', he was deep in thought.

"Well, I think it's time to collect that champagne I had put on ice, don't you?" Mike suggested. "After all, I promised we'd celebrate, didn't I?"

Neither Graham nor Melinda answered him, but that was no deterrent to Mike. As he walked over to the bar, Graham smiled at Melinda for the first time that evening, albeit a little sadly.

"That was all a bit traumatic, wasn't it?" he said.

"I'm sorry, Graham. I was asking too many questions. It's nothing to do with me."

He didn't answer—couldn't answer. It wouldn't be fair to give her any idea of how he felt about her, not now. "You think it's all a bit sudden, this pregnancy, don't you?" he asked instead.

"Don't you?"

"It's unexpected, but no, I can't say it's sudden. I don't know how Stella's going to cope with being a mother, mind you. It's going to come as a shock to her when she has to put a baby's needs before her own."

"And how do you feel about it?"

"Don't go there. It's done now. I've no choice but to accept it."

"We all have choices," she murmured.

"Not where a child is concerned, we don't. I was brought up in a series of foster homes. I've no intention of letting any child of mine go through anything like that."

Melinda sat back in her seat with a sigh. So that was it. No matter what doubts she put in his mind about this pregnancy, he wasn't going to listen. Because of the way he'd been brought up, he was tied to Stella for life, and Stella probably knew that—knew exactly what she was doing.

***

It had never been in Jack Sullivan's life plan to work on a provincial local newspaper. When he first went into journalism, he'd thought he'd end up on one of the big national newspapers, but life had conspired against him. He'd married too young, got caught up in a messy divorce and ended up back home with his elderly, widowed mother with the rest of his siblings relieved to hand the reins of her care over to him as the newly single child.

Still, he was working in a job he loved, had good friends on the paper and more or less free choice on the hours he worked and the stories he covered. Sometimes, though he longed for a story he could get his teeth into—something more meaty than missing dogs and cats and potholes in the road.

Consequently, when the editor called him into the office on Wednesday morning, he was expecting another dull assignment—certainly not the one he was presented with.

"It's an old story that's raised its head again," Bob Stewart began. "Baby stolen from the hospital about nineteen years ago. The mother's decided she finally wants to have a push at finding her daughter. Apparently, she's got the backing of the hotel where she works, and they're thinking of offering a reward for any information. It's got the potential to be a big story and I know you'd like something a bit heavier to go at. Reckon you could handle it?"

"What do you think? It's what I've been waiting for all these years!" Jack grinned.

"Right then. I've set up an initial interview with them for this afternoon, which'll be my last bit of input for now. I know I can trust you with this one. Just make sure you've got all the facts before you go to print with anything."

Intent on being prepared for that interview, Jack went down to the basement where all the old papers were kept on microfilm and searched for the reports on the stolen baby, nodding in satisfaction when he found one, but it hadn't been published. The magistrates had slapped a gagging order on the paper—Jack guessed it was to protect the mother—and the details were patchy, but he established which hospital the baby was taken from and that they'd put new security measures in place soon after. There was also a bit of information about the police's futile search for the baby. It would all help to give some body to the story, and he made various notes before heading back to his desk.

"What's got you all fired up?" the sports reporter asked. "It's more than a missing cat, judging by the look on your face."

"Missing child. In fact, you'll probably remember it—nineteen years ago, baby stolen from the hospital?"

"Nineteen years ago, I was more interested in girls and football than missing babies."

"Well, apparently the mother's trying to find the baby."

"Not easy after all that time. It could be a flop or it could be the biggest story this paper's had in decades."

"I'm hoping for the big one. With a bit of luck, it'll go even further than here," Jack said with a grin.

It could be the opportunity he'd been looking for. If any of the big nationals picked it up, it might be his route down to London and the kick-start his career needed.

Chapter Fifteen

Gladys Sullivan scowled at her son when he shot through the door at lunchtime.

"Have you got my prescription?" she demanded.

"Not yet. I'll collect it on my way home."

"Home? Why, where are you off to now?"

"I've got an interview to do over at the Riverside Hotel. Shouldn't take long. About a missing baby."

"Bit careless of them, isn't it, losing a baby?"

"This one was stolen from the hospital nineteen years ago."

"Oh, I remember that." That piqued Gladys's interest. "Terrible, it was. Poor young girl must have been devastated."

"She's trying find her daughter."

"Taken her long enough to miss her," she muttered acerbically, her brief show of compassion over.

Jack didn't have time to argue with her and was already on his way out of the door.

***

Jack did a double-take at the reception committee waiting for him at the Riverside. He'd expected to be meeting the woman who'd had her baby stolen not half the hotel's staff. Looking at the three of them, he wouldn't have cared to say which of the two women had lost the baby; neither seemed particularly upset, although the man stood stiffly to one side and seemed very uncomfortable.

"Hi." Jack smiled. "I'm here to see Carol Marsh."

"That's me," one of the women said.

Jack focused properly on her then. If he'd had any prior expectations of who he'd be interviewing, it wasn't this attractive, middle-aged woman who offered him a nervous smile.

"Hi there, and...?" He gestured at the other two.

"Peter and Valerie, the owners of the hotel—"

"And friends," the other woman added firmly. "We're here for moral support."

That made sense. Hadn't Bob said something about the hotel giving their backing to the appeal? Presumably, that meant they wanted to keep tabs on what Carol told him.

He took the seat they offered, and Jack observed Peter relax, though only slightly.

"Okay, can you give me a bit of background? What happened? What are you hoping to achieve?"

Carol gave him a brief outline of what had happened and what she wanted to do, and Jack made notes, aware all the while of Peter's brooding presence. Of the three of them, only Valerie seemed at ease, and when Carol had finished explaining, Peter asked curtly, "So can you help at all?"

"We can certainly put out an appeal for information, but...I'd like to do something a bit more in-depth than that so we can get over to people how you really feel about all this."

"How do I feel?" Carol echoed. "I feel as though I want to find my daughter. What more is there to say?"

"What about the father? Where is he in all this?"

"He never knew I was pregnant."

Out of the corner of his eye, Jack saw Peter tense. The reporter in him sensed something deeper than what Carol was telling him, and he was immediately determined to ferret it out. If he wanted to kick-start his career with this story, he'd need all the help he could get. He needed to talk to her on her own.

"I wonder if you could come to the hospital with me at some point, Carol? The woman you spoke to might be able to give us some idea of what it was like for the maternity ward staff."

"You mean get a human angle on it?" Valerie asked, and Jack nodded, grateful after all that she was there. She'd know exactly what to say to persuade Carol to go along with his idea.

"Do we have to?" Carol asked.

"If you want a chance of finding her, we need to put a big story out there."

"Okay then. Fine. But I can't go now. I have to work."

"Neither can I. I've got a prescription to pick up for a lady waiting anxiously at home. How about tomorrow? I could pick you up about eleven?"

"Go on, Carol," Valerie encouraged. "The sooner you get this moving the better."

Carol looked from Valerie to Jack but avoided looking at Peter, who was keeping quiet. Finally, she nodded. Jack grinned.

"Great. I'll see you tomorrow then."

As he left, he resisted the urge to look back, but he could guess Peter was still playing his version of statues. If that was moral support, Jack would hate to see him when he wasn't helping someone out.

***

As soon as Jack had left, Peter made as if to go to the office, but Valerie stopped him, refusing to let him escape so easily. Carol wished she'd just let him go.

"Right," Valerie said, "now we've set the wheels in motion, we need to start thinking about a reward for information. I didn't say anything to the reporter, but I think we need to do it."

"And how, exactly, is Carol going to find the money to pay a reward?" Peter asked. "Honestly, Val, it's a bit of a big ask."

"We can fundraise—give the hotel some publicity at the same time. I was thinking of a sort of gourmet dinner one evening."

"You'll not get our guests to fork out extra money for a fancy dinner. They think they pay over the odds as it is."

"We wouldn't involve our usual guests. We'll invite the local bigwigs, sell them a table, run a raffle, that sort of thing."

"And what's this raffle prize going to be?"

"A luxury weekend here."

"And of course I'll do the cooking," Carol added. "That way, I won't feel quite as guilty about you doing all this for me." Not that she should, considering Peter was the child's father, but she'd promised to keep him out of it. Still, it was only one evening of fundraising.

"So when do you want to do this? Bearing in mind we're full this week," Peter pointed out.

"Well, of course we can't organise it in a couple of days," Valerie said with surprising patience. "I was thinking maybe a Wednesday—it's rare for us to have anybody in then. In fact, why don't you go and check that now?"

Muttering darkly to himself, Peter walked out of the lounge.

Valerie rolled her eyes and smiled at Carol. "Honestly, he's like a bear with a sore head lately. I don't know what's got into him."

Carol had a good idea. It wasn't her fault if he couldn't cope with all this.

"Anyway, enough about that weird husband of mine, how do you feel, now you've started the ball rolling?"

"Glad in one way, scared in another. I'm worried about the reporter wanting to make a big thing of it."

"Well, let's forget about that for now and think about this gala dinner, shall we?" Valerie suggested, and Carol nodded her relief. Catering was safe ground. It would keep Valerie's mind off the possible identity of the child's father and give Peter a chance to calm down away from them both.

***

"How did it go then?" Gladys asked as soon as Jack arrived home. "What's she like?"

"She's very nice. Very nervous about doing this."

"I should think she would be. It's going to be a shock to her daughter if she ever does find out her mother finally got her finger out and looked for her."

"Don't be too hard on her, Mum. There's a lot more to this than she's letting on."

"Oh, really? Do tell." Gladys folded her arms and gave him the eye.

Jack could have bitten his tongue out. The last thing he wanted was rumours spreading amongst his mother's cronies before he'd even got the story down on paper. Already he could see her brain working, her anticipation growing as she waited for him to say more.

"Come on, lad. You can't leave it at that."

"I can."

She glared after him as he walked across the room. "And I'll bet you've forgotten to pick my prescription up," she muttered. "Useless, that's what you are."

"It's on the table, Mum. And now I'm going to get some tea ready for us. Do you want anything in particular?"

"I'm not that hungry," she claimed listlessly.

Jack sighed and went into the kitchen. These days, it was like walking on eggshells with her. One minute, she'd be as bright as a button, but gainsay her on anything and she'd turn into a harridan. No wonder his brother and sister were so relieved when his marriage broke up and he came back home.

"I hope you aren't going to be out more than usual while you're doing this thing," Gladys commented, following him into the kitchen.

"There's no reason why I should be."

"You know I can't manage here all day on my own."

His temper flared then.

"Why can't you? You're not disabled. Some of your friends are in a much worse state than you, and they live on their own. And you know I'm only here until I get myself sorted out with a place of my own."

"You'll never do that—not while you can live here rent-free. Worse than having you at home when you were a teenager, it is."

"Well, with any luck, I'll get the break I want from this story. And, believe me, Mum, if I get the chance to go down to London, I'll be off like a shot."

Her eyes narrowed as she looked at him. "So what is it that's so big about it?"

"It's a human interest story."

"Bah. Human interest. There's stories like that in the papers every day. It must be something else for you to get so fired up about it. Still, if you don't want to tell us about it, that's fine. No doubt I'll have to wait to read it like everyone else."

Jack slammed the oven door.

"You damage that oven and you'll be paying for a new one."

Leaving that final shot ringing in his ears, his mother turned on her heel and stomped out back to the sitting room.

***

The following morning, when Jack walked into the hotel, Carol took one look at him and asked, "Do you have a problem with this? Only if you do, it's okay if the paper don't want to cover it."

"No, I've no problem with it," he replied shortly. "Shall we go?"

She followed him down the path to his car, practically running to keep up with his long strides. "I don't know that I want you to be driving me anywhere in this mood," she said breathlessly as she finally caught him up.

"What? Oh, hell." He groaned. "It's not you, I promise."

"Even so, you're no ray of sunshine this morning, are you?"

He ran a hand through his hair and shook his head. "I'm sorry. I'm having a few problems at home."

"With the lady who was waiting for her prescription? Your wife?"

"No, my mother. I'm divorced."

"I see. You're your mum's carer, are you?"

"Sort of. She doesn't need looking after, but as the years go on, she will do, and I don't know that I'm the right person to be doing it. She's got me running round in circles like a terrier chasing his tail."

Carol chuckled. "Oh, dear. I understand why you're in a bad mood now."

"Yeah, well, maybe I'll meet somebody else I can't live without and she'll drag me away from the apron strings." He sighed, already feeling better now he'd voiced his feelings.

It was the first time he'd actually admitted to anybody that he didn't see himself as his mother's carer and dreaded the prospect of doing it for the rest of her life. It felt as though a lead weight had been lifted off his shoulders. If only his brother and sister knew how he felt, it would make life a whole lot easier. They seemed to be working on the theory that if they didn't ask, they didn't need to know about it and, therefore, wouldn't have to face up to the responsibility of caring for their mother.

"Come on then," Carol jollied him along. "We've covered the trials and tribulations of parents. Time to go now."

Jack drew a deep breath, released it and smiled. "It is. So, first of all, have you made any attempts to trace your daughter before you contacted us?"

"Only the trip to the hospital which I told you about."

"Are we wasting our time going back there today?"

"I don't know. That nurse, Amy, who worked there when my baby was stolen—she remembered quite a lot about it."

"And do you think she'll let me interview her?"

"I don't see why not. She was willing enough to talk to us."

"Us?"

"I took one of the waitresses from the hotel with me. Just for moral support."

"You're pretty keen on moral support, aren't you?" he mused seeing potential problems ahead of him from well-meaning friends.

"It's not easy doing this after so many years."

"What is it you're scared of, Carol? Is it in case the baby's father sees the story, realises it's his child we're looking for?

Or is it something else that's frightening you? Maybe the reaction from your daughter if we do manage to find her?"

Carol thought for a long time before she answered. "This is a big thing for me. You understand that, don't you?"

"Of course I do. I don't think I'd have the courage to do it if it was me who'd lost a child."

"Have you got any children?" she asked him, and he winced, giving her the answer before he actually spoke.

"Two. A boy and a girl. And, no, before you ask, I don't have any contact with them. They're totally on their mother's side in all this."

"How old are they?"

"Too old for the courts to get involved. Late teens, early twenties."

Jack had noticed Carol was adept at turning the discussion away from herself, and he'd given her yet another opening. He was beginning to realise how difficult this whole thing was going to be. Had he done the right thing, letting Bob know he wanted a challenge? There again, if he ever got down to London, he was going to have to learn to keep his private life just that. Private. He certainly shouldn't have revealed as much as he had to her that morning.

It wasn't just Carol who had a task on her hands here.

Chapter Sixteen

AFTER THE DISASTROUS start to the day, things improved for Jack once he and Carol arrived at the hospital. Amy was as eager to talk to him as she had been to Carol and Shona, and he managed to extract even more information from her. In his mind, he'd already decided the culprit was Mary—the nurse who'd left abruptly after the theft. But he couldn't go on his gut instinct. He needed to know if the police had interviewed her or if she'd already gone before then.

The baby had been stolen at night, and it had taken a good few hours before anybody realised she'd gone—hours during which Mary could have got a long way, even left the country. She'd been an agency nurse, which explained why the hospital had no employment records for her and why Amy didn't know her surname.

Unfortunately, the trail had gone cold after that. The agency had closed down a few years after the theft, which meant Jack had no chance of finding any records. It was frustrating, but it wasn't the end of the world. He was here to write a story, not do the police's job for them, and if they'd messed up, it would add even more impact to the appeal. He'd certainly have no compunction at all about asking Mary to come forward.

He and Carol had enjoyed a leisurely lunch together after that, ostensibly so he could get to know her better, in reality because he found her fascinating and was attracted to her. He doubted if he could have shown the strength of will she had after all she'd been through, and having talked to her, he could understand why she'd suddenly decided to try and find her daughter again. He knew all about loneliness since his divorce and losing touch with his own kids. All right, he had his mother and his siblings, but it wasn't the same as having a child. Yet there was no bitterness in Carol; she didn't even seem to bear any hatred for the woman who'd taken her baby, convinced it was someone desperate for a child of her own.

"So are you saying you weren't desperate?" he asked, and she smiled at him and shook her head.

"I was young. While I wanted to bring my baby up myself, I still thought that I'd get married, have other children. It just didn't happen."

"Why not? You're a very attractive woman. You must have had plenty of boyfriends after that."

"I did but nobody I cared enough about to marry."

He'd wondered then, and had asked tentatively, whether the man she'd loved had been the baby's father, and her face had clouded. She'd shaken her head, reiterated the statement that she hadn't known him well, that they'd already split up before she found out she was pregnant, and Jack had known—reporter's instinct—that she was lying. Known it and let it go. He already had his suspicions about Peter Clarke, but he wasn't going to push her on it. He could always find an excuse to speak to the other man on his own at some point.

***

All the euphoria of the day disappeared as soon as Jack saw his sister's car parked outside his mother's house. Lucy was a rare visitor and wasn't known to interrupt her working day to call round, which meant something was wrong. He didn't bother to lock his car, racing into the house to find his mother and sister sitting together on the sofa.

Lucy turned an accusing glare on him. "Where've you been?" she demanded.

"Working. Why?"

"Mum's had a bad turn and you weren't here."

"I told you, I was working."

"That's not good enough. You can't leave her on her own all day and go swanning off."

"I've just told you I was working," he gritted out. "What bit of that don't you understand?"

"I don't understand how you can look after Mum properly and work as well."

"That's enough, you two," their mother cut in. "I'm fine, and I don't want him under my feet all day long." Her gaze settled on Jack. "It was just I needed somebody here, and when you weren't around, I thought I'd better ring Lucy. I knew she'd come straight away if she knew I wasn't well."

"I've given you my mobile number, Mum. You could have got hold of me on that."

"I can't be paying big bills for ringing mobiles. Not on a pension, I can't."

"You can if it's an emergency, Mum," Lucy soothed with another slightly accusatory glance at her brother. "I'm sure Jack can afford to pay the bill for you."

Their mother smiled and patted Lucy's hand. "Anyway, lad, now you've decided to come home, you can put the kettle on. Poor Lucy'll be desperate for a cup of tea when she's come all this way to sit with me."

To Jack's mind, Lucy looked more inclined to make a dash for the door than sit and have tea and biscuits with them, yet some inner devil made him agree with his mother and set off to the kitchen before she could get to her feet.

Despite his amusement at seeing his sister's day disrupted, for once he was concerned about his mother. To his knowledge, she'd never had any sort of illnesses before, and it must have panicked her if she'd called Lucy. His mother might not want him looking after her all the time, but she wasn't the sort to make a fuss, especially with her daughter. Lucy was always her favourite and as such could've got away with murder.

It didn't surprise him when his sister followed him into the kitchen, a frown creasing her forehead.

"You calmed down?" he asked her.

"I suppose so. I'm sorry I had a go at you. I know you have to work, of course I do. God knows I couldn't stay here with her all day, but maybe you should organise a carer or someone to sit with her while you're out."

"Okay. Let's go back a bit here. What happened today? So far, all I know is she had a bad turn. What was it?"

"I'm not sure. When she rang me, she sounded panicky, said she'd passed out."

"Did you call a doctor or an ambulance?"

Lucy shook her head. "By the time I got here, she seemed okay again."

Jack folded his arms and leaned against the worktop, watching his sister and the slow realisation dawn on her.

"Oh my God. You think she was lying, don't you?"

"Not lying, exactly. I don't think she would do that—definitely not to you—but we need to know how bad it is. Maybe get her checked out by the doctor."

Lucy sighed impatiently. "Don't start that 'you're the favourite' thing again."

"Well, you are!"

"It doesn't look like that from where I'm standing. She used to let the two of you stay out all night, *and* she never even batted an eyelid when you announced you were getting married at twenty-one. When I told her I was marrying Bill, she had a fit!"

"That's right, sis. Bring up my failed marriage, why don't you?"

"That's not what I meant and you know it. Favourite, indeed. But whatever, whether she's laying it on or not, you're right. She should see a doctor."

And the problem of what to do whilst he was working still remained. He could do a lot from home but nowhere near enough to enable him to be here all the time, and anyway, as he'd confessed to Carol, he didn't want to be a full-time carer.

"Maybe she could go and sit with one of her friends," he thought aloud. "She's a hell of a lot more mobile than they are."

"And how's she going to get there?"

"I can drop her off. What's the alternative, really?"

Lucy raised her eyebrows at him, and he shook his head.

"I'm not doing it, Lucy. I'm not giving up my job to look after her. I'm only here until I get a place of my own, both you and Stan know that. As soon as I get my break, I'm going down to London, and the caring will fall on you two then whether you like it or not."

Lucy stared at him in patent disbelief. "You selfish bastard."

"Oh, no. Not me. As soon as I came back here, you and Stan disappeared into the woodwork. I'm not the selfish one here, sis. I'm the one you two thought had come to your rescue, let you off the hook."

"But we've got families. We can't just drop everything to look after Mum."

"And you think I can? Who's to say I won't meet somebody else, get married again? Or aren't I allowed to do anything while she's alive? Are you expecting me to put my life on hold for the next however many years while you and Stan carry on visiting once a month if she's lucky? Sorry, your happy-ever-after isn't going to happen at my expense. I'm as entitled to a life as you two are."

It was the first time he'd voiced all this, and Lucy looked stunned. To give her credit, she clearly hadn't thought about it before, as her next words demonstrated.

"I'm sorry, Jack. We've been selfish, passing over the responsibility to you. It isn't fair. But what are we going to do about her? I mean, she's all right now, but what about in a few years' time? What if she does need looking after? I can't do it. For one thing, Bill and I can't afford for me to stop work, and you know what Clara's like. She struggles to look after Stan and the kids as it is. She'd never cope with Mum too."

"Let's cross that bridge when we come to it, shall we?" Jack said with a sigh. "For now, she's okay. I'll get the doctor to come and see her—that should scare her into behaving herself for a while."

"And if her funny turn was genuine?"

"Then at least we'll know where we stand."

***

Jack had deliberately omitted to tell his mother he'd been in touch with the doctor. Consequently, when the knock came on the door that evening, she looked at him with a frown.

"It's not the night for the window cleaner to come for his money, is it?"

"No. You stay there, I'll go."

"Whoever it is, get rid of them. I can't be doing with any visitors after the day I've had."

"Oh, you'll need to see this one," Jack muttered as he walked out of the room.

"What did you say?" she called after him, and he smiled to himself as he let the doctor in. There was obviously nothing wrong with her hearing.

His mother bristled when she saw the doctor standing in the doorway with Jack.

"What are you doing here?" she demanded.

"I hear you've had a bit of a nasty turn, Mrs. Sullivan. Can you tell me what happened?"

"I don't know. I went a bit dizzy, fainted, that's all. I'm fine now. No need for you to be bothering with me."

"There's every reason. Your son was quite right to ring us. We can't have you fainting for no reason, can we?"

Gladys shifted in her seat uncomfortably and looked at Jack.

"Right, you've got him here now, you can go. Don't want you knowing my business."

Jack did as he was told and spent an anxious thirty minutes sitting in the kitchen waiting for the doctor to come out. As soon as he heard the sitting room door open, he was on his feet.

To Jack's enquiring look, the doctor said, "Come and sit in the car with me for a few minutes," and didn't say any more until they were in the vehicle, at which point he turned and looked at Jack.

"I don't know what's going on here, but I can assure you that your mother is in very good health."

Jack nodded. "To be honest I can't say I'm surprised. She called my sister because she had this turn, but we weren't sure what was wrong with her."

"We do have a name for this condition. We call it EAS."

"EAS?"

"Elderly Attention Seeking. I've had a word with her, so she won't be happy with any of us for a while, but I hope she'll have more sense than to do this again."

"I'm sorry we called you out."

"I'm not. It's put your mind at rest, which is the main thing. Why don't you see about getting her to a day-care centre a couple of times a week? It would get her out of the house and give you a break. She doesn't need a full-time carer even if she thinks she does, but no doubt she gets lonely, hence the EAS. Call in at the surgery and have a word with the receptionists, they'll have all the information you need."

Feeling thoroughly chastened, Jack was more than ready for the tirade which greeted him when he walked through the door. He let his mother have her say then sat beside her on the sofa and took her hand in his.

"Right, Mum, that's enough. We need to talk about this. It's no good you going off on a rant because the doctor's told you there's nothing wrong with you."

"He said nothing of the sort! Of course there's something wrong with me."

"What?"

"I'm old."

"Well, if that's all that's wrong, you should be grateful. Look at the rest of your friends—some of them aren't even mobile anymore."

"You don't know what it's like being stuck here day after day. It gets lonely."

"So let's do something about it. How about a day centre?"

"What? Sit with a load of old fogies? Playing bingo and doing jigsaws? I'd rather be dead!"

"But it's an option, Mum," he said, struggling for patience. "It would get you out of the house a couple of times a week, get you some company."

"I've got enough friends. I don't need to go there."

"Okay, so how about if I drop you off at one of your friends' houses sometimes when I'm going out to work?"

"I can find my own way there. I've got my bus pass."

"So basically you don't want me to do anything for you. Is that it? Fine. That's the way we'll play it."

"You won't have to worry about me anyway," she muttered.

"What do you mean?"

"You said you couldn't wait to get out and go down to London."

"This is about our argument yesterday?"

"What'll happen to me then, Jack? Your brother and sister will shove me in an old folks' home and leave me to rot. They won't do what you've done for me."

Jack looked at her in amazement. Of all the things he'd expected to hear, it definitely wasn't this. His mother showing appreciation for what he did and practically in tears as she faced the prospect of him going to London?

With a sigh, Jack put that particular dream to one side. It had all been pie in the sky anyway. Maybe it was time for him to settle down here. Unbidden, he thought of Carol and sighed again. Not the best idea—to get involved with her. Better to concentrate on the appeal and have done with it.

"Okay, Mum, forget about that argument. It was stupid, and we both said things we shouldn't have done. I can tell you Lucy is worried about you, as am I, and there's no way she and Stan would abandon you or dump you in a nursing home. Okay?"

She managed a smile and a nod and then astonished him again by offering to put the kettle on herself. "It's about time I got my finger out," she added, leaving him wondering what the doctor had said to her.

Chapter Seventeen

VALERIE WAS IN her element planning her gala evening. She spent her days surrounded by telephone directories and sample menus, her evenings getting Carol to try out at least one of the proposed dishes on their guests.

"This must be costing us a flaming fortune in ingredients," Peter grumbled, and his wife glared at him.

"Carol needs to know she can cope with the menu we've come up with."

"It strikes me we're bending over backwards for Carol on this, and it's not as though she's even family."

"And it strikes me that you've suddenly turned on a very good friend of ours, and I'd like to know the reason why," Valerie retorted.

Peter shrugged, but he mentally pulled himself up short. He was obviously going too far in his efforts to show that he didn't care about Carol, didn't know anything about her baby beyond what she'd told them. If he wasn't careful, Valerie would cotton on by his attitude alone.

"I'm sorry. It just seems like a lot of fuss to be making, that's all."

"I know, but it's for a good reason, isn't it? I mean, it isn't as though Carol's got anybody else to help her with this?"

"No, of course she hasn't. I suppose I'd better apologise to you both."

"It'd be a start, especially where Carol's concerned."

"Right then. I'd best go and start mending some fences."

Valerie smiled as she watched him go.

Poor Peter, he must have thought they were taking shameful advantage of his good nature, but the last thing they needed was a bad atmosphere in the hotel, especially with the guests walking around as though they had the weight of the world on their shoulders.

***

Stella was miserable. Holidays to her involved quite a lot of social drinking, and this pregnancy farce was playing havoc with that. But no matter how desperate she was for the odd gin and tonic, she daren't give Graham any reason to doubt her story. His silence was hard enough to tolerate; the only time he showed any signs of animation was when they were with Mike and Melinda, and she thanked her lucky stars that she'd thought of doing this. It was so obvious now that he had feelings for the other woman—a woman who showed every sign of being as unhappy as he was.

Melinda wasn't just unhappy, she was desperate. Mike was playing the role of attentive husband to the hilt, and it was driving her up the wall. She could cope with him taking her for granted better than this continual fawning over her. A few days ago, she'd complained that he never asked for her opinion about anything; now she wished he'd just leave her alone. She didn't want to have long conversations with him, she wanted to be left alone with her thoughts, her misery. How could Graham have led her to believe his marriage was on the rocks when he and Stella were trying for a baby? Why hadn't he been honest with her and said he was only looking for a quick fling, a holiday romance?

Yet, even as she thought that, she knew it wasn't true. Graham had given her no indication at all that he was looking for an affair; he'd been honest with her all along. If anything, it was Stella who was being dishonest, not him.

With the growing tension between them all, it was inevitable that things would come to a head at some stage, and it was a chance remark from Shona of all people which triggered it.

Carol and Valerie had decided to try out a shellfish starter on their guests that night, which Stella had had before at a restaurant and loved it, but as soon as Shona asked if they would all give it a try, Graham shook his head.

"Three of us, yes, but Stella had better abstain."

"What on earth for?" his wife demanded.

"We don't want you having any sort of allergic reactions in your condition do we darling?"

"What condition?"

"Er, pregnant?" Melinda said.

"For God's sake, I'm not ill. Of course I can try the starter, and as I'm probably the only one here who's ever had it before, I'll be able to give an informed opinion."

"Actually," Shona said, "it might not be a good idea. Like your husband says, you don't want to take any chances, and I think shellfish could be a problem for someone who's pregnant."

"And what, might I ask, has a private conversation got to do with you? We'll all have the starter, thank you," Stella declared icily.

Shona flushed, and Graham smiled at her apologetically.

"Ignore my wife, she thinks she's above everyone else because she's pregnant."

As soon as Graham had spoken, he could have bitten his tongue out, especially when he saw the expression on Melinda's face. How could he have been so crass, knowing what she'd gone through with her own miscarriage? Not that he had a chance to apologise. Stella was on her feet and resting her hands on the table as she glared down at him.

"I'm not going to stay here to be insulted by you or anybody else. Send that waitress to get me when the starters arrive."

As she stormed out of the room, Melinda leaned over and touched Shona's arm.

"Are you okay, love? Try not to take it personally. I suppose her hormones will be all over the place."

"It won't just be her hormones when I get hold of her," Graham muttered.

"Now then, it wouldn't look good if you were to murder your wife and unborn child, would it?" Mike laughed in a vain attempt to defuse the situation.

"So it's definitely four of the starter then, is it?" Shona asked, ignoring their attempts to cover for Stella's behaviour.

"Yes, I suppose so…" Graham's voice trailed away as a scream echoed around the hotel.

Chaos immediately broke out. A serving dish crashed to the floor in the kitchen, and Shona dropped her pad as she dashed out of the dining room, Peter hot on her heels as he abandoned the bar. They found Stella at the bottom of the stairs, her leg twisted under her, pain etching her face into harsh lines.

"What happened?" Peter demanded.

"I tripped on the stairs. I'll be all right in a minute," she gasped.

"Shall I call an ambulance?" Shona asked anxiously as Graham joined them, closely followed by Mike and Melinda.

"No, I'll be fine." Stella groaned.

"We can't take any chances," Peter said. "It's an accident that's happened on our premises, and we need to make sure we've done everything to help you."

Graham knew he should be comforting his wife, but looking at her lying there, he felt nothing beyond a vague sense of concern for the child she was carrying.

Things happened rapidly after that, too rapidly for Stella's liking. Within half an hour, she was at the hospital, biting her lip more from anxiety than pain as there was talk of X-rays followed by the inevitable question.

"Is there any chance that you could be pregnant?"

With Graham standing beside her, she had no choice but to nod, her heart sinking at the next question.

"How many weeks?"

"I'm not sure. I only just realised a couple of days ago."

"She hasn't seen the doctor about it yet," Graham added. "We're here on holiday."

"Well, we'll do a test before we go any further, just to make sure," the doctor said briskly.

In that moment, Stella knew the charade was over. She wasn't going to be able to keep the result from Graham; he'd know as soon as they sent her for the X-ray. She couldn't ask them not to say anything, and they certainly wouldn't lie for her. With a sick certainty, she knew then that she'd lost him. There was no way he'd tolerate her lying to him about something as important as this.

***

Melinda picked at her food and reflected on the possibility that Graham and Stella would decide to cut their holiday short in view of her fall.

Mike, intent on giving a good judgement on the starter, paid her little attention, inspecting his food, finally ready to deliver his verdict.

Shona looked at Melinda's practically untouched plate with raised eyebrows as Mike noticed for the first time that his wife wasn't eating.

"Well, I found it very good. Mel? Didn't you like it?"

"Oh, no, it was fine. I'm just worried about Stella."

"She's fallen, that's all. It's not exactly life-threatening, is it?"

"She might lose her baby."

"Ah, yes. Of course. Sorry," he muttered then made the situation worse by explaining about Melinda's miscarriage to Shona.

"Why did you have to tell her?" Melinda hissed as soon as the waitress had gone.

"I had to explain why you hadn't touched your food, didn't I?" he blustered.

"That's typical of you! Make sure everyone else is happy and don't worry about me!"

He frowned, perplexed at this unexpected attack from his usually mild-mannered wife. "God, I just don't know what to say to you anymore. I'm doing my best to be the perfect husband here."

"Well, you're not doing very well at it, are you?" she snapped back.

"You know what, Melinda? I think I'll stop trying. Let's just carry on as we've always done, shall we? It's obvious that you just don't want to know anymore, that you've had enough of me."

If he expected her to disagree, to plead, it didn't work. She just sat and stared at him until he finally picked up his wine glass and drank, wishing he'd just left things as they were.

She laid a hand over his, forced a smile. "I'm sorry, Mike. I know I'm being a bit of a cow, but just let's get this holiday over and see what happens when we go back home, shall we?"

"I thought you were about to say you were leaving me."

"No, of course not. And, anyway, where would I go if I did?"

He caught the hint of sadness in her voice and frowned, but where Stella had guessed what was going on between Graham and Melinda, Mike had no idea. As far as he was concerned, it was still only his gambling that was the problem here.

***

Graham stared at the nurse in numb silence as Stella was wheeled away for her X-ray. Had he heard right? Had she just said that Stella wasn't pregnant? Had never been pregnant? Had this young nurse taken on the guise of an angel, rescuing him from the hell he had been thrown into just a few short days ago? Had she offered him the lifeline he'd been longing for?

"Are you all right, Mr. Cox?" she asked anxiously. "I realise it's probably disappointing news for you and your wife, but I'm sure there'll be other chances for her to have a baby."

"No doubt there will be, but it won't be with me."

"Oh, no, please don't do anything hasty. She's going to need your support with this. It must be a terrible blow to her as well."

"You don't understand. You'd have to know my wife to realise what's going on here."

"Well, you know, when someone really wants a child, they can make mistakes about whether or not they are pregnant."

She could have added that Stella was probably beginning to feel anxious because she was in her late thirties—always a bad time to be thinking about starting a family. It was quite understandable that every period she missed would be the one when she was pregnant. Instead, she sighed and shook her head. She had enough to do without sitting with this man while he waited for his wife to come back. If she hung around here any longer, she'd have the ward sister after her.

***

Graham walked slowly out of the hospital, without Stella, his mind in a whirl as he tried to take in what had just happened. Thank God he hadn't got round to calling Darren and telling him their plans were all off. His whole life was suddenly opening up in front of him again, and at the centre of it was Melinda. Was there any chance at all for them? She'd warned him that Stella could be lying to him, and he'd refused to listen to her, had been wrapped up in his own past, in his determination to sacrifice himself, his happiness, for his child. Would she understand why he'd done that? Why he'd been prepared to see her walk away from him with Mike? If the situation were reversed, he doubted he'd have understood, but he owed it to himself to give it a try. With a new spring in his step, he pulled his mobile out of his pocket, carefully composed his message, and pressed send. All he could do now was hope.

***

Melinda read the message on her mobile and frowned.

"Bad news?" Mike asked.

"I don't know. It's Graham. He says he wants to talk to me about something. Alone."

"Is it about Stella? Something to do with the baby?"

"I don't know. He doesn't say."

"It sounds like it to me. I'll bet she's lost it, and he wants another woman to talk to her about it."

Melinda sighed and shook her head. How could Mike be so obtuse? Couldn't he see how she felt about the other man? Was she really such a good actress? And, for that matter, why hadn't he realised that nobody would ask a woman who'd lost her baby to talk to someone else who'd just gone through the same thing? It was yet another example of his insensitivity.

"So where is he now?" he asked.

"On his way back here. He wants me to meet him outside."

"Well, it's a good job we've finished eating, isn't it? I'll tell you what, I might have a walk into Chester. I could do with some exercise, give you a chance to talk to him privately. That okay with you?"

"I suppose so."

"Right. I'll be off then. See you later."

He kissed her cheek and hurried out of the lounge before she could warn him about gambling.

Hadn't he said to her after they'd had their starters that things would carry on as they always had? It wasn't a lie. He had to do something to stop this craving for the big win, and if he came good, they could really make a new start.

***

Mike didn't have as good a night as he'd hoped. He wasn't winning on the fruit machines, had drunk too much wine at dinner and was generally fed up. His footsteps echoed on the pavement as he set off back to the hotel, as hollow as he felt inside.

All he needed was one win, just enough to lift his spirits. On impulse, he called in at a late-night newsagent's, bought a couple of scratch cards and stood outside as he checked to see if either of them was a winner.

He had to read and re-read the numbers on that card, and when he read them a third time and they stayed the same, he whooped in delight.

It didn't matter that it was far too big for him to collect there and then, he was quite happy to wait and submit it through the official channels. This was just the boost he and Melinda needed to get them back on track. She'd be as excited as him and would finally accept that his gambling wasn't a bad thing after all.

***

Melinda was stunned. She stared at Graham as he sat opposite her in the lounge, shaking her head as he revealed the depth of Stella's dishonesty. And then, suddenly, he stopped talking about his wife, moved to sit beside her and took her hand in his, startling her into complete stillness.

"Melinda, this leaves me free. It allows me to walk away from the marriage because I can't live with someone who's done this to me. But I don't want to walk away alone. I want you to come with me. To leave Mike and his gambling behind, have a new start, a fresh start. I can't give you everything Mike does money-wise, but I can give you the love and respect that you deserve, hopefully the happiness, take your worries away from you because I can promise you one thing: I'd do nothing without discussing it with you first. All right, the new business is a bit of a gamble, but Darren and I know it's going to work, and I want nothing more than you at my side when it takes off."

"I can't."

"Yes, you can. There's no reason—"

"I promised Mike I wouldn't leave him, and I can't go against that."

"But you were talking about leaving him. You said if he didn't stop gambling—"

"He said he'd stop. He's really been trying hard today. I can't let him down. I have to support him through this."

Graham's heart was pounding like a drum. She couldn't do this to him when he was so close to winning her. Surely common sense told her that Mike was an addict. He couldn't stop gambling, not even for her. With a supreme effort, Graham bit back his words. It wasn't up to him to say anything. She'd accepted his decision to stand by Stella; he couldn't accuse her of throwing her life away now. But he wasn't about to give in either.

They were still sitting chatting quietly, carefully skirting around the subject of her leaving Mike, when Stella arrived back from the hospital. She hobbled into the lounge with her ankle firmly strapped up, an unusually humble expression on her face for once.

"It's not broken then?" Graham asked. "The ankle, I mean."

"It's badly sprained. Where's Mike?"

"He went into Chester," Melinda replied, offering no other explanation.

"So you've let him go out alone?"

"Oh, I think he's old enough to look after himself, don't you?" Melinda replied coolly.

"Well, I hope he isn't gambling all your money away for you again."

Melinda smiled and shook her head. "He promised me he wouldn't do any more gambling."

"And you believe him? How very trusting of you."

"At least Melinda knows when her other half is lying to her. I wasn't quite so lucky," Graham interrupted bitterly.

"Still defending your little friend against all comers, darling?" Stella drawled, her humility already forgotten.

"You'll be wanting a gin and tonic, will you, now that the pregnancy fiasco is over?"

"It wasn't a fiasco," she retorted hotly. "I genuinely believed I was pregnant."

"Of course you didn't. You were lying through your teeth to get your own way, Stella, and it's backfired on you. I'll buy you a drink, but I'm warning you here and now. It's the last thing you'll ever get out of me."

The argument might have raged on even longer if the door hadn't opened to admit Mike, his face wreathed in smiles as he waved a scratch card in the air triumphantly.

"Mel, my darling, all our worries are over. I've won."

"How dare you!" Melinda spat. "How the hell dare you go out and gamble when you promised me you'd stop. I trusted you tonight, and this is what you do. Stuff your bloody scratch card, I don't want to know anymore."

He was still gasping like a landed goldfish as she pushed past him and raced up the stairs.

"Well, well!" Stella said. "It seems the mouse has suddenly found her backbone."

"Leave her alone!" Graham snapped. "At least she isn't a liar like you."

Stella sighed dramatically as he, too, walked out of the room before she turned to Mike with a smile.

"Well, it appears you and I are in complete disgrace."

"In which case, I suggest we have a drink together and let them both cool down."

***

Furiously, Melinda threw clothes into her suitcase. She was going home, wouldn't stay in this hotel a moment longer than she had to. It had been a disaster from start to finish; she should never have given Mike another chance—another chance to add to all the others he'd had and thrown away.

Graham stood outside the Lands' bedroom door and hesitated. What did he do now? Did he take advantage of Mike's latest slip, or did he do the decent thing and walk away? Why should he walk away? Both Stella and Mike deserved all they got now.

Melinda didn't hesitate when she answered his knock. With a little sob, she flew into Graham's arms and he held her there, kissed her, gave her all the love she'd wanted from Mike. No matter what happened now, they would be together.

Chapter Eighteen

Carol frowned the following morning as she walked past Room One. The door was firmly closed, the 'do not disturb' sign on the handle. She was certain they hadn't had any new guests in last night, so who was in there? Surely Peter and Valerie hadn't had a row? If they had, it could only be over her and the baby.

She smiled in relief when she found them both in the kitchen, sitting at the table and drinking coffee, chatting quietly.

"Hi, there. Anything wrong?"

"Not really, except that Stella Cox asked to be put in Room One last night. Claimed she couldn't manage the stairs," Peter said with a shrug.

"Have you moved them both in there?"

"No. Her husband's still in their original room. Mind you, by the time she and the other chap went to bed, neither of them could walk. I don't mind the guests staying up late, but it was nearly two when they ordered their last drinks, and I had to tell them I was closing the bar. God knows what time they finally turned in." Peter groaned, rubbing his eyes.

"You should have had a lie-in this morning," Valerie ticked him off lightly. "I said so, didn't I?"

"I slept okay once I eventually got to bed. I'm sorry I disturbed you as well."

"So the chances are, that we won't see two of them for breakfast then," Carol mused.

"Well, at least it'll be smoother without the Cox woman," Valerie pointed out. "But maybe we should be ready for her appearing at the last possible minute and demanding a full English."

"I'll keep some stuff ready just in case."

As it turned out, there was no sign of any of them until almost nine when Mike arrived in the dining room looking, to Valerie's mind, extremely hungover. He sat down and stared at her out of hollow, haunted, eyes.

"She's gone," he muttered.

"Who has?"

"Melinda, my wife. Gone."

An icy chill feathered along Valerie's spine. Dear God, this was all they needed, a dead body in the hotel! Whilst she wanted to run to Peter for support, she knew she had to find out more details first, tactfully.

"Do you know what happened?" she asked.

"Of course I don't bloody know. She'd gone when I went upstairs last night. Just—gone."

"And you've no idea what happened or why?"

"No. I mean, I wouldn't have cared so much if she'd left a note, at least told me why, but she didn't."

This was getting worse by the moment. Not just a body but a suicide.

"Look," he said suddenly, "is there any chance of a black coffee, please? Just to get my head in order."

Valerie was only too happy to escape, scurrying back to the kitchen, gasping out Mike's request for coffee as Carol looked at her in alarm.

"Whatever's the matter?" she asked.

"Where's Peter? I need to get him to ring…someone. The police, I suppose."

"The police? Why?"

"We've got a dead body on our hands."

"What?! Who?"

"Melinda Land. When her husband went up to bed, she was dead."

"Last night? What's he done all night then? He can't have slept with a dead body, can he?"

Valerie halted in the doorway and stared at her. "But he said she'd gone…"

"*Gone.* But not dead. How do you know she hasn't just left him?"

"He said she didn't leave a note or anything."

"So you thought she'd committed suicide?"

"Oh, hell." Valerie gasped in a mixture of dismay and relief. "She's walked out on him, hasn't she?"

"Maybe we should be checking if the other one's husband is still here. They were pretty close, weren't they?"

All Valerie's relief at Melinda not being dead vanished. She certainly didn't want to be the one who had to tell Stella that her husband had gone off with another woman if that was what had happened.

***

Despite the pain from her ankle, Stella had slept well, telling herself it was because she wasn't disturbed by Graham's snoring, and hobbled out to the dining room even as she wondered why he hadn't bothered to knock on her door on his way downstairs.

As there was only Mike sitting in there, she automatically gravitated to his table, looking at him with raised eyebrows.

"No Melinda?"

He shook his head and gave a shuddering sigh. "She's left me."

"Oh, no! When?"

"Last night. She'd gone when I went up to bed."

Stella's eyes narrowed as a dreadful suspicion hit her. Imperiously, she beckoned a reluctant Valerie over. "Has my husband been down yet?"

"No, Mrs. Cox, he hasn't."

"I want someone to check our room, make sure he's there."

"We don't tend to disturb the guests—"

"But I want, *demand*, that you disturb him. *Now*!"

"I'll get my husband to check." Valerie sighed.

Mike was shaking his head as though to clear his brain. Why did she want to know if Graham was there? Of course he was, where else would he be? Unless…

"You don't think they've gone together do you?"

"Don't you think it's a bit obvious that they have? In their eyes, we both did something wrong. All they were waiting for was an excuse."

"She wouldn't do that," Mike mumbled.

"Why not? She's a woman, and even if I do say it myself, my husband is something of a catch."

"Don't be ridiculous. She's already got everything she needs. Doesn't have to work, can do whatever she wants all day—that's going to be a hell of a comfortable lifestyle, thanks to that win I had last night."

Stella's lip curled at his conceit. She could have mentioned the age difference between them, the fact that he treated Melinda more as a child than his wife, but before she could speak, Valerie was back with the news that Graham had indeed gone.

"Maybe he's gone out for a walk," Valerie added brightly.

"Please don't bother to patronise me. I know exactly where he's gone," Stella retorted. "Wait!" she said as Valerie turned away. "I would like some breakfast, please."

"They stop serving at nine-thirty," Mike pointed out.

"And?" Stella replied with delicately raised eyebrows. "I'll have the full English, please, without the sausage."

***

"Well!" Valerie expostulated when she went back into the kitchen. "It looks as though her husband going off with another woman hasn't quelled her appetite after all."

"Maybe you need to actually care about someone besides yourself for it to affect your appetite," Carol remarked.

"It's certainly knocked the other poor chap for six."

"Yes, but he didn't really care about his wife either, did he? He's just shocked that she's actually left him, although from what Shona said, they were all scrapping in there last night at dinner before Stella Cox fell."

"Hopefully she'll decide to go home herself today after this."

"How?" Carol asked. "She can't drive with that ankle, and especially as they'll have taken her husband's car. I reckon we're stuck with her till she can arrange some sort of transport home."

Valerie groaned and dropped her head into her hands. This was going to ruin all their plans. They couldn't arrange the gala evening with that woman still in the hotel, and she was going to want them all running around after her more than ever as long as she had that bandage on. Right then, Valerie could have happily throttled Graham Cox for her! He could at least have taken her home before he went off with Melinda Land.

***

Shona halted on the stairs as she heard her mother's voice. Being a one-sided conversation, she knew she was on the 'phone and that she shouldn't be eavesdropping, but it was obvious her mother was discussing a job of some sort, which had to be a good sign. She'd said the night before that she was thinking of applying for a part-time job, but Shona had taken it with a pinch of salt. There had been plenty of moments over the past few weeks when her mother had come out with various wild suggestions, but this time, it definitely sounded promising.

"I have experience, yes, although it's a long time ago. To be honest, I haven't worked since my daughter arrived, so it's been about nineteen years."

As the conversation came to an end, Shona continued down the stairs, calling out a greeting as she headed for the kitchen. Her mother followed her, telling her almost as a throwaway comment that she had an interview that morning.

"Oh, right. Where?" Shona asked, equally casual.

"Just in an office. Receptionist."

"What time's your interview?"

"Ten-thirty."

"Don't forget to take your certificates with you."

"What certificates?"

"Your typing and shorthand ones. Do you want me to fish them out for you before I go to work?"

"I'm quite capable of getting them myself, thank you. I'm not a child!"

"Fine, I was only trying to help," Shona muttered.

***

"Boy, am I glad to see you," Carol greeted Shona when she arrived at the hotel, which was a scene of chaos, with Stella Cox holding court in the lounge.

"What's going on?"

"Oh, it's absolute pandemonium here. You know Mrs. Cox fell down the stairs? She's sprained her ankle or something, so she asked to be moved into Room One because she couldn't manage the stairs, and in the meantime, her husband's gone off with Melinda Land. She's just furious, and the other chap's in pieces. We can't get anything done in the hotel because she's taken over the lounge, and we can't get the other chap out of the dining room."

"Where are Peter and Valerie?"

"Mrs. Cox has got Peter trying to find out where her husband is, and Valerie's feeding the other chap tea and sympathy."

"Okay, what can I do?" Shona asked, her mother's job interview forgotten.

"You can come and help me in the kitchen. I suppose the other guests will still want to eat tonight even if those two don't. Mind you, thinking about it, it certainly hasn't put her off her food. She put away a full English earlier."

***

Mike hadn't thought again about his lottery win since he woke up that morning, but now, as Valerie sat with him so patiently, assuring him that there was no need for him to leave the hotel until he was ready, he realised he owed this woman, this stranger, a huge debt of gratitude. To Mike, debts like this were repaid in monetary terms.

"I'm sorry, I've taken up your whole day here, haven't I? And you must be busy."

"We are, but it can wait. The only thing we're really busy with is trying to arrange this fundraiser for our chef."

"You never did tell us what it was all about when you had us tasting those dishes for you."

Briefly, Valerie explained about Carol's daughter, and Mike shook his head when she finished.

"So how much do you want to offer for this reward?"

"As much as we can manage to raise."

In that moment, Mike knew exactly what he was going to do. If Melinda had left him, there was no way he was going to hand over any of that win to her and Graham Cox. He'd give the scratch card to the hotel chef, let it go to a good cause, to someone who deserved it. For him, the pleasure had all been in the winning anyway, and there'd be plenty of other chances for him, especially now there was no need for him to give up his gambling.

***

Carol was puzzled that evening when Tina reported Mike wanted to speak to her. So far as she knew, there was nothing wrong with the food, and anyway, he wasn't the type to complain, so why did he want to see her of all people?

"Is he with the other woman?" she asked.

"Oh, yes. Anybody would think it was them two having the affair, not the other pair."

"Well, let's see what it is he wants, shall we? Can you two cope for a few minutes in here?"

"I promise we won't burn anything," Shona said, laughing.

If Carol had expected a complaint, she was stunned when Mike handed her a scratch card instead.

"I gather you're trying to trace your daughter, and I'd like you to have this to help you offer a reward for information."

Stella snorted her disapproval, but Mike had no links to her, and he could ignore her.

Carol gasped. "I can't take this. It's fifteen thousand pounds! We wouldn't dream of offering that big a reward—we'd have every gold digger in the country contacting us."

"Then take her on holiday when you find her, take the time to get to know each other. I've got no need for it now."

"At least let me think about it and give you a chance to be sure."

"That's fine. I'll be leaving in the morning. Give me your answer then."

As a stunned Carol left them, Stella immediately launched into her attack.

"You must be mad! She's a stranger to you. For all you know, she's lying about trying to find her child. She'll take your money and squander it for you."

"And if I keep it, Melinda can claim half of it, and I don't want her to squander it with *your* husband," he retorted. "And believe me, I'll be getting rid of a lot more than that before she can come knocking on my door demanding a divorce."

"Well, I can think of better ways of doing it than handing it to that woman."

Mike sighed and shook his head. "You know what, I'm not too bothered about what you think, Stella. If I were you, I'd look after my own problems—like how you've allowed your husband to get away from you—and leave me to mine."

"if you don't want my advice—"

"I don't. Let's enjoy this meal together, and then I'm going to pack and get ready to leave in the morning."

***

Tina looked at Carol curiously as she walked back into the kitchen, worried that Stella had complained about her again. Judging by the chef's shocked expression, it seemed all too likely.

"I don't believe it," Carol muttered.

"Go on, what am I supposed to have done this time?"

"What? Oh—no. Nothing. It wasn't a complaint or anything."

"Don't say they wanted to compliment you on the food?" Shona teased.

Carol shook her head. "That chap, Mike Land? He's just given me a scratch card to help out with the search for my daughter."

"Oh, is that all?" Tina collected her pad and pen from the table. "I guarantee it won't be a winner."

"It's a winner, all right. Fifteen thousand."

"How much?!" Tina squealed, making Carol momentarily thankful that she hadn't been holding a tray full of food as the pen clattered to the floor.

"Oh, Carol, that's brilliant!" Shona said.

"You know I can't possibly take it, don't you?"

"Why not? It's only like getting a tip, isn't it?" Tina reasoned as only Tina could.

"With the best will in the world, Tina, I don't think any of us have ever been offered that size of tip."

"So you've said no."

"Of course I've said no, not that he took that as an answer. He said he's leaving in the morning and I've got to tell him then whether I accept or not."

"More fool you if you turn him down, that's all I can say," Tina muttered as she walked out of the door.

Shona was more reasonable. She knew how desperate Carol was to find her daughter and this was the sort of opportunity she needed to help her to do that. It would certainly make it a lot easier. There'd be no need to fundraise and no need to worry about the bills for the private detective she might need.

"You know if you did accept, there's nothing to stop you offering some of it as a reward and maybe giving the rest of it to a charity."

"I know, but surely that's up to him to do, not me. I mean, he's the one who's won it, not me, and he's just lost his wife. Maybe he's in shock, doesn't know what he's doing."

"The best person to talk to is Valerie," Shona advised. "She's been stuck with him all day, hasn't she?"

Relief surged through Carol. Of course Valerie would know what to say to him, how to point out that he couldn't possibly do this, couldn't give this amount of money to a stranger.

Chapter Nineteen

VALERIE WASN'T SURPRISED when Carol told her about Mike's offer. Whilst she'd been sitting listening to him through the day, he'd gradually come round to the idea that his wife had left him because of that scratch card. It had been the final straw for Melinda, and while he didn't understand, he had to accept it.

That evening, Valerie looked at Carol steadily and tried to find the right words. "For his sake, I think you have to accept it, but if you don't want to spend it all, why not donate some of it to charity?"

"That's what Shona said as well."

"And which charity did she suggest?"

"We didn't get that far. Why?"

"Well, because of the way this has affected two marriages, I reckon you should donate some of it to Gamblers Anonymous."

"Is there such a thing?"

"There'll be something like it. They have charities for everything. Ask Jack, he's sure to know."

Carol nodded thoughtfully. It occurred to her she should ask Mike if she could include what he was doing for her in the newspaper feature, perhaps mention that if Melinda saw it, she might think again about leaving him. That way, he'd be more likely to agree, which seemed a bit underhand, but it was all publicity to help with her search, wasn't it?

***

Jack whistled quietly to himself as he tapped away at his computer keyboard. He loved it when a story came together almost of its own accord. Already he'd managed to feed in a lot more detail than he'd originally hoped, but he wanted to go further. He sat back in his chair and steepled his fingers under his chin. How much of her background would Carol be prepared to reveal? Would she let him say how young and vulnerable she'd been when her baby was born? Could he persuade her to reveal the father's identity? Did she share the inherent distrust most people had of journalists? If that were the case, it wouldn't matter whether Jack promised to keep the father's name out of it, she wouldn't tell him the truth. In fact, why did he want to know anyway? If he was keeping it out of the story, it was nothing to do with him.

He sighed and closed down his machine. His mother would be shouting for her tea any second now, and with things a little better between them of late, he didn't want to upset her. She was doing more around the house and pretty much taking care of herself—except for meals. For some reason, she didn't seem to have any interest in food, and it was taking all Jack's skill to get her to eat anything at all, although she wasn't losing weight, he didn't think. He didn't notice these things—one of the reasons his marriage had failed, according to his ex-wife, who accused him of not caring how she looked. To him, she was just Rose and he'd loved her; that was all that mattered. But she'd sought continual reassurances about whether he still found her attractive and worried when she put on the odd pound or two.

They were halfway through their meal when his mother suddenly cleared her throat, and he looked at her in alarm, panicking she'd got some food stuck, but no, she was preparing to say something.

"How's that story going about the baby?"

"Not too bad."

"Have you met the mother yet?"

"I have, and she's very nice."

"Nice? A woman who hasn't bothered to look for her child for so many years?" she scoffed.

"It takes courage to do this, Mum. She's going to be facing all sorts of people—people like you who will condemn her for something she didn't do. It's not going to be easy facing all that."

His mother shrugged but didn't apologise or revise her opinion.

"I hope you're not getting too attached to her," she said instead. "I'd have thought you'd have learned your lesson about women after that wife you had."

"Don't call Rose 'that wife', Mum. It wasn't her fault things went wrong. We were both to blame."

"Don't you dare be taking any of the blame for her. She was the one who had the affair, not you."

There was a gentleness to her voice that startled Jack. He was used to the sharpness and certainly hadn't found any sympathy here when his marriage broke down. Again he wondered at this new vulnerability his mother occasionally showed. He found it slightly worrying.

"When are you talking to her again then?" she asked.

"Tomorrow morning."

"Well, I'll be out in the morning, thought I'd go round to see Ethel. She's not too good at the moment, so if you need to bring her here to talk, you can do."

Jack grinned at her but shook his head. "Thanks for the offer, but we thought we'd have a chat at the hotel. That way, it's easier if I need to talk to any of the other staff." Not to mention that his mother would no doubt change her mind at the last moment about visiting Ethel, just so she could get a look at Carol. For some reason, his mother saw every female who crossed Jack's path as a threat these days, and the last thing he wanted was her scuppering this story before it got going...or picking up on his growing affection for Carol.

***

Mike was down for his breakfast early, sitting at his usual table, and smiled at Valerie when she took his order. He wanted to ask her what Carol had decided, but he didn't. Carol might not have told her boss about his offer.

"If she's not too busy, could I have a quick word with your chef?"

"Yes, of course you can. I'll send her out to you."

Carol knew what was coming and looked at Valerie nervously. In the space of the next few moments, her search for her daughter would become a reality. Was she ready for this? As soon as she accepted Mike's gift, they could go ahead; by the end of the week, she might have made her first contacts, and she was frightened and hopeful in equal measure.

"Go on, it'll be fine," Valerie urged her. "Just remember what I said last night."

Mike indicated the chair opposite him and Carol sat down all too willingly; her legs were in imminent danger of refusing to support her.

"So have you made the right decision?" he asked.

"I don't know if it's the right one, but I've decided to accept your offer—your very generous offer—but there are a couple of conditions."

His eyebrows rose as he listened to her fumble her way through her explanations, and then he sat back and nodded thoughtfully.

"I've got no objection to you giving some of it to charity," he said, "but I don't want any publicity."

"Then I can't accept."

"Why do you want to tell people about me? Why do you think I'd want people to know my reasons for doing this?"

"Because this is the turning point for you. I don't think you'll gamble again. You've learned your lesson, and if your wife sees that, realises what you've done, she might realise she's made a mistake by leaving you."

Mike laughed then, the same deep laugh they'd heard at the beginning of his stay but less and less as the week went on.

"You know what? If it means you'll accept the scratch card, do it, but even if Melinda sees the paper, I'll not be taking her back. She's made her decision and that's an end to it."

"That's up to you at the end of the day. Yes, I accept, and thank you so very much. You don't know what this means to me."

"I can guess. And it means something good has come out of this mess." He sighed and smiled wistfully. "Now, back to that kitchen or I'll be having to eat with Stella again, and I'd like to be on my way before she makes an appearance."

Carol could understand that. Given the choice, she'd be avoiding that lady as well.

Clutching her precious scratch card, she shook Mike's hand and went back to the kitchen, where she was met by Valerie's enquiring gaze.

"Yes."

"Fantastic!" Valerie gave her a quick hug before collecting Mike's breakfast and hurrying out to the dining room.

Valerie was pleased for Carol but sad that all her work on the fundraiser had been in vain. On the plus side, Peter would be happy they were shelving that idea. Now it was a matter of waiting for the funds to come through, although if need be, she and Peter could advance the money to Carol to settle it if anybody came forward. Valerie just hoped she could persuade Carol not to go overboard with the charity side, to keep some of it for herself—hadn't she said she needed to do some things to the house? This was a much-needed windfall for her.

***

Jack was well used to the goalposts changing every time he saw Carol. At the rate they were going, they'd need a special edition of the newspaper to cover everything she wanted to include, but even he was stunned to hear about Mike's gift.

"The man must be mad," he muttered.

"No. I think he *was* mad on gambling, and now he's finally realised. He's lost two wives because of it and he's finally come to his senses, which brings me to something else. Is there any chance we can mention him in the article? Not the amount, of course—that could lead to all sorts of problems—but that he's given me a winning scratch card to go towards the search."

These sorts of stories were the icing on the cake for journalists, and Jack had no hesitation about agreeing.

"You're sure he won't object to us naming him?"

"Not at all. Mind you, I did say I wasn't prepared to take the card off him unless he agreed," she added with a smile.

"Dodgy. What would you have done if he'd said no?"

"Carried on with Valerie's ideas for the fundraiser."

"I thought you'd want to get this moving quickly."

She bit her lip anxiously, and he looked at her curiously.

"What's wrong?" he asked.

"Oh, you know… It's all happening a bit quick now."

"It's taken nineteen years for you to get round to this. That's not quick from where I'm sitting."

"I know. But it's only a few days since I told Valerie, and suddenly it's all getting out of hand, if you know what I mean."

"You want a bit of breathing space," he guessed. "Well, it's still going to take time for me to write the story—it's certainly not going in this week's edition—so it'll be a couple of weeks at least before we publish. How does that feel?"

"It feels…wonderful," she admitted.

"Okay. So let's see how we can get this chap's name in there, shall we?" he continued briskly, slightly unnerved by the smile that lit up her face. In that moment, he found her too attractive for his own good.

Before he could get himself into any more hot water, they were joined by Peter and Valerie with a welcome tray of coffee. Jack subtly observed Peter, who greeted him with a polite nod, seemingly more at ease today. Not that it alleviated Jack's suspicions of him. After that first meeting, it didn't matter how amenable Peter was; he'd already given Jack the wrong impression.

"I don't suppose there's a lot we can do, now that Carol's been given the money for the reward, is there?" Peter said.

"We can still support her," Valerie remarked snippily.

"Well, yes of course, I know that. Carol knows that, don't you, love?"

It was that moment, when Carol winced at the casual endearment, Jack knew his suspicions were right. Peter Clarke was the father of her missing child, which was why Carol had waited so long to do this. She was protecting him, and the callous bastard had let her do it. He'd deprived her of the chance to find her child. He didn't deserve to be kept out of this.

"So how soon do you think you can get the story out?" Valerie asked.

"There's a few loose ends to tie up yet. I've just been telling Carol—it won't be this week. Maybe next."

"Oh, that's a shame. I thought it would be quicker than that, now we don't need to do the fundraising."

Jack smiled and shook his head, explaining smoothly about the deadlines on the paper, making sure he kept Carol's feelings out of it. He wasn't giving Peter Clarke the satisfaction of knowing how nervous Carol was about her story being out there.

Unaware Jack had already made the connection, Peter glanced shiftily at Carol and asked, "How do you feel about it taking so long?"

Jack baulked at the audacity of the man.

"I think she can wait a bit longer, considering how many years she's kept quiet about this, don't you?"

Peter blinked at the abruptness of Jack's tone, and Jack kicked himself for losing his cool. Hoping the women hadn't noticed the tension between him and Peter, Jack pressed on.

"I don't think we can do any more here today. We've covered the donation bit. I'd still like to include a bit more about you, Carol, so—"

"You don't need to know any more about me," she interrupted. "It's my daughter we're looking for. She can find out all about me once I've met her."

Right on cue, Valerie added, "Actually, Carol, I think Jack's right. If you don't have some public sympathy, you'll only end up with money-grabbers coming forward. And he's not going to press you about the baby's father, are you?"

"No not at all," Jack assured her with a sideways glance at Peter. "I don't think he deserves any involvement anyway, after what he's done to you. So yes, I just want a bit of the human side—how you felt at the time, why you didn't feel able to do something until now. That sort of thing."

Carol shrugged uneasily, but she didn't refuse, looking to Valerie for guidance. So *that* was why Carol was protecting the father or, rather, his wife. Carol was sacrificing her happiness for the sake of her friend's.

Chapter Twenty

THE COLLEGE WAS surrounded by students when Tina arrived, but she had no trouble spotting Kelly and Tracey. As always, her friends were standing slightly apart from everybody else and deep in conversation. It wasn't surprising. At school, the three of them had always been together, rarely allowing anybody else close. Maybe that was why Tina found it so hard to make friends now: her social skills had purely been connected to Kelly and Tracey.

Kelly was the first to see her, squealing her delight as she waved Tina over, causing more than a few heads to turn in the process. Aware of the smattering of interest from some of the lads, Tina tossed her hair and took her time walking past them. College could be quite interesting after all.

"What are you doing here?" Kelly demanded.

"I've decided it's about time I did a course so I can help to run the hotel," Tina replied, forgetting for a brief moment how well her friends knew her.

"You mean your parents have put their feet down and told you to do one," Tracey teased.

"I had a bit of trouble. One of the guests complained about me—mind you, she complains about everybody, does that particular one, but still. I ended up having a blazing row with my dad, and he threatened to sack me."

"He can't sack you! it's a family business!" Tracey laughed.

"Do you think I didn't tell him that? Apparently, it's their business, not mine, I'm just there on sufferance."

"So have you left home as well then?" Kelly asked.

"No. Luckily I found something out. It doesn't matter what it was, but it means I can keep my dad exactly where I want him."

"Ooh, go on, tell us," Tracey squealed. "It sounds like blackmail, does that."

Tina smirked, revelling in being the centre of attention and knowing she'd have to give them something or they'd lose interest.

"Let's just say that he did something he shouldn't have done before I was born."

"Oh, right. He had an affair then, did he? And what about your mum? Does she know?"

"Of course she doesn't. I wouldn't have anything over him if she did."

"Will you tell her?"

"Nah. I don't want to rock the boat, do I? That hotel will be mine someday, so I don't want them two getting divorced or they'd have to let it go. I'm quite happy with the way things are. He knows he can't get rid of me, and basically, whatever I want at the moment I can get. Can't go wrong!"

"Still, I never thought you'd want to come to college," Tracey said.

"It gets me out of some of the chores at home, and look at us! The terrible three back together again!"

"So what course are you going to do?" Kelly asked.

"Something to do with the business, I suppose. What are you two doing?"

"Health and Beauty."

"I could do that. We could have a salon at the hotel."

"No, you can't. It's already over-subscribed."

"Oh, right. Looks like it'll have to be something boring then."

"Ours isn't exactly a barrel of laughs, is it, Kelly?"

"No. We've got an absolute cow of a tutor. Right old-school, she is. 'Sit there, don't say a word, listen to me.' I tell you, if it wasn't for the practical side of it, I'd be out of here like a shot."

***

The careers officer had never been faced with the likes of Tina before. Usually, young people arrived in her office looking for something to do with their lives; very few of them were already involved in a business of some sort. Yet, looking at this girl, the woman could see there were going to be just as many problems with her as there were with any of the students.

"We don't actually do any courses in hotel management, but I can suggest a couple of others that might be what you're looking for. How about a small business modular course? That covers most of the things you'll need."

"It sounds like hard work. I was thinking of just one course," Tina said.

"Oh, don't worry, it won't be too strenuous for you," the careers officer replied drily.

Tina managed to miss the hint of sarcasm in her voice, frowning when she saw the topics she'd be studying, none of which were exactly inspiring.

"Of course, it's up to you," the woman continued, "but I can't see the point in you doing anything else, not if it's meant to tie in with the family business."

"Okay." Tina shrugged. "I'll see if I can get on them."

"I can sort that out for you now."

***

Half an hour later, Tina had signed up to three different courses and was already wondering if she'd made a massive mistake by agreeing to this. Should she have held out with her father? Surely she could take on the hotel when the time came without all these qualifications? It wasn't as though she had to prove anything to anybody. Then she mentally squared her shoulders. She'd get out of doing a lot of work at the hotel thanks to this lot, and that was all she'd been trying to do. It didn't matter whether she passed or failed; the hotel would still come to her in the end.

***

Carol smiled at Jack as she settled herself in the passenger seat of his car. With his promise that they wouldn't be discussing the story, she could relax, enjoy his company. She had a feeling she could get to like this man given time—not in a romantic way. She was much too old for that now, but he would make a good friend. Carol sometimes felt that she needed new friends.

"So where are we going?" she asked brightly.

"I thought we'd try a little pub I know just outside Chester. That suit you?"

"Lovely. And no chance of meeting anybody we know."

"Does it worry you, meeting people you know if you're out with me?"

"No, of course not. Sometimes it's nice to chat without being interrupted, isn't it?"

He didn't reply, and she wondered if she'd given the wrong impression. She didn't want him to think that she was attracted to him and was looking on this as some sort of a date. His next words soon set her mind at rest.

"You know we aren't going to be able to avoid talking about the search, don't you?"

"I know. It's the only thing we have in common."

"At the moment, yes. But I thought we could perhaps decide how we're going to do this so I can put it to bed over the weekend. That okay with you?"

"Will I be able to read it before you publish?"

That was one question Jack had been dreading. He never allowed anybody to read a story before it went to print, and the last thing he wanted was someone pulling the whole thing apart once he'd written it.

"Do you know why I'm asking?"

"Because I'm a journalist. We're not all the same."

"No. But can I really trust you?"

"I'd like to think so."

"Then let me read it."

He sighed, accepting there was no way around this one, which put more pressure on him to do a good job on the story.

"You're not wanting to do this so you can delay publication a bit longer, are you?" he asked.

"Well, I can't delay it forever, can I?"

"Okay then. I'll try and have it ready by the end of the week. If you look at it over the weekend, I should be able to get it in the paper next week. That okay with you?"

"Yes. And thanks."

He shrugged. He didn't want thanks; he wanted her trust but accepted he had to earn it. She'd spent a lot of years on her own, and it was going to be bad enough for her meeting her daughter without him complicating matters further.

Despite her fears, Carol enjoyed her lunch. Jack was good company—more so once they moved past her story and focused more on general things. He told her about some of the crazy stories he'd covered for the paper: the odd bequests in wills, the 'alternative' weddings. She learned more about their area than she could ever have imagined, and then, not surprisingly, he drifted onto his failed marriage.

"You miss your wife," she observed.

"Not exactly. I miss my kids, but Rose? No, I don't think so. I've put the marriage behind me. We were too young when we married, and she had an affair, but I can see why she did now. Neither of us had had a chance to find ourselves before we got married. Maybe if we'd been better advised by our parents... mine were more concerned about my sister than me. But what about you? You said you'd never been tempted to tie the knot."

"No. I don't know why. It wasn't that I was madly in love with my baby's father. I think I just realised that men aren't to be trusted. As soon as something happens, they turn elsewhere for comfort. Sorry, do I sound cynical?"

"Maybe. We aren't all shallow bastards, though."

"Ouch. I deserved that, didn't I?"

"Not at all. It sounds like it's all mixed up with the baby being stolen. From what you've said, you didn't have much support—not even from the hospital or the police. It seems to me they were more concerned with covering up the hospital's shortcomings than helping you."

Carol had never looked at it like that, but she nodded in acceptance. He was probably right. If the baby had been taken from outside a shop or something, they'd have gone all out to find her, but because it had happened in a supposedly secure environment, they'd covered it up, protected the hospital at her expense.

"Was there any press coverage?" he asked idly, as if it were of no real concern.

Carol shook her head. "Which is why this is such a big thing for me."

"Right." So how had his mother heard about it? Even as he changed the subject, Jack made a mental note to ask her that evening.

***

Shona felt like she had a permanent frown on her face. There was something that bothered her about the way her mother had reacted when Shona offered to dig out her certificates. Maybe her mother didn't have any qualifications, but that was nothing to be ashamed of. After all, Shona was in the same boat since she'd given up uni.

As she walked down the road to the hotel, she vowed to bring it up with her mother later, reassure her that she was proud of her for going out there and getting a job, whatever it was. But still, she couldn't help thinking her mother was covering up for something. Maybe she'd been sacked in the past?

The hotel was deserted when she walked in. Even Carol was missing, although as Shona put the kettle on, Tina breezed into the kitchen.

"Hi, there! All on your own?"

Shona couldn't resist making a show of looking around before she nodded and asked, "Do you know where Carol is?"

"Out with her fancy man."

"What fancy man?"

"That reporter. He was here this morning. I reckon he's got a thing for her. I'll bet any money they've gone off somewhere together."

"Don't be daft. Carol's only interested in finding her daughter. She's certainly not up for any sort of a romance."

"Pity she didn't think that years ago, isn't it?" Tina muttered, and Shona threw her a puzzled look.

She couldn't possibly know what had gone on between her father and Carol, could she? Neither of them would dare trust Tina with that sort of information. Had she guessed? Or maybe she just meant because Carol had been a young, unmarried mother.

Before Shona could speak, not that she'd planned on challenging Tina's comment, Tina said, "Anyway, we'd better make a start on the evening meals. I'll peel the spuds if you can find out what we're doing tonight."

"Be the normal menu, I suppose. We can't cope with any specials if the chef's not here."

"Should we give her a ring, check she's all right?" Tina asked.

"Do you know her number?"

"No, but Dad'll have a record of it in the office."

"Right. Do you want me to go and see?"

"I'm keeping out of his way at the moment, so yes, you'd better."

***

Peter looked round in surprise when Shona arrived in the office, automatically thinking something was wrong. After all the trouble with Tina, the last thing he needed was a problem from Shona as well.

"Tina and I were wondering if you knew Carol's 'phone number."

"Why?" he asked, instantly suspicious.

"She's not here yet, and we're a bit worried about her."

"Oh, right! She went out to lunch with that reporter chap—I'm sure she's fine. If you two can make a start, she'll be here soon enough."

After Shona left, he glanced at the clock and frowned. It was almost five o'clock, so where the hell was Carol, and what was she telling that reporter? She was vulnerable, desperate to find the child she'd lost all those years ago, and Jack was an experienced journalist who knew how to wheedle information out of people.

Peter couldn't begin to fathom what she'd gone through, and he was angry on her behalf about what hadn't been done to find her baby. Even so, it wasn't like her to turn up late for her shift. She'd never once let them down in all the years she'd worked for them, would have called if she couldn't make it in for any reason.

Unless that reason was Jack. He could have sown all sorts of seeds in Carol's head by now. Peter should never have let her go with him.

He pulled himself up short then. He had no hold over Carol. She was free to do what she wanted, see who she wanted. Simply because he'd found out she was the mother of his other child—a child he'd known nothing about—it didn't give him the right to tell her what to do, who to see. He was absolutely powerless.

Chapter Twenty-One

TERRY STARED AT his wife with a mixture of dismay and disbelief fighting for supremacy in him. Of all the things he'd expected to hear, that she'd got herself a job was not one of them. Mary had never shown any inclination to go back to work since Shona, and now his daughter was asking questions as well. Difficult questions he didn't want to answer.

"So what have you told Shona about this job?" he asked finally, when the shock wore off.

"Not a lot. She thinks I'm a receptionist."

"If you'd told her the truth—"

"How do you think she's going to react if she knows?"

"Sooner or later, she's going to find out what this job is, and it's better she finds out from you. You don't have to tell her which department you were in—just tell her you thought she knew. Put the girl's mind at rest. You owe her that much, at the very least."

"I don't owe her anything!" she snapped. "If you hadn't walked out on us, this would never have happened."

"How do you make that one out?" he asked wearily.

"She wouldn't have had to come back from university, would never have met that woman who's looking for her daughter—would never have started asking questions about us, about her background."

Terry wasn't having that one for a moment. He hadn't been the one to bring Shona home, to refuse to say anything about where she'd come from. That was all down to his wife, but that was by the by. He wasn't about to let her change the subject from her new job.

"Look, do me a favour, okay? Come clean and tell her what the job is. Knowing Shona, she'll let it drop."

"She's been to the hospital already," Mary said quietly.

"What? Why?"

"She went with that chef from the hotel, didn't she? To see if the staff remembered anything about her baby…who was stolen from there."

Terry had heard people say their blood ran cold but had never experienced it for himself until now. He sat and stared at her, shock coursing through his veins, panic clutching at his throat.

"Did they get anywhere?" he finally managed to ask through parched lips.

"They talked to a nurse who remembered someone called Mary working on the maternity unit."

In that moment, Terry couldn't have spoken if his life had depended on it.

As soon as Mary told Shona she'd been a nurse, she was going to guess the truth. There'd be no keeping it from her.

"So now do you see why I had to lie to her about the job?" Mary asked quietly.

"I don't see why you had to apply for it in the first flaming place," he retorted.

"Because I need to get out of this house. It's not good for me sitting here day after day with nothing to look forward to and nobody to talk to, and it isn't as though you're prepared to come back to us, is it?"

"Cut the blackmail, Mary, it doesn't wash. You know and I know there's no going back now. This is about Shona, not us."

"So what do you expect me to do?" she asked. "Was I supposed to get shop work or something? Something to keep our daughter happy?"

"That's just it, isn't it, Mary, She isn't *our* daughter!"

They'd come in a massive circle and ended up back where they'd started—back with no answer to the mess Mary had created. Back to the point of no return. Yet Terry knew she was going to continue with the lie, hoping Shona never discovered the truth, and he supposed, deep inside himself, he couldn't blame her for that. He didn't want his daughter to know the truth either.

***

Gladys seemed in a reasonably good mood when Jack arrived home that evening, and he wondered if he should chance asking her what she knew about Carol's baby. She came into the kitchen as he was preparing their evening meal, filling the kettle and glancing at him every so often.

"You've been out all day," she observed.

"Mm. Did you get round to see Ethel?"

"I did, and she's in a right state. That daughter of hers hasn't been near all week, not even brought her any shopping in. Poor old soul. I don't know how she copes on her own like that."

"She's lucky she has you to go and see her."

"She's not as lucky as I am though, is she?"

Jack didn't reply, and Gladys nudged him playfully.

"Come on, lad. Can't you take a compliment anymore? Really knocked the stuffing out of you, has that wife of yours."

For once, Jack didn't warn her to keep quiet about Rose, maybe as a result of talking to Carol about her, but his mother did seem glad that he was moving on at last—just as long as it wasn't towards another woman.

"You know you said you remembered the baby being stolen?"

"Mmm?"

"How did you know?"

"I suppose I just heard it from somewhere. Why?"

"From what Carol said, the police kept it as quiet as they could."

"Well, I must have heard it from somewhere." Gladys shrugged.

"Local gossip?"

"It was nineteen years ago, Jack. How do you expect me to remember so far back? Why is it so important to you anyway?"

"Just curious, that's all."

Gladys let it go and turned away to make the tea.

To her, it was unimportant, but Jack still wanted to know who'd told her. It could be a vital lead that would take them to someone who knew what had happened to Carol's baby.

***

"Where the hell have you been?" Bob Stewart demanded as he stopped by Jack's desk in the office the following morning. "I asked you to cover a story not drop off the face of the planet."

"I've come in now to pull it all together," Jack replied calmly, knowing better than to be ruffled by the editor's bad temper.

"No, Jack. You've come in to help put the paper to bed for the week. You don't concentrate on one thing and to hell with everything else. You know how this paper works. Unless it's something massive, I expect all hands on deck on a Wednesday. I'm not impressed."

"Now, hang on a minute!" Jack protested, finally riled. "This could be the biggest thing this paper has covered for years…"

"Bollocks." Bob was already on his way back to his office. "It's a story about a kid who was stolen nineteen years ago. A mass murderer is a big story. This is small fry."

"Not when the father of the child has made the mother keep quiet to protect his marriage, it isn't," Jack muttered.

Bob stopped in his tracks, turned and came back to his desk. "What did you say?"

Jack groaned. Now he'd done it. He hadn't meant to say it out loud, but he couldn't take the injustice of that attack on him. Nor could he come up with a convincing story, and Bob was still waiting.

"My office, ten minutes," Bob barked and stalked off once more.

Ten minutes. As if that was going to save him.

***

Bob leaned back in his chair and looked at Jack enquiringly. "Right then, shall we start from the beginning?" he asked.

"Beginning of what?" Jack asked innocently, back to being calm and in control.

"That statement about the father of the baby. I take it you've met him, got permission to include him in the story?"

Of course! This was Jack's way out. He'd forgotten how keen Bob was on protocol. He would never allow anything to go to print which might lead to a lawsuit.

"The mother has asked me to keep his name out of it."

"In other words, we're back where we were with a bog-standard story. Look, I'm sorry, Jack, but I can't leave you on just this one job. We haven't got enough stuff for this week as it is, and it doesn't sound as though this story will be ready on time. Or am I wrong?"

"Next week," Jack admitted.

"Right then, put it on ice for now. I need you to get down to the school on Weston Road. They're running a road safety initiative, and they've asked us to put something in this week."

Jack knew better than to argue. He was in enough hot water, and if he wasn't careful, Bob would insist he put the story in this week. He couldn't let Carol down when he'd promised he wouldn't publish without her reading it first.

***

It was beginning to irritate Peter and Valerie that Stella Cox was still staying with them. Neither of them could see any reason why she was still there. Granted, she still had her ankle bandaged, but surely she could have taken a taxi to the station and gone home by train. But no, she seemed intent on getting every last ounce of sympathy out of them. It wasn't even as though she had a claim against them. She'd already had a loss adjuster out to the hotel, who'd assured her there was nothing wrong with the staircase or the hotel in general. If anything, he'd said, she was lucky how much effort they'd taken to accommodate her after her fall. Peter had hoped that would be the end of it and she would leave, but then she'd announced her intention of staying for another week—"Just until I'm mobile again." Now, to add insult to injury, she'd decided she needed someone to go with her to the health centre.

"I need some more painkillers," she told Peter, "and with the state I'm in, I'd prefer not to go alone. I've booked a taxi, and I thought one of those waitresses could go with me. I don't know the area, you see, and as I had the accident in your hotel, I feel you should be helping me as much as you can."

Personally, he felt they'd given her enough help already, never mind letting Shona go with her, assuming by 'one of those waitresses' she didn't mean Tina. Still, it was only four o'clock, and they could spare someone for an hour. Whether Shona would actually agree to go with Stella was another matter. If she said no, he supposed it would be left to him or Valerie to do it.

To his relief, Shona jumped at the chance.

"Are you sure you don't mind?" Peter asked. "It's not in your job description, playing nursemaid to the guests."

"It's okay. I don't mind. Honestly."

"Well, just remember she's not the easiest woman to cope with."

"Don't worry." Shona smiled. "I won't give her any more cause for complaint."

"That's why I asked you, not Tina. Knowing my daughter, there'd have been murder before they reached the health centre, and I wouldn't like to guess at whose."

Shona laughed. "At least it would get rid of Stella once and for all."

"Don't even go there." Peter shuddered. "That reporter of Carol's would have a field day."

***

The health centre was as busy as any GP's by the time Shona and Stella arrived.

"You have an appointment with the nurse, Mrs. Cox," the receptionist greeted them.

"I want to see a doctor, not a nurse," Stella demanded.

"I'm sorry, but you did say you only wanted the dressing on your ankle changing. That doesn't need a doctor to do it."

"But what if there's something wrong with it? It should be healing by now, shouldn't it?"

"If you're worried, you should go over to A and E, I believe that was where you said you were treated in the first place?"

Stella had met her match with this woman, and Shona hid a smile as she watched the verbal battle. Peter and Valerie would be envious of how the receptionist was in charge—in this environment, the 'customer' had no rights at all.

With Shona's help, Stella eventually hobbled her way to a seat, continuing to mutter darkly about complaints to everyone from the practice manager to the GMC. Shona said nothing, waiting with much more patience than her companion, but it wasn't long before they were sent through to the nurse.

***

Mary's face paled when her daughter helped her next patient into the treatment room. This wasn't supposed to happen! Shona never came here. Their GP was close to where they lived, not over here, on the other side of Chester. There should never have been a reason for her daughter to come here.

"I need my ankle re-strapping," Stella declared, unaware of the tension between mother and daughter. "I would have preferred to see a doctor, but they seem to think I'll be okay with a nurse instead. Are you actually listening to me?"

"Yes. Of course!" Mary smiled, pulling herself together, indicating the treatment couch.

"You can go now," Stella told Shona. "This nurse will help me back out when she's finished."

***

Numbly, Shona sat in the waiting area, jumbled thoughts careering around her head. Even with her doubts about the coincidence of her mother's name and that of the woman who'd worked in the maternity unit when Carol's baby was taken, there'd still been a hope at the back of her mind that she was seeing connections that weren't there. Now she was faced with the very strong possibility the mysterious Mary in the maternity unit had been her mother.

Her mother who ended up with a child that was never officially adopted.

Chapter Twenty-Two

CAROL LOOKED CURIOUSLY at Shona as she walked into the kitchen after her trip to the health centre with Stella. The girl was paler than usual and collected her pad and pen, moving towards the door without saying a word.

"Wait a minute."

Shona stopped and turned back but wouldn't meet Carol's eyes.

"How did it go with Stella Cox?"

"Fine. She wasn't too happy when they made her see the nurse rather than a doctor, but she seems fine now."

"So if she was okay, what's upset you?"

"Lies. Deception. Parents. That enough for you?"

"Sounds heavy. Want to talk about it?"

"I don't know." Shona sighed. "I certainly don't want to talk to my so-called parents about it anymore."

"Right. Give me a shout when you're ready for someone to listen. I promise not to judge anybody, to give you whatever support you think you want."

Shona blinked back tears and hurried out of the door.

***

It was much later that evening before Shona and Carol could sit down together. Carol broke her usual rules and got them a couple of drinks from the bar.

"You look as though you need this," she said.

Shona nodded and took a few sips, setting her glass down before she spoke. "You know when we went to the hospital and found out about that nurse, Mary, who'd left?"

"The agency one? Yes."

"Well...my mother has just got herself a job." Shona swallowed hard. "At the health centre as a nurse."

Carol frowned and shook her head, not yet grasping what Shona was trying to say.

"Her name's Mary as well, Carol. She and my dad told me a few nights ago that I was adopted, but when I tried to trace my birth parents, the adoption agency didn't have any record of me. They said it was probably a private arrangement between my parents and my birth mother, but when I asked them they said it wasn't, and—"

"Just a minute," Carol interrupted her. "You're not getting around to saying you think I'm your birth mother, are you?"

Shona gulped, nodded and licked suddenly dry lips.

"No." Carol shook her head. "It's too much of a coincidence. There must have been lots of nurses in that hospital called Mary, and why on earth would they steal you?"

"Somebody did," Shona said. "And if they didn't, why can't they tell me who my birth parents are? If I wasn't officially adopted, they must know them."

"Maybe they're trying to protect you? For all you know, your birth parents could be in prison or something. There's all sorts of reasons why your mum and dad wouldn't tell you."

"Including that my mother might have stolen me..."

Carol wanted to believe it with all her heart. To finally have an answer to what had happened to her baby without putting something in the paper and owing Valerie and Peter, and she couldn't ask for a better result than Shona being her daughter, but she didn't dare hope. She had to keep her feet on the ground for both their sakes, wait and see what came of the press appeal first. Maybe it would prompt Shona's parents to tell her the truth, and if they did, and it turned out Shona was Carol's daughter... all well and good. But she wouldn't hope—couldn't face the disappointment of them both being wrong.

***

Jack hadn't been expecting to hear from Carol until the weekend, when he planned to take the finished story over to the hotel for her to check through before it went to press. He frowned at the message she'd sent, asking to see him. It must be urgent, whatever it was; she'd even given him her address and requested they meet there rather than at the hotel. Surely she hadn't changed her mind after all this? Apart from the amount of work he'd put into the story, he wanted to help her find her daughter, get her life back on track.

By eleven o'clock on Thursday morning, he was sitting in her kitchen with a cup of coffee and listening to her relate the conversation she'd had with Shona the evening before.

Like Shona, Jack arrowed straight to the fact that Mary hadn't been telling her daughter the truth all along. There had to be a reason for that, something she was trying to cover up.

"Don't say it," Carol warned, seeing his expression.

"We have to talk to Shona's mother. You do know that, don't you?"

"No. Look, I told Shona it's a coincidence, and I'm still sticking to that. Don't you see, Jack? If it was a perfect world, Shona would be my daughter, and I don't mind telling you, I'd be over the moon about it. But if I've learnt anything in this life, it's that coincidences don't happen and the world isn't perfect, at least not for me."

"You ended up working for Peter Clarke."

"Meaning what?" Carol asked, her face flushing with colour.

"He's the baby's father, isn't he?" Jack said.

For a moment, Carol looked as if she was going to deny it, but Jack knew he was right. Eventually, she sighed. "Off the record?"

"You have my word."

Carol nodded. "Yes, he's the father. We had an affair, and Val doesn't know. So you see? It wasn't a coincidence. I'm a chef, and I was already working at the hotel when they bought it. They asked me if I'd stay on, and I couldn't see any reason not to."

He'd assumed she'd applied for the job with Peter and Valerie after the baby, which meant she was right; he couldn't put that down to coincidence.

"What about Shona? Are you going to let me talk to her?"

"She won't be able to tell you anything."

He sighed, losing patience. This was ridiculous. Carol was determined there could never be a happy ending for her. She hadn't struck him as some sort of martyr, yet she seemed to be punishing herself for not trying to find her baby sooner. Or was she afraid of the repercussions if Shona did turn out to be her daughter? Maybe she couldn't cope with it being so close to home and would be happier if there was no link, no matter how tenuous, to anyone that she knew. The journalist in him was warring with the male psyche which, at that moment, wanted to protect her at all costs and make it come right for her.

"You don't understand," Carol said with a smile. "No matter what happened in the past, those people have raised my daughter for nineteen years. They must love her or they wouldn't have done it. You've got to see it from both sides, haven't you?"

"Not really, but you're obviously determined to do so. I'm sorry, love, but I see these people as criminals. They could have adopted a child through the proper channels, but they didn't. They chose to break the law, to do something morally wrong. I can't understand why you don't want them found and prosecuted."

"Prosecuted?" she asked in alarm.

"You didn't think they were going to get away unscathed, did you? Not once this comes out. At the very least, the police will re-open the case—they won't be able to ride the publicity if they don't."

Watching Carol's face, Jack knew he'd gone too far. She was on the verge of saying she wouldn't go on with this search. For reasons he couldn't comprehend, she was now intent on protecting not only Peter Clarke but the people who'd stolen her baby.

He could only think of one person in that moment who could talk sense into her.

"Get your coat. We're going out," he requested crisply.

"Out where?"

"To visit someone."

***

Gladys's eyebrows rose when her son walked in with a woman she'd never seen before. He hadn't done that for years—bring a new girlfriend home to meet her. In fact, she hadn't been aware he was seeing anybody, and his opening words sent a shiver of dismay down her spine.

"Mum, I've brought someone to see you. This is Carol, the lady whose baby was stolen."

Gladys sniffed and looked her up and down before waving her to a seat.

"So you're the one who couldn't be bothered looking for her daughter for nineteen years," she said bluntly.

Carol blinked. She hadn't been expecting that. She looked at Jack for help, but he said nothing, leaving his mother to get the message across for him.

"Why has it taken you so long?" Gladys continued, albeit surprised that her son wasn't saying anything.

"It hasn't been easy," Carol said.

"What hasn't? For God's sake, whoever it was that stole your baby broke the law, and you've sat back and let them get away with it. Your daughter isn't going to be happy about that, is she?"

Nobody had pointed out that Carol may be the one in the wrong here. So far, she'd had nothing but support from everybody around her, but Gladys was turning the whole argument on its head.

Again, Carol looked at Jack.

"Not considered it from that angle before, have you?" he asked quietly.

Gladys smiled, out of relief as much as anything else. "Oh, I see what you're playing at now. You've brought her here for me to knock some sense into her, have you?"

"Somebody has to. The trouble is, Mum, Carol has got it into her head that she has to protect everybody except herself. She doesn't want the people who stole her baby to be prosecuted. She doesn't want the baby's father to be named in case it breaks his marriage up—"

"And what about your daughter?" Gladys asked sharply. "Don't you think she deserves to know the truth?"

"She's happy with the parents she's got," Jack replied on Carol's behalf. "She won't want to know the truth."

"Stop it!" Carol begged, finally. "You've made your point. You're right. I haven't looked at this logically. I'm not the one in the wrong here, they are."

Jack sighed. "Thank God for that. Now, are we going ahead or not?"

"Yes. Of course we are."

"And you'll let me name this Mary in the article?"

There was only the briefest hesitation before Carol nodded.

Gladys patted her hand. "That's a good girl. You find your daughter and put things right once and for all."

***

"So was your friend all right when you dropped her off?" Gladys asked when Jack returned home alone later that evening.

"Yes, she was fine. She needed someone to show her the other side of the coin."

"You mean you needed someone to tell her how it is and you thought I was enough of a dragon to do it for you," Gladys retorted.

"It worked, didn't it?"

"She's a nice woman. She doesn't deserve this. Poor lass has spent all these years thinking about everybody but herself. It's no way to live your life, isn't that."

Gladys had always maintained that Jack was too good for most of the women who were out there, but a brief chat to Carol had made her wonder if she could be right for him. He needed someone in his life, and if it was someone who worked locally, there was less danger of him moving away. As for Carol: she deserved a bit of happiness after all she'd been through. It sounded like she had few friends and even less support. Same as anyone else, people were happy to offer support, but ask them to put themselves on the line and they'd run a mile.

Decision made, Gladys smiled at her son. "You can bring her for tea next time. I'd like to get to know her better."

Jack stared at her, startled. "Why would you want to get to know her? I'll not be seeing her again after this."

"Then you're a bloody fool! Can't you see what's under your nose? That girl dotes on you—I saw the way she looked at you—and, as for you…well, you wouldn't be getting this involved if she was a woman like your Rose was."

"I'm not involved."

"Aren't you? Then why are you running round after her? Getting into bother because you aren't doing the job you should be doing at the paper? I'm not daft, lad, even if you are. You like her, and it's time you moved on with your life."

It was a complete turnaround for Gladys. So far, she'd fought tooth and nail to keep him single and with her, but it was time he moved on.

"Has Lucy been round?" he asked.

She chuckled. "Your sister's not daft. She's a lot like me, tells it as it is. I've been a bit of a selfish old woman, and it's not fair. I'll not be here forever for you, and what will you do then? Grow into some crusty old bachelor living alone? I don't want that for you, lad. Don't you miss out on happiness like poor Carol has had to do."

"She might not even be interested."

"And she might be. At least give it a try."

***

Mary was quietly dreading the weekly paper coming out. She knew she wouldn't have a chance to get rid of it before Shona arrived home, and anyway, what would be the point? It would be the subject of the day at the hotel when the story about the chef's baby came out—the story Mary had never wanted telling. But as it was, she got a reprieve that week: there was nothing at all in the paper about it, and for a brief couple of hours, she could hope there never would be. Until Shona came home.

"Is that the local paper, Mum?"

"It is. Why? Did you want to look at it?"

"Not really. Carol's article isn't going in it until next week—Jack's agreed to let her have a look at it first, and they go to press on a Wednesday, so it was all a bit tight in the end."

"So it's definitely going in then?" Mary asked, piling on the agony.

"It is. Why? Is there something you want to tell me?"

As challenges went, it was too direct for Mary to ignore. She drew a deep breath, remembered Terry's words, and decided to tell Shona the truth—or some of it.

"I was working in the hospital when it happened, but I only vaguely remember it. You know how big that place is… We didn't get to mix much with the specialist units."

"So you weren't working in maternity?"

"No. Why do you ask?"

"Because you've been so cagey about being a nurse. I mean, why didn't you just tell me you'd got a job at the health centre?"

Mary shrugged. "I didn't think it was important."

"Not important? I'd have been so proud to know you're a nurse, Mum."

Again, Mary shrugged then turned away. "Well, you know now, don't you?"

"So that's the end of it? I know now, so we don't need to talk about it anymore?"

Mary knew then she had to pull herself together. If this was how she reacted to a simple conversation with Shona, how on earth was she going to cope when the story actually came out? Her eyes drifted to the letter for Shona, which had arrived that morning. It was from the university, and Mary had deliberately kept it from her. But maybe now was the time to persuade her daughter to go back, if not for good then at least to see what her options were. Maybe at the end of next week... But, in the meantime, she had to get Shona's mind off her nursing career, and in Mary's opinion, the best form of defence was attack.

"Oh, for heaven's sake. So I was a nurse! Big deal! It wasn't as though I even worked at one specific hospital. Most of us were agency nurses in those days." She turned away to fill the kettle.

"Like the one called Mary who worked on the maternity unit?" Shona said.

Mary's hands shook as she switched off the tap. "Do you want a cup of tea?" she asked.

"No, thank you. I'm going to get an early night." Shona sighed. "Good night, Mum."

"Night, love."

Mary leaned heavily on the edge of the sink as the door closed behind Shona. The way her heart was pounding...if she hadn't known better, she'd have thought she was having a heart attack.

Chapter Twenty-Three

Shona had assumed she'd never hear from the university again after she left. She'd made it clear to her tutor she didn't think she'd be coming back, but now they'd written to her asking her to get in touch and review her options. The last thing she wanted was to let anybody down. She'd come back home for her mother's sake but Mary had a job now; maybe she could cope on her own again. As for the hotel—at the end of the day, it was just a job, and if she left, Peter and Valerie would need to find another waitress, which wasn't going to be too difficult.

As always, it was Carol to whom she turned for advice, and who was as encouraging as ever.

"If they want to see you, you have to go. What does your mum say about it?"

"She thinks I should go as well. Says she feels guilty about me giving up uni for her."

Carol pursed her lips but said nothing. It was probably lucky Jack wasn't around to hear that; he'd instantly decide it was suspicious.

"They want me to go and see them as soon as possible."

"Well, that's not a problem, is it? Peter may want you here at the weekend, though. How about if you go over there next week?"

"Oh, no. I want to be here for you when the story comes out in the paper."

"I've got Peter and Valerie, and I suppose I've got Jack as well. I don't want you missing this chance for me. After what I said about your parents forcing you to come home, I'd be a right hypocrite if I asked you to ignore that letter for my sake, wouldn't I?"

Shona bit her lip anxiously. She'd resented having to give up her course for her parents, but this was different. She wanted to be here for Carol because there was no predicting what the reaction would be to that story, how many crank calls may come in. Carol was going to need a friend. Peter would have his own problems to cope with when it broke, although his loyalty would be to his wife, not his one-time mistress.

"I'll not forgive you if you refuse to go, you know." Carol carried on as though she could read every thought that was going through Shona's head.

Shona smiled and hugged her. "You know what? I really, really hope you are my mother."

"So do I, love," Carol replied huskily. "Maybe if this was a fairy story…but it's real life, and that can be cruel at the best of times."

***

Jack had taken his mother's words on board, and when he dropped the story off for Carol at the hotel on Friday morning, he tentatively asked her if she'd like to go out with him for the day on Sunday—"We can discuss any problems you've found in the article over lunch somewhere."

"Yes, why not. That would be nice," Carol said.

He could have kicked himself for making it sound as though he only wanted to discuss the story, but she'd agreed. She might've refused if he'd made it sound more like a date. He'd have to see how it went—there was nothing to say he had to bring up the story if things were going okay.

"Getting a bit close to him, aren't you?" Tina remarked after Jack had left.

Carol smiled at her. "Do you have a problem with that?"

"Nothing to do with me, but I wouldn't have thought you'd have trusted him, being a reporter and all."

"Well, Tina, I'm getting quite good at knowing who I can and can't trust nowadays."

"No, you're not. In fact, you'd be surprised if you knew who you should really be trusting in all of this."

Carol shook her head as the girl flounced off. That chip on her shoulder was no smaller even though she'd got herself into college now. It was a lot calmer around the hotel through the day, but they all knew about it when Tina returned home. Her anger at her father seemed to be growing rather than fizzling out, and Peter had taken the route of 'least said soonest mended', leaving everyone else to cope with it.

Unlike Tina, Valerie was delighted when Carol told her she was going out for the day with Jack.

"Don't rush back. I'm sure we can cope for an odd evening without you being here. It's going to be quiet anyway—there's only Stella Cox eating here every night, and the other guests won't be as difficult as her."

"Well, I'll prepare as much as I can before I go," Carol promised.

"No, you won't. We'll run like we do on a Tuesday, when it's your proper day off. Look on this as a holiday—we'll even pay you!" Valerie laughed, and Carol smiled and nodded.

"It isn't a date, you know," she said. "He's only suggested this in case I find anything wrong with the story."

"Of course he has," Valerie tormented. "If you want to believe that, you go ahead. I won't argue with you."

"I'm too old for dates anyway."

"Too old, my foot! We're never too old for a bit of romance. You get off and enjoy yourself, my girl."

The last person to call Carol 'girl' had been her mother many years ago, but she had to admit it didn't sound too odd in some ways. She often felt she had allowed her life to pass her by after Peter. She hadn't had many dates, definitely no serious relationships. She was in her forties, not old, and certainly not too old for a fresh start in her life. Her heart lifted, and she smiled at Valerie.

"You know what? Maybe I will have a good time. You never know, do you?"

"He's a nice man, Carol, and an honest one...if a journalist can be honest. He won't let you down or mess you about."

Carol studied Valerie for a moment but concluded it was an innocent comment. Sometimes she suspected Valerie knew about her and Peter, but no. Carol had always maintained the father had left her before she knew she was pregnant, which was kind of true. As for Jack—he was definitely an honest man; he'd proved that by the story she'd read. Everything she'd asked him to do was in there, and he'd kept the rest out like she'd asked. It probably meant it wasn't as powerful as she'd have liked, and he still had to get it past his editor, who may want it altering, but she was happy with it.

***

Stella's lips tightened as she banged her 'phone down. So Graham had already put the house on the market, had he? *Her* home! The man was making it blatantly obvious he had every intention of going ahead with all his plans, including moving in with that woman, breaking up their marriage. It was definitely time for her to go home, to sort this out before it could go any further.

Peter was delighted when Stella announced her intention of leaving the hotel. He'd begun to think she would be staying with them forever.

"If you'll prepare the bill, I'll take it for my husband to settle," she said.

"No. I'm sorry. You need to pay it in full before you leave."

"I don't think so..."

"Mrs. Cox, those are the terms of the hotel. I can't waive them for one person."

"And where am I supposed to get that sort of money from?"

Peter didn't reply to that rather silly question. She was the type of woman who'd walk round with credit and store cards; she'd certainly have a card for their joint account, and even if her husband had frozen it, Graham was an honourable man who would know this bill had to be paid.

"I'll have to contact my husband before I can settle it."

"That's fine. I'll have it ready for you."

"I must say, I'd have expected more understanding of my situation," she snapped as she hobbled back to her room.

Peter sighed, shook his head. How on earth had that poor chap managed to live with her at all?

Valerie and Carol were equally delighted when he told them their guest was finally leaving. Her temper had got worse as the week went on, and they'd all had to bite their tongues as they struggled to cope with her. The sooner she went the better for all of them.

"Tina'll be sorry not to have had a chance to say goodbye to her," Valerie joked.

"Don't even go there!" Peter warned. "It's best if she's out of the way. I wouldn't put it past the woman to refuse to pay her bill if she was reminded about the complaint she made about Tina."

"Do you really think she's forgotten?"

"I hope so. I'm going to have enough problems getting her to pay as it is."

He explained about the argument with her over the bill, and Valerie shook her head. She might have known they weren't going to get rid of her that easily. Stella was bound to try and wriggle out of paying.

***

The conversation with Graham was brief and bitter on both sides, but he insisted she pay the bill out of their joint account—whether out of a sense of responsibility or to prevent her using her credit card, she didn't know. Any other woman would have realised there could be a problem with the cards, but not Stella. He wouldn't dare cancel them without talking to her first. He, in his turn, was determined to get her back home before he told her what measures he'd already taken to dissolve their marriage. Unknown to her, there was a solicitor's letter waiting for her when she got back. He had no reason to delay things. There would be a divorce, and after that, he intended to marry Melinda. Life, for Graham at least, was looking rosy.

***

Peter rubbed his hands in delight when Stella's taxi drove away from the hotel. The nightmare was finally over. She'd paid her bill, albeit reluctantly, not leaving them a tip even though they'd bent over backwards to accommodate her after her fall. In truth, the 'tip' for Peter was the fact she'd finally gone. Both he and Valerie had been thinking she'd stay with them as a permanent guest if they weren't careful.

"She's gone then?" Valerie asked when he went back into the office with a smile on his face.

"She has and good riddance."

"Don't be too cocky. If her husband's sold the house, she might end up coming back."

"Oh no she won't. We've got no vacancies as from now if she rings us."

"And what do we do if she turns up on the doorstep?" Valerie teased.

"We'll still be full."

"You couldn't turn a guest away if you tried. I'll bet if that woman comes back, you'll give her a room just like that." She clicked her fingers at him and laughed.

"You can make your bet, but you won't win," he retorted with a show of determination she'd rarely seen before.

Maybe Peter had finally learnt his lesson about letting people stay when they were full. What she didn't tell him was that, despite her attitude, she actually felt a little bit sorry for Stella Cox. It had been a cowardly way for her husband to leave her, going off when she needed him beside her. And she did. Despite everything, a fall like she'd suffered meant she'd needed support from someone other than strangers. Even Mike Land had refused to stay and support her, running off with his tail between his legs as soon as he realised he'd lost his wife as well. They were a totally selfish pair, but they didn't deserve that sort of treatment. Nobody did.

Watching his wife's face and guessing her thoughts, Peter smiled and patted her hand. "Come on. The whole lot of them have gone now. They're not our problem anymore."

"I know, but if only Stella Cox and Mike Land had listened to their spouses, this wouldn't have happened, would it? Mike's wife told him she'd leave if he didn't stop gambling, and Stella Cox did such a vile thing pretending to be pregnant—she must have known she'd lose him when the truth came out."

"They were two people who didn't think things through before they did them. There's plenty of them around." Peter shrugged, well aware that his own actions of nineteen years ago still had the potential to lead to repercussions for him if Carol didn't keep her word or Tina refused to keep quiet.

Sometimes he felt as though he was walking on a knife edge between the two of them, although, to be fair to Carol, it was his daughter he was most worried about. As long as he kept out of her way, he felt reasonably safe, but how long could he do that? Certainly not for the rest of his life. He loved his daughter despite all the problems they had with her, and he wasn't prepared to lose her over this. Wouldn't it make more sense to come clean with Valerie and take the consequences whatever they might be?

Almost as though he'd conjured her up out of thin air, Carol breezed into the office, smiling at them both and sharing a joke with Valerie, and he knew he couldn't do it. He wasn't bothered for himself, but he couldn't bear to see these two women lose their friendship. He'd caused enough problems for Carol over the years, whether he knew about them or not, and he couldn't put her through more grief now.

"What's wrong?" she asked, noticing his expression even as he struggled to smile at her.

"Nothing. I'm just a bit concerned about that payment of Stella Cox's," he hedged.

"It went straight through, didn't it? If it was a cheque, yes, but not with a card." Valerie laughed. "You just can't believe she's actually gone at long last."

"I suppose so."

"Anyway, we've got more important things to talk about than her. Carol won't be working on Sunday, so we need to make sure we've got a menu on that I can cope with."

Peter looked at Carol with raised eyebrows, and she blushed slightly.

"By the look on your face, I'd hazard a guess you're off out with Jack."

"It's not a date," Carol said, like she'd done with Valerie.

Valerie laughed and shook her head. "Basically, she's in denial. Can't believe a man might want to take her out just for herself without an excuse."

"He was the one who said it was so we could discuss the story," Carol protested.

"Only because you'd have refused to go if he said it was a proper date."

"I give up. You've already made your minds up, the pair of you."

Peter laughed. "Don't be tarring me with Val's brush, lady. I haven't actually said a word, have I?"

"You wouldn't dare," Carol retorted, coming the closest she'd ever been to blurting out the truth about their affair.

"Anyway," Peter said, "can I leave you two to decide on a reduced menu for Sunday? I need to get down to the bank."

Valerie winked at Carol as her husband left them. *Typical man*, that wink seemed to say, *scurrying off as soon as the discussion got too heated.*

***

It was many years since Jack had felt nervous about going out with a woman, but on that Sunday morning, he felt like a teenager all over again. The only consolation for him was the expression on Carol's face when she opened her door to him.

Carol had spent hours wondering what to wear, finally deciding that casual was best. She'd also read the story five times in an effort to pick up on something, anything, they could talk about and was still trying to convince herself this wasn't a date.

Jack smiled his relief and shook his head. "You look as uneasy as me if that's at all possible."

"I know. This feels odd, somehow. Does it to you as well?"

"Contact with any woman other than my family is odd for me these days. Sorry, that came out all wrong, didn't it?"

Carol laughed and invited him in for coffee before they set off. If nothing else, she knew quite categorically now this was a date, like Valerie had told her it was. She'd been in Jack's company enough to be able to chat to him about anything and everything, so why on earth did they both feel uneasy now?

In Jack's case, it was his mother's doing. She'd made such a big thing of this day, he felt as though he was supposed to be proposing at the end of it, not just seeing how he got on with Carol. In her case, it was mostly down to Valerie's continual teasing. The truth was, neither Jack nor Carol was ready to be pushed into a relationship, but it showed how attracted they were to each other that they were actually going out together.

By the time they'd drunk their coffee and were sitting in the car, their initial awkwardness was gone and they were once again chatting easily to each other. The time flew by, and it was only as they were strolling around Conway's picturesque little harbour that Jack brought up the subject of the story. He'd deliberately avoided it until then, but time was passing and he needed to know at some point if Carol wanted to make any changes. He certainly didn't want to have to wait for another week before it went to press and almost glowed with delight at her praise—and sighed his relief—when she said there was nothing she wanted to change.

"So it's going to be in the paper next week," he said.

She nodded and smiled. "I'm ready for it."

It was time to find her daughter.

Chapter Twenty-Four

It was rare for Gladys to take any interest in Jack's reports in the newspaper, but this was a special week and she could scarcely wait for it to come through their letterbox on Friday morning. She'd already told all her friends to look out for it, making sure they knew how big a story her son had been asked to cover. As soon as she'd read it for herself, she waited for the 'phone to ring, and when nothing happened, she put on her coat and set off to see Ethel. Of all her friends, Ethel was the one who'd shown the most interest when Gladys had told her what was going on.

It was Gladys who made the tea for them both; her friend was struggling more each day to get around, and Gladys feared Ethel's daughter would put her in a nursing home soon rather than take the responsibility for her care on her shoulders.

"Have you read the paper then?" she asked once they were settled with their cups of tea.

"Aye. It's a good story that your lad's done. I'll tell you what, though, I already know all about it."

"How could you? It wasn't reported when it happened."

"Didn't need to be. I was a cleaner at the hospital. Don't you remember me telling you about it?"

Gladys didn't remember, but she nodded slowly anyway. Jack had asked her how she knew about Carol's baby; it must've been because Ethel had mentioned it at the time, and it had stuck in her memory all these years.

Now, Ethel frowned as they pored over the paper. "She was a right rum 'un, was that Mary, you know. Didn't have any time at all for us cleaners, not like the regular staff. And it was weird because they didn't usually put agency nurses on the maternity unit."

"Why not?" To Gladys, a nurse was a nurse; surely she should be able to do her job in any department.

"They were specialised in maternity. I suppose they had more training to work in there, I don't know, but I do know we couldn't understand what she was doing there."

Gladys didn't say any more about it, sipping her tea and wondering if her old friend was in the early stages of dementia. No hospital would have allowed an untrained nurse onto a ward and especially not a maternity unit.

***

Jack was intrigued when Gladys reported on her conversation with Ethel. Whilst his mother didn't put too much credence on Ethel's words, he wasn't so sure. From what he'd seen of his mother's friend, there was nothing at all wrong with her mind. She was as bright as a button in that respect.

"All right, what's on your mind now?" Gladys asked sharply, and he realised he'd been fiddling with the pen he kept with him at all times. He put it back in his pocket.

"I think I need to talk to Carol."

"I should hope you do, now that you're courting."

"Not for that reason, and like I said before, we aren't courting, we're just good friends. I need to talk to her about what Ethel said. In fact…do you think Ethel would talk to me and Carol?"

"I don't see why not. She'll be glad of the company, I should think. Why?"

"I don't know. I'm getting more and more intrigued by this Mary. She crops up so much in all of this I'm beginning to wonder if she really was the one who stole the baby."

"And you think the police didn't catch on to that at the time?"

"Maybe they didn't find her. Who's to say she was a genuine nurse at all?"

"If you ask me, your imagination's running away with you," Gladys retorted. "You've always been the same—get an idea in your head and you don't know when to stop."

"Which is why I do the job I do, Mum." He grinned. "If nothing else, I need to be able to look deeper into things than most people do."

She sniffed but said no more. She'd never thought journalism was a proper career. He should have done as his father had wanted and followed him into the insurance business. It was much more secure than being on a newspaper. But Jack had been his own man, had known what he wanted to do, and there'd been no gainsaying him. Journalism was what he loved, and that was an end to it.

***

Tina couldn't quite hide her little smirk of triumph as her father set the paper down with a sigh.

"So, Dad, how does it feel now it's all out in the open?"

"Nothing to do with me, is it? I don't see any mention of the father of the baby in there, do you?"

"I don't need to read it. I already know the truth."

"You know some of it, yes. Not all, by any means. So, did you want something, Tina, or are you here to cause trouble?"

"I need to know what's happening with Shona. Is she coming back or will you be looking for another waitress? Because if you are, Kelly could do with a part-time job."

"I don't know whether Shona's coming back or not, and I certainly don't want one of your friends working here."

"Do you think you've got a choice? If I want Kelly working here, I think it'll be fine. Don't you, Dad?"

"Oh, no. I won't be blackmailed by you over who works at the hotel. After all, do you want it going downhill before you get your hands on it? Because it will with the likes of Kelly working here."

Tina pursed her lips but had to admit he could be right. Kelly would exactly give the right impression of the hotel; her dress style and attitude were just two of the reasons she hadn't been able to get herself a job anywhere else.

"Okay. I'll concede on that one. But we do need to know if Shona's coming back because it makes it a hell of a lot harder for me and Carol with only one waitress."

"It's been two days, Tina. I'm sure you can cope for another evening between you," he snapped.

"And what about the weekend?"

"Your mother'll help out."

Tina frowned. That wasn't ideal. She was used to being able to pick and choose who she served, and with her mother there she wouldn't have any choice. She'd actually have to pull her weight for once.

Tina wasn't the only one missing Shona. Carol had to admit, she wished she hadn't insisted that Shona go to the university. She wanted to talk to someone about the story, and Jack wasn't coming over until Sunday, which meant she had to get through two days on her own. She wouldn't know if anyone had made contact with the newspaper until she saw him—it was unlikely anyone would turn up unsolicited at the hotel, and they'd deliberately left her telephone number and address out of it. Jack didn't want any cranks knowing where she lived or who she was.

Peter had been uneasy ever since the news broke, and Carol could understand why but didn't want to say too much about it in case it upset him even more. And then, of course, there was Tina. Because Shona wasn't there, she was having to work more, and now Peter had refused to let her friend come and work for them. Whilst it was a relief to Carol that he'd done that, he'd still be worried about what Tina might do. It wouldn't take much for her to suddenly decide to break her word and tell Valerie what she knew. Of the three of them, the only one who was carrying on with her life placidly was Valerie, and that was only because she didn't know about the past and what was hanging over them all. Yet.

Carol was brooding on the hornet's nest she'd opened up when Jack arrived at the hotel, asking if he could have a quick word with her. It was Valerie who came to find her, telling her smugly that her 'boyfriend' was here.

"Take him in the lounge and I'll bring you some coffee through," Valerie offered.

Carol tried, and failed, to hide her delight that he'd come, and Valerie grinned as she watched her scurry away. If nothing else came out of this, there might be some happiness at the end of it for Carol, thanks to her meeting the reporter.

Jack smiled and kissed Carol before guiding her to a seat.

"Have you heard something?" she asked eagerly.

"Not at the newspaper, no, but I have heard something from my mother." Briefly, he related her conversation with Ethel, and Carol gasped, sat back in her seat.

"Oh God. It's the Mary thing again, isn't it?"

"Looks like it. Listen, I thought it might be worth us contacting some of the nursing agencies, see if we can track her down—find out why they did put her on maternity."

"What about the hospital? Should we contact them again?"

"I don't know. There's only that one woman who remembered her, isn't there?"

"I wasn't thinking of asking on the unit itself. Maybe we should write to them. At least that way, we should get further than the receptionists, shouldn't we?"

Jack frowned. That would take time, and he wanted quick results for Carol's sake.

"Okay. Leave it with me," he finally said. "I'll try the agencies and, like you say, write to the hospital."

"What about this Ethel? Do we talk to her as well?"

"Yes, I think that might make more sense. I guess Mum shut her up before she got too far into the story. I know she didn't believe her, so I reckon we go and see her. Tomorrow?"

"Tomorrow." Carol nodded. "Although will she not have family visiting her on a Sunday? If she has, we shouldn't disturb them."

"Not according to my mother, she won't. Apparently, the daughter doesn't go near unless she has to," Jack replied grimly, thinking of his sister but aware it could just be the opinion of two elderly ladies unhappy with their offspring. Still, they could always leave if Ethel did have visitors.

"Do you think she might have seen it?" Carol asked; Jack didn't need to ask to know she meant her daughter.

"She may have, but it all depends on how honest her parents have been with her, doesn't it?"

"Would you have told your daughter if she wasn't yours?"

"I'd have told her she was adopted but probably not more than that. They're not likely to admit to stealing her. Of course, there's always the possibility your daughter already suspects—"

"No," Carol interrupted. "I told you. It'd be too perfect. Besides, I can't see that the woman who stole my baby would stay in Chester. She'd move away, cover her tracks."

"Maybe. People do strange things. But I suppose you're right. For all we know, Shona's parents took on some family member's child and were sworn to secrecy for whatever reason."

Carol was a little disappointed he'd found a logical explanation. For as much as she kept saying it was coincidence, she still held a small hope she was wrong.

"Out of interest, is Shona here?" Jack asked.

"No. She had to go to the university, decide what she's going to do about her course."

"You get on well with her, don't you?"

"I do, and she offered to stay, but I couldn't let her do that for me. I've said often enough that her parents were wrong to bring her back home when their marriage broke down. It would have been hypocritical of me to put the same sort of pressure on her when she isn't even related to me."

Jack didn't say anything, but he stored that bit of information at the back of his mind.

There were always reasons for marriages breaking up.

***

In all fairness, Jack didn't think he'd get a response from the hospital or the nursing agencies. He'd told Carol he'd write to them, but he was too impatient to wait.

Experience suggested the best time to approach the hospital was at the weekend when the skeleton admin staff and visitors mingled together, the admin staff easily identifiable by their badges. He glanced round the coffee shop before he decided on the most likely person to approach. She was in her fifties, killing time as she chatted to one of the cleaners, who finally glanced at her watch and left her. With a smile and a nod, she indicated the seat opposite when he asked if it was free.

"I should be getting back to the office, but it's so boring being in on your own as cover."

"I can imagine," he said. "Beryl—you don't mind me calling you Beryl, do you? I'm Jack, by the way."

"You visiting someone, are you?"

"Do you want the tactful answer or the honest one?" he replied with an engaging smile.

"Let's go for the honest one, shall we?"

"I'm trying to trace a missing baby."

"Not the one that's in the paper?"

"Yes. I wrote the story."

Beryl's eyes widened, and she leaned forward slightly in her seat. Here was a woman who clearly loved a good gossip, but Jack couldn't afford to be choosy.

"There was a nurse here at the time who worked for an agency, but there's no trace of her in hospital records, and I need to talk to her."

"Oh, that's nonsense!" she said. "No computerised record, maybe, but she'll be there in the archives, you mark my words. In fact, we could have a look now if you want?" She was already on her feet. "I know we've only ever used a couple of agencies, so she had to come from one or the other of them."

Jack followed her along the corridor to some offices and beyond them what looked to be an old ward stacked floor to ceiling with shelves and boxes of paper, which Beryl sifted through at speed. In some ways, she reminded him of a younger version of his mother, eager to help if it led to a bit of company and, hopefully, some gossip she could pass on to her colleagues on Monday.

Two hours later, they sat back and looked at each other, thoroughly baffled. They'd gone through all the records of agency staff who'd been employed at the hospital over the last twenty years. Nowhere was there any mention of a nurse called Mary who'd come from an agency.

"Maybe they used another agency," he mused aloud, searching for answers.

"It wouldn't matter," Beryl said. "We'd still have to have the records. With medical issues, things can blow up years after treatment, so we'd definitely have it. Are you sure you've got her name right?"

Jack nodded grimly. "I've spoken to two people who worked with her. She was here, and she was on the maternity unit at the time the baby was stolen."

Beryl looked at him wide-eyed. "You think she took the baby."

"I don't want to jump to any conclusions," he replied hastily.

Already he was regretting all he'd said to her and hoped desperately she didn't contact the paper. If she did, his job could be on the line. He'd broken the golden rule of not speaking to anybody about an ongoing story. If it hit the social networks before they'd completed it, he'd definitely be for the high jump.

Chapter Twenty-Five

Ethel loved having visitors. As she got older and less mobile, a knock on the door was the highlight of her day, and she welcomed Jack and Carol warmly. Just like Gladys had done, Carol made the tea for them all, guided by Ethel's shouted instructions from her chair. Once they were settled, Ethel looked from one to the other of them brightly.

"I bet you've been talking to your mum about what I told her, haven't you?" she asked Jack.

"You remember her coming then?"

"Of course I do. It was only a couple of days ago. I'm not senile yet, you know," she retorted with a twinkling smile. She looked at Carol then. "And you, I'll guess, are the young woman who had her baby stolen."

Carol nodded.

"Gladys has already met you, hasn't she? Seems to think you two'll be getting married sooner or later." Ethel followed that up with a chuckle at the outraged looks on their faces. "We have to talk about something, and there's not a lot happening in our own lives. Anyway, you're not here about that, are you? What do you want to know?"

"This nurse who was working on maternity—you told Mum you couldn't understand why she was there?"

Ethel nodded and pursed her lips, well aware that Gladys hadn't believed her and wondering if she should say anything, not wanting Jack to be dismissive of her opinions as well.

"It was strange, that's all. They didn't usually allow agency nurses to do anything other than the normal wards."

So far, Jack hadn't said anything to Carol about his meeting with Beryl the day before, but it felt like an appropriate time to tell them what he had, or rather, hadn't found out.

"Well, I can't say as it surprises me," Ethel said while Carol gasped—more at the fact he'd kept his visit to himself than anything else. "I said to Gladys that she seemed a bit strange. It makes sense she'd have pretended to be a nurse if she wanted to get close enough to steal someone's baby for her own."

"So you don't think it was a spur-of-the-moment thing?"

"No. I'd say she knew exactly what she was doing."

"But surely the police would have realised that?" Carol interrupted them. "Why didn't you tell them?"

"They didn't interview me. I was just a cleaner. We came and went, more or less invisible to the doctors and nurses, and I wasn't working on maternity when the baby was stolen."

"Not exactly thorough, were they?" Jack remarked.

"Things were different back then."

"It's no excuse. It was Carol's baby. She had as much right as anyone else to expect they'd do their best to find her daughter."

"Jack, we're not here to talk about what went wrong," Carol cautioned quietly, "we're here to see if Ethel can point us to where Mary might have gone."

"Sorry. Yes, of course." Jack forced himself to calm down and addressed Ethel again. "So what can you tell us about her?"

Ethel sat back to make herself more comfortable. This was what she loved: a chance to reminisce, relive her younger years.

"Well, now, she appeared on the ward a few weeks before your baby was stolen—not every day, mind. Just a couple of times a week. They reckoned she was being brought in when it was particularly busy..."

"Who were they?" Jack asked.

"Just the other staff—you know, people you asked while you were working."

"So nobody knew why she was there?"

"No, but we didn't know every member of staff who came and went, but we knew people, could tell what they were like, and that woman was no nurse. Nurses care about their patients. All she cared about was what happened to the babies that were born, and especially the ones who belonged to those poor single mums."

"I know," Carol agreed quietly, and they both stared at her. "She had a go at me because I wouldn't have my baby adopted, said I was being selfish, not thinking about her future."

Ethel pursed her lips, shook her head. "As if she knew what was best for them poor little babies. I mean, look at you! Nineteen years later and you still want to find your daughter."

"I *have* to find her. Now more than ever because, if she was the one who stole her, how can I be sure she treated her right? What if she was insane?"

"She definitely wasn't right in the head."

"Now come on," Jack cautioned. It was a short trip down the road to the libel courts from there for a reporter, and the last thing he wanted was to land these two women in trouble. More than that, Carol would only torture herself with the what-ifs.

***

Carol was quiet in the car on the way back, and Jack threw her an occasional worried glance. He was regretting a lot of things lately but none more so than taking her to see Ethel. He'd hoped they'd get more information about the mysterious Mary, but instead it had opened another can of worms which he couldn't seem to put the lid back on no matter how he tried. It was bad enough this woman may have stolen Carol's baby, but if there was something wrong with her mentally, what harm could she potentially have done to the child?

"You're worrying about what Ethel said, aren't you?" he asked her as he drew to a halt outside Carol's house.

"Wouldn't you be?"

"I don't know. Look, this may sound awful, but you've got to remember how old Ethel is. I appreciate she seems bright enough, but she can't remember what things were like back then, or not clearly. For all we know, this Mary was just desperate for a baby. That doesn't make her insane. Maybe 'wrong in the head', like Ethel said, but definitely not mad."

"I suppose you're right," Carol conceded with a sigh. "I'm seeing the black side of everything at the moment."

"Understandable. The longer this goes on, the worse you're going to feel. Which, my lady, is where I come in. I know you have to go to work now, but how about if I pick you up later? We could go for a drink somewhere, have a chat—not about this but other things. Suit you?"

Carol nodded and blinked back sudden tears. It sounded wonderful. Exactly what she needed.

***

Shona heaved a sigh of relief as she opened her front door. It had been good going back to the university, seeing all her friends again, but she hadn't felt as though she belonged anymore. Everyone had moved on, relationships had failed and formed elsewhere, the work they were talking about was far advanced from where she'd left it, and she felt as though she'd been caught in a sort of limbo which wasn't helped by her tutor going over what she'd missed so far.

Afterwards, she'd gone back to the room she'd shared with one of her friends, and they'd talked long into the night, but Shona had already concluded she couldn't do this any longer. There was too much hanging over her, too many things she'd learned about her life. Until she found out the truth of how she came to be with her parents, she wasn't going to be able to concentrate on her studies. Her friend had tried to persuade her otherwise, but Shona had already made her decision. She wouldn't be coming back.

There was no sign of her mother, and Shona walked slowly around the house, trying to look on it as her home still, trying to get rid of the feeling she belonged even less here than she did at the university. Just at the moment, she didn't actually feel as though she belonged anywhere. She'd told Valerie she wouldn't be back at work until Tuesday, and now she wished she'd said today—at least it would give her something to do. Of course, she could still go in; they'd certainly be glad to see her. Impulsively, she rang Carol, asked if she could go in to work.

"Of course you can. But why? I thought you'd said tomorrow."

"Oh, you know. There's nobody here, and nothing feels right at the moment."

"You have said you'll go back to university, haven't you?"

"Not really. I'll explain when I see you. An hour, okay?"

"Fine. We'll have a talk when you get here."

Shona groaned as she ended the call. Carol was obviously in training for being a full-time mother. Some girl was going to get very lucky when she was reunited with a mother who cared about what she did, about her future. *If only it could be me.* But, as Carol had said, that only happened in fairy tales.

With a sigh, Shona went to unpack and get changed so she could keep her promise of being there within the hour.

***

Carol wasn't sure how she was going to play things. Shona's call had put a sick knot of dread in her stomach, the cause of which she couldn't quite put her finger on. Was it hope or fear? Clearly, Shona's tutor's advice hadn't changed her mind, and she wasn't getting any help at all from her parents. Her friends at university would have moved on in their lives already. Carol had no qualifications whatsoever to advise the girl, but someone had to. Someone had to stop her throwing her future away.

"You okay?" Peter asked as he brought the clean tea towels into the kitchen.

"Yes, I'm fine. But can I ask you something?"

He looked at her warily and glanced over his shoulder, making sure they were alone. "What?"

"I've had a call from Shona. She's decided to come in to work. I think it went pretty badly at the university for her. She sounds as though she's decided not to go back."

He drew a relieved sigh and sat down at the table. "Sorry. For a moment, I thought it was something to do with...us."

"That's all in the past, isn't it?"

"Fair point. So what do you want to talk about? Not thinking of interfering, are you? Surely that's up to her parents, not you."

"It sort of ties in with her parents. They told her recently that she was adopted, and it's thrown her."

"I can see why. You don't wait nineteen years to tell someone she's been adopted, do you? So I suppose she's not talking to them at all."

"Not from what I can tell. I don't want her to waste her life working here—sorry, I don't mean to sound ungrateful, but waitressing isn't a career, is it?"

"Try telling Tina that," Peter muttered.

"She's pulling herself together now, though, isn't she? Going to college and everything."

"For as long as it lasts."

Carol could have pulled the conversation back to Shona without too much effort, but she thought better of it.

As Peter left, he passed Tina in the doorway. She watched him go and then grinned at Carol. "Moaning about me again, is he?"

"He worries about you, Tina. There's a big difference between moaning and worrying," Carol retorted sternly.

"Whatever. So Shona's decided to come back a day early, has she?"

"Yes. But I'm concerned she's giving up her university course for the sake of it."

"It's nothing to do with you though."

"No, but she's a friend of mine, and I've always tried to look out for my friends."

"It's a shame her dad didn't talk to you instead of me."

"What?"

Too late, Tina realised she'd let it slip, and now Carol was waiting for an explanation.

"It was when he came looking for her one morning. Nobody but me was here, and he…well…I think he thought I was her friend."

"And of course he had no help from you coming to that conclusion."

"He might have. Anyway, I wished I hadn't said anything when he told me what he did."

"Which was?"

"Apparently, she's not their daughter."

"Oh, she's known for a while now," Carol replied, relieved it hadn't been anything worse.

"What, all of it?"

There was something about the incredulity in Tina's voice which put Carol on alert. "What else did he say?"

Tina opened her mouth and shut it again as Shona breezed through the door.

The moment was gone.

Chapter Twenty-Six

SHONA HAD THOUGHT she was prepared for Carol's 'advice', but within minutes of them sitting down to 'discuss' what had happened, she realised she wasn't. Considering Carol had never been to university herself, she seemed to know an awful lot about it, and all Shona's arguments for not going back were being shot down in flames.

"I won't go back till I know the truth about where I come from, meet my birth parents," she finally declared stubbornly, at which the chef sighed.

"So you're going to put your whole life on hold, are you? Throw your future away for what—a whim?"

"Is it a whim that's got you looking for your daughter?"

"Ah, but I haven't put my life on hold, have I? I've got on with things, got the qualifications I needed to get a decent job, waited until I was in a good place to look for my daughter—"

"And avoided ever getting married, going into a relationship after she was born, after—"

"Shush! I don't want Tina hearing us," Carol warned.

"I couldn't care less if she hears us. At least Tina's got the courage to stand up to her parents, do what she wants to do, and that's what I'm going to do. I'm grateful for the advice, Carol, but at the end of the day, this is my decision, nobody else's."

The firmness in her tone told Carol there was going to be no swaying her. Shona had been forced to grow up a little too quickly with all she'd learned about her background, but it still wasn't any excuse for her to give up her place at university. Surely someone could convince her not to do it.

"Anyway, have you had any response to the newspaper story?" Shona asked, moving the conversation on.

"Yes and no. Nobody has come forward with any information, but Jack's mother has a friend who was a cleaner at the hospital."

"And?"

Shona waited, but Carol didn't elaborate. Why was she being reticent all of a sudden?

"What aren't you telling me?"

"Oh, it's silly, really. Just the ramblings of an old woman, I suppose. She knew who Mary was, but she didn't think she was a nurse—reckons she went in with the deliberate idea of stealing a baby for herself."

"She must have had some nursing qualifications though, or she wouldn't have got away with it, would she?"

"I know. Like I say, I think she was embellishing the story a bit."

"Sounds like it," Shona said. "And how's it going with you and Jack? I assume you went to see this woman together?"

Carol flushed slightly, shrugged. "Oh, you know, we're good friends…"

"And the rest," Shona teased. "I'm really happy for you. He's just what you need."

"I don't know about that. He comes with almost as much baggage as me."

"You mean his mother?"

"Mother, ex-wife, two grown-up kids…"

"It could be worse. At least he won't be having the kids on a Sunday with all the other divorced dads."

"I don't think they get on with him."

"So another case of the ex-wife getting it all her own way," Shona muttered and left the kitchen.

Carol sighed at the cynicism in the younger woman's voice. A year ago, Shona would have been happy, secure in her life, not for a moment thinking it would all be blown apart when her father walked out of the door. The only positive was that she didn't blame her father as much as she had done at first. Maybe someday Jack's kids would find out the truth about what happened to his marriage and they just might get in touch with him, start to heal the rift the divorce had created.

***

The more Jack thought about what was going on, the more convinced he was that he needed to talk to Shona's mother. If nothing else, he wanted to put his mind at rest about her—make sure Shona wasn't that missing daughter of Carol's. What he really wanted to do was go and interview her, but that would be impossible, which left him with rather limited options. Of course, he could approach Shona, ask her if she wanted any help tracing her parents. Carol had mentioned that Shona had drawn a blank when she'd approached the adoption agencies and was now trying to get information out of her parents without any success at all.

When he suggested his plan to Carol, she looked at him suspiciously. "Why would you want to do that? You're not doing this because her mother's called Mary, are you?"

He sighed and shook his head. "My God, you should have been a journalist, woman. Wasted, you are, working as a chef."

"Well," Carol continued, glossing over the compliment, "I think she'd probably agree. Shona isn't thinking along the lines that you are. She's already made her mind up that her mother wasn't the woman who stole the baby, so there's no harm in it, is there? Just don't put any ideas into her head."

"Of course I won't, but by the same token, I wouldn't be offering to do this if I didn't think there was a link to your story."

She held her hands up to silence him. "No more. I don't want to think about it."

It was frustrating, but he could appreciate how she felt. She'd already admitted to him that in a perfect world, Shona would turn out to be her missing daughter, but it still didn't mean to say it would work out for them. Nobody knew what Shona's reaction would be if her parents were arrested, and no matter what Carol thought, the woman who stole her baby should be brought to justice. Nobody, and especially Carol, could prevent that from happening.

***

Shona couldn't hide her excitement from her parents. Terry was becoming a more frequent visitor at their house, and she seemed pleased to find him there when she arrived home after talking to the reporter.

"Guess what!" she said.

They both looked at her warily. She hadn't been very forthcoming with them since they wouldn't help her to get to the bottom of her adoption, and Terry hoped this was to do with her going back to university.

"You know that reporter who covered Carol's baby being stolen? Well, he's offered to help me to track my birth mother down."

They were both aware of her watching for their reactions, and it was Mary who recovered first. She shrugged and shook her head.

"What's wrong with that man? I thought he was a reporter—don't they have to look for stories that are of interest to people?"

"It's of interest to me!" Shona snapped. "You could both just tell me the truth and have done with it!"

"That's enough," Terry cut in. "I haven't come over here to watch another battle between you two. Your mother says you've decided not to go back to university, I was hoping you were about to tell us you'd seen sense and decided to go back after all."

"What's the point? I need to know who I am, where I come from before I can concentrate on anything else."

"No, Shona. You need to get your future sorted out. All of this is in the past. It's not important."

"It might not be to you, Dad, but it is to me."

Her defiance shocked him, and he glared at Mary as she stood up. "Where do you think you're going?"

"To make us a cup of tea."

"Don't you think it would be a better idea to sort this out once and for all?"

She looked at him steadily, calmly, and then walked out of the room, making it clear she wasn't going to sort anything out and especially not concerning her daughter's questions.

As soon as Mary had left them, Shona looked enquiringly at her father, and his heart sank like a stone.

"So are you going to tell me the truth, Dad?"

"I'm sorry, love. I can't. It's not up to me."

"It's up to Mum? But why is it? You're both my parents. You both adopted me. It's not some one-sided affair. I mean, you did both want me—didn't you?"

"Yes. Of course we did."

He was aware of Shona looking at him steadily and his heart sank even further.

"That adoption agency were right, weren't they? There was no official adoption. This was something Mum did off her own bat, and you had no say in it. My God, it's worse than buying a flaming kitten!"

"Of course I had a say!" he blustered. "She wasn't just going to bring you home, was she? Even unofficial adoptions have to be agreed to."

"You're lying," Shona accused. "Don't you see, Dad? This is why I can't go back to uni—why I can't get on with my life. I don't understand why you're protecting her. You'd already left!"

***

Jack wasn't surprised when Shona rang him; nor was he surprised she'd been crying.

"They won't tell me anything," she said. "It's like they've built this wall around themselves and I'm not allowed to go inside it."

"Okay. Don't get upset. I promise you we will get to the bottom of this. Can you come over to Carol's place at about eleven on Wednesday? We'll have a chat about what to do next."

"Why not sooner?"

"I want to do a bit of digging first."

The time had come to uncover the truth once and for all because Jack knew exactly what this was all about. Now he needed to prove it and make sure both Carol and Shona got the happy ending they deserved.

Chapter Twenty-Seven

TINA STARED AT her tutor in amazement as he sang her praises in front of the class. Did he really mean her? Was he really saying she was his star pupil? All right, she was enjoying the course—more than she'd thought she would—but it wasn't as though she was trying hard. She frowned and shook her head. After all this time, had she finally found something she could do, wanted to do?

"Anyway, enough about Tina," the tutor said briskly, "let's get down to some proper work."

She was still stunned when she met up with Kelly and Tracey at lunchtime. Kelly, ever quick to sense her mood, looked at her curiously.

"Not been thrown off your course, have you?" she asked.

Like Tina, she couldn't see any of the three of them doing well at college.

"No. My tutor reckons I'm his star pupil."

"Get out of it, he's having you on. Probably fancies you or something "

"Don't be daft. He's nearly sixty! He told the whole class how good I am. Says I've got a natural aptitude for business."

"Bloody hell. And you didn't even want to do this in the first place!" Tracey marvelled.

"Just think," Kelly added a little slyly, "if it wasn't for your dad playing away, you wouldn't even have looked at doing something other than waitressing."

Tina stared at her friends, realising there was a hint of jealousy for all she had and they didn't have. After all, she would have her own business someday—something neither Kelly nor Tracey would get unless it was by their own efforts. They must have thought she had everything, and Kelly was right. If Tina's dad hadn't sacked her after the complaint from that Cox woman, none of this would have happened. She certainly wouldn't be sitting here realising she really did want to move on, help them out more in the hotel, be a proper member of the family business.

Family.

Thank God she'd never carried out her threat and told her mother about Carol and her father's affair. Her whole life would have been over when, in fact, it was just beginning.

***

Instinct told Jack he had to get Ethel and Mary together somehow, but he was damned if he knew how to do it. he wasn't even sure how he was going to get near Mary because, from what Shona had said, her mother wasn't prepared to talk to anybody about this, which was a sure sign of guilt in his book, not that he'd said that to Shona, of course.

In the end, it was Gladys who threw him a lifeline.

"Ethel needs to go to the doctor's in the morning, although how they expect her to get there I've no idea, but as it's just for blood tests, they won't come out to her."

Jack's ears instantly pricked up. "Which doctor's?" he asked as casually as he could manage.

"The health centre."

As he'd suspected. He could hardly believe his luck. "I'm down that way myself tomorrow. I can give her a lift if she wants."

"What are you there for?"

"Oh, I'm…covering a community story."

"You'd have to help her in to see the nurse if you do take her. She's not too good on her legs at the moment."

"No problem."

"And you'd have to take her with you to cover your story."

"It'll be a bit of a trip out for her."

"Well, I can't say she won't like that. Poor old soul doesn't get out all that much these days. I'll give her a ring and tell her, see what she says."

***

Ethel wasn't quite as convinced as Gladys had been by Jack's reasons for taking her to the health centre, and her first question the following morning was what he was really up to.

"Does your lady friend you brought to see me know what you're up to?"

"I shouldn't think so. No."

Ethel frowned, and Jack sighed. He'd been hoping to see her reaction when she saw Mary without her knowing why he was there, but he'd already made her suspicious.

"The nurse at the health centre—I think she might be the one from the hospital when Carol's baby was stolen."

"That Mary one?"

"Yes."

"I'll not lie if it isn't her."

"I wouldn't want you to, Ethel, but I also don't want her to know that you recognise her if you do."

"Then it's a good job you've warned me," she parried. "The last thing you want is me walking in there and giving your game away."

"It isn't a game," he protested.

"I know it isn't, lad. At least, not to you, but like I said when your young lady came round, any sort of excitement is a game to me these days."

Jack couldn't argue with that. He had no idea how lonely Ethel's life really was, but Gladys had been right about Ethel's daughter leaving her to cope on her own.

"You know, lad," she said as though she'd read his mind, "it shouldn't be you having to bring me to see the nurse, it should be that daughter of mine doing it."

"Do you see her often?"

"She comes over when she can, but you know, it's difficult for her."

"Why?"

"She's got a family of her own."

"So has my sister, but she gets over to see Mum as often as she can."

"No, she doesn't. Gladys has told me how often your brother and sister visit her, and that the pair of them are quite happy for you to be the one who's there all the time, doing everything for her, keeping her company."

"That's a bit harsh."

"Might be harsh, but you know it's true."

She fell silent then as Jack wondered if Gladys had told her Lucy and Stan didn't visit often to make her feel a bit better. It was certainly the sort of thing a mother would do.

***

Mary looked at the list of patients coming to see her that day and noted there were only three blood tests and a couple of blood pressure checks. That was a shame. She'd have preferred to be busy and keep her mind occupied.

The longer the situation with Shona went on, the more it worried her. She had a terrible feeling that at some stage, Shona would find out the truth for herself or Terry would break his silence and tell her. He'd got it into his head that she had to go back to university, carry on with her education, although why he was so fixed on that idea, Mary didn't know. It wasn't as though she was guaranteed a job at the end of it. Maybe she'd be better going to college, training for a career that would do her some good. That way, she might not be so fixated on her past.

Mary sighed and glanced at the clock. Her first patient was due any minute, and it wouldn't do for her to be thinking about her own problems while she did a blood test.

***

Jack was undeniably nervous as he sat beside Ethel in the waiting room. His mind was in turmoil. If his suspicions were proved right then the search was more or less over—apart from the small fact that Mary still wouldn't admit to what she'd done, but he was convinced they could wear her down to a point where she gave in. And if not? He decided not to think about what came next—about the fact they would have to involve the police and reopen a long-ago investigation, which would lead to its own problems.

Before he could go any further down that route with his thoughts, Ethel was called through to the treatment room, and he smiled at her reassuringly as she leaned heavily on his arm.

"Remember, not a word until we're back in the car," he whispered.

She dimpled at him, and he realised he didn't need to worry. The old lady was enjoying every minute of this subterfuge.

Jack sat quietly at the back of the room as the nurse did the blood test. She was quick and efficient, obviously well trained, and his lips tightened as he realised they were looking at a qualified nurse, not somebody who'd scammed her way into a hospital to steal a baby. He had to be wrong about her.

Ethel was chatting away to her brightly, leading Jack to conclude she hadn't recognised her or she'd have been quiet, thrown by it, no matter what she'd said beforehand, and he accepted it was probably time to put this particular notion to one side. Carol wasn't going to get her happy-ever-after ending to this story after all.

"Well, that was a surprise," Ethel declared when they were back in the car.

"What was?" Jack replied, only half listening to her, still disappointed that his theory had been shot to pieces.

"I reckon I were wrong about her not being a proper nurse."

"What? You mean it was her?"

"Oh, aye. Not a doubt," Ethel replied smugly.

"But the way you were chatting to her…" Jack was perplexed.

"Well, you said not to let on that I knew her, didn't you? What should I have done? Sat quaking in my boots because she was sticking a needle into me?"

"I think I would have done."

"I'm too old to be worrying about little things like that. So what do you do now?"

"Now I have to tell Carol and Shona that we've found the mysterious Mary—not that it means she was the one who stole the baby, of course, but…"

"But it's looking pretty certain?"

"Yes, I think it is."

***

Carol and Shona were rendered speechless when Jack told them he'd found the mysterious Mary.

"I can't believe it," Shona finally whispered.

"Oh, I can," Jack said. He'd seen enough over the years to know how low human beings could sink if they wanted something badly enough, and for some women, a baby was the fulfilment of their lives.

"What do we do now?" Carol asked.

"We have to get some sort of proof."

"A DNA test," Shona suggested. "That would show if I was Carol's daughter, wouldn't it?"

"To be honest, I'd rather we got Mary to admit the truth herself," Jack replied. "I think she owes you two that much."

"And risk jail? I can't see her doing that," Carol demurred.

Shona gasped, and Jack could almost see her mentally backing away from them, retreating to the safety of what she'd always known.

"Carol doesn't want her arrested," he said hastily.

"You don't? Why not?"

"Because whoever she is—and she may not even be the thief—she's brought up my daughter for me. It's going to be bad enough having to tell the girl the truth without her mother being arrested as well." Something was niggling at the back of Carol's mind. Something Tina had said. Something about...

"Shona, did your dad talk to Tina?"

"Yes. He's an idiot."

"But she's never said anything to you?"

"No."

"And she's been a lot nicer to you lately?"

"I suppose so."

"We need to talk to her."

"Why?"

"She said the other day she knew something. When I mentioned you were adopted, she asked if your parents had told you everything. I think she knows more than we do."

Jack gave Shona a moment to assimilate that and then nodded. "It's no good me approaching her. I think it has to be you, Shona."

"No problem. I'll ask her tonight."

"Just be careful she doesn't go over the top," Carol warned. "You know what she's like for being a drama queen."

"Oh, don't worry, I'll be able to work out what is and isn't true," Shona assured her.

***

Following her rather strange epiphany at college, Tina made her mind up to turn over a new leaf. It was high time she grew up, got her life back on an even keel. For the first time, she felt equal to Shona, who'd gone to university, and accepted that she too was clever, albeit in different ways. She remembered what her parents had said about it being her own fault she hadn't gone there herself and finally admitted they were right.

Her parents were astounded but delighted by the change. All the bitterness seemed to have seeped out of her, and already they were seeing the benefits. Tina was cheerful, pleasant to the guests and far more approachable with the staff, and Peter began to hope she would keep his secret safe for him.

All of which was fine until Shona asked her what Terry had told her.

"Carol said you already knew everything," Tina replied.

"I know they sort of adopted me, but I can't find out anything else, and I wondered if he'd said something to you that he either can't or won't say to me."

A week ago, Tina would have jumped at the chance to cause trouble and wouldn't have thought twice about blurting out the truth, but tonight, she decided to be more cautious, to think before she spoke.

"He said your real mother abandoned you."

"Right. So they must know who she is."

"Your mother found you."

"Found me? Where? You don't just find a baby!"

"I don't know. He said she came home with you, and they took you in. That's all I know."

It might be all Tina knew, but it was more than enough to convince Shona that Mary had stolen her from the hospital. Stolen her from Carol, her true mother.

Chapter Twenty-Eight

Mary looked uneasy as Shona sat opposite, staring at her as though she'd never seen her before. She was going to have to say something, but fear niggled at her.

Shona slowly drank her tea, put the empty mug down, cleared her throat. "Where did you find me?" she asked bluntly.

Mary paled. This was the one question she'd always dreaded and had convinced herself she'd never hear. She had to buy herself some thinking time.

"What do you mean—'found you'?"

"I've been talking to Tina. Dad told her you came home with me, you found me somewhere."

"You were abandoned at the hospital. I couldn't bear to see a little baby, a defenceless child, left without a mum, so I brought you home."

"What did the police say?"

"The police?"

"You must have told them. It wasn't as though you were bringing a stray dog home, was it? I mean, didn't the neighbours notice when you suddenly had a baby?"

"We were in the middle of moving house," Mary replied, trying to avoid the question about the police. But Shona was nothing if not persistent, and she went straight back to it.

"What did you tell the police?"

"We didn't actually contact them," Mary admitted reluctantly.

"So somewhere, there might have been a young woman needing medical attention after she 'abandoned' her baby, and you didn't think to tell the police about it? Seems a bit odd for a nurse."

Mary shrugged uncomfortably. Where was Terry when she needed him? He was the one who'd told that girl about this. He was the one who'd brought her to this point, and now he was nowhere to be seen as usual.

"Don't you think it's time to tell me everything? It might make us both feel better," Shona coaxed, but Mary shook her head, as stubborn as ever.

"There's nothing else to tell you."

Shona stood and sighed. "Oh, Mum, I wish you'd tell me the whole truth once and for all instead of leaving me to find out bits and pieces for myself."

As Shona left the room, her shoulders slumped with weariness, and Mary felt an unaccustomed pang of guilt.

It would be best if she could tell her everything, of course it would, but the lie had gone on for so many years. She was too afraid of the results if she did tell her. She'd already lost Terry; she couldn't bear to lose Shona as well. What would she do with the rest of her life with neither of them? But there was no choice about what would happen to the rest of her life. As soon as Shona found out the truth, it was all pre-ordained. She'd be arrested, charged, would most likely spend the rest of her days in a prison cell, kept away from the other prisoners because of what she'd done to protect her safety. She couldn't, wouldn't let Shona find out the truth. There had to be a way to stop her. The need for self-preservation at all costs was growing in Mary.

***

"Shona's not coming in tonight," Peter told Valerie. "Apparently, she's not too well."

His wife frowned. The girl must be really ill if she was letting them down. She never did that—they'd had to send her home on more than one occasion when she wasn't fit to work.

"Did she say what was wrong with her?"

"No. Her mother rang in for her."

"Her mother? Just how bad is she if she couldn't do it herself?" Valerie asked in alarm.

"I've told you, I don't know. So are you going to tell Carol or am I?"

"I will."

***

Shona closed her eyes against her mother's concerned gaze. She didn't want to eat, didn't want anything else to drink. Everything which passed her lips made her feel even more ill. All she wanted to do was sleep, allow her body to heal itself.

"Come on, sweetheart, at least try to drink something. I don't want to scare you, but if you don't drink, your fluid levels will fall, and that's when this will get really dangerous. You don't want to end up in hospital, do you?"

Shona did her best to sip at the fruit juice Mary held to her lips. At least then she knew she'd leave her in peace for a while.

"I'll have to let them know at work," she whispered.

"It's all right, I've done it for you. There's nothing at all for you to worry about. You just sleep now."

Mary looked back at her daughter as she lay in her bed and sighed. If only Shona had kept quiet, had believed what she told her, hadn't insisted on asking all these questions. It had all been such a waste. All those years of looking after her, and for what? Nothing.

***

Tina considered Carol, not sure what she should do for the best. She had an awful feeling Shona had confronted her mother about what she'd told her, and whoever had heard of an illness which meant you couldn't ring in to work yourself? Even if you had flu or something, you could manage to make a call on your mobile. Of course, she could send Shona a text message, make sure she was all right. They were friends now; Shona was bound to answer her. And if she didn't? Well, then she may have to say something to someone about what Shona's dad had told her. But not until she knew Shona wasn't all right. She was determined not to cause more trouble for anybody.

***

Ethel frowned as she replaced the telephone receiver. She'd been waiting for her blood test results for a few days, and now they said they'd misplaced them.

Gladys sipped her tea and looked at her curiously. "What's up?" she asked.

"They've lost my blood tests. They're sending one of the doctors out to do them again."

"That's odd. I'd have thought they'd have sent the nurse. She must be the one who's lost them."

"Apparently, she isn't there. Her daughter's ill, and she's looking after her."

"She's lucky they'll let her do that."

"Well, I suppose it's with her being a nurse and all," Ethel replied absently.

But something was wrong. She knew it was. She looked at Gladys and decided it was time to confide in her friend. Jack had said not to say anything, but had to get a message to him somehow. Get him to make sure that girl was all right.

***

Even if Shona had heard her mobile ring, she couldn't have answered it. She no longer had the strength to sit up unaided or think for herself. She was totally reliant on her mother, who urged her to drink more juice, which was the only thing she could swallow now. She didn't have many lucid moments, but when she did she would wish her father would come, that both her parents were here with her, but he never did, and that was how she knew she would get well again. If this was something serious, her mother would have sent for him by now or called the doctor.

***

Carol watched Tina in alarm as the girl wiped away a tear mid peeling potatoes. She'd never seen Tina cry in all the years she'd known her, and she moved over to her, placing a gentle arm around her shoulders.

"Leave that, come and sit down."

Sniffling, Tina obeyed, and Carol placed a cup of tea in front of her, then sat beside her at the table.

"What's the matter?" she asked.

"It's Shona. I'm scared for her, Carol. I've sent her text messages, but she's not answering them. I even tried ringing her, but her mobile is switched off."

"Well, I suppose that's because she's not well…"

"No. I told her what her dad said to me, and I think she might have asked her parents about it—I don't know what they might have done."

"What exactly did you tell her?"

"What her dad told me—that her mother found her."

Carol shivered, remembering what Ethel had said about Mary not being totally sane. What if she'd done something to Shona? What if she was desperate to escape justice? Would she hurt the child she'd raised all these years? The child she'd claimed to love?

"You sit there and drink your tea, love. I'm going to give Jack a quick call."

It turned out Jack was already aware of her concerns, and as soon as Carol told him what Tina had said, he asked, "Do you know where Shona lives?"

"No, but Peter'll have her address. I'll ask him."

"Okay, I'll pick you up in ten minutes."

Carol was hovering anxiously near the front desk when he arrived, and he tried to offer her a reassuring smile, which didn't work at all.

"You know something else, don't you?" she asked.

He nodded. "Mary hasn't been in to work for a while. Says she's having to stay home to look after Shona."

"Oh God. There's something really wrong, isn't there?"

He didn't reply, and that alone was enough to convince her they were about to find something dreadful going on.

***

Mary's lips tightened when she saw Jack and Carol standing on her doorstep, but she didn't come to the door. The curtain dropped back into place.

"She must be there if Shona's ill and she's looking after her," Carol reasoned.

"Oh, she's there, all right," Jack said. "Don't look, but she was just at the window. However, if she won't open the door—"

"We have to do *something*," Carol said desperately. "Can't we call the police?"

"We don't know that she's actually doing anything wrong. Unless…hang on a minute. Shona's ill, and her mother rang into the hotel, so as a concerned employer, yes, of course we can. Follow me."

They returned to the car, and he drove around the corner. He didn't want Mary guessing what they were about to do.

It was obvious how worried Carol was about Shona now. There was no more talk of avoiding having Mary arrested when it came to the girl's safety, and he smiled grimly to himself. He should have known that when push came to shove, there would be no leniency offered.

Chapter Twenty-Nine

TERRY HELD HIS daughter's limp, almost lifeless hand in his and looked up at Carol helplessly.

"I can't believe I didn't know, didn't realise how unhinged she was," he whispered.

It wasn't the first time he'd said that over the past few hours, and Carol had long since stopped trying to reassure him or even sympathise with him.

He must have known there was something not right about his wife. He'd covered up her crime, had only told Tina half the truth, and it was that omission which had led them to where they were now—waiting, praying for Shona to recover from the poison which Mary had been pouring down her throat.

The only saving grace was that Tina had finally come clean about what she knew, and it had saved Shona's life. Another day and it would have been too late.

Carol shuddered at that thought and turned her attention back to Terry—the man who'd helped his wife to keep Carol's daughter away from her all these years. He was as upset and shocked as the rest of them by what his wife had done, but that was no excuse for him having gone along with it. The police would want to talk to him, and Carol wondered why he hadn't left, got as far away as he could.

As though he could feel her gaze resting on him, Terry turned to look at her and forced a smile to his lips. "You're wondering why I'm hanging around, aren't you?"

"Of course I am."

"For all that she isn't my true daughter, I've loved Shona as though she were. I know Mary shouldn't have brought her home like that, but…well, I'll admit I went along with it—"

"She didn't *bring her home*. She stole her. From me," Carol said.

"Oh, no. You're not putting the blame for that on her. You didn't want that baby. You told her you were going to leave her and walk out of the hospital."

As Carol opened her mouth to protest, Jack held up his hand and moved to sit beside Terry.

"We need a chat."

"What about?"

"About your wife and what she did. This could keep you out of jail, my friend. Carol, can we leave you here for a while?"

"Of course. I'm going nowhere," she replied and watched them leave. No matter what Terry said, he had, at the very least, known that they were bringing Shona up illegally. Mary was out of the equation now; she'd tried to murder Shona to protect herself, and none of them could let her get away with that, but by the very fact that Terry was still waiting here for Shona to come round, he was proving how much he cared about her. He certainly wasn't concerned about his wife, who was being held at the police station until she could be questioned and transferred to prison.

***

Jack watched Terry stirring his tea, his brow furrowed.

"I still can't believe she actually tried to kill Shona. She loved that girl. She wouldn't have hurt her for the world."

"But she did," Jack said. "There's no doubt about it. I went down to the police station this morning, and she's admitted to everything—from stealing her as a baby to trying to poison her now."

"She told me the girl didn't want the baby."

"And you believed her. You didn't think there was anything at all suspicious about it?"

"She worked on the maternity unit. She'd been nursing the girl in there. Of course I believed her."

"So you genuinely thought the hospital authorities would let her bring the baby home?"

Terry shrugged uneasily. "Well, of course I thought it was a bit odd, but she said the girl had agreed to it."

Jack shook his head. "God, what a bloody mess. When Shona wakes up, she's going to have to be told Mary tried to kill her, that Carol's her true mother, and that you didn't know the whole story. How do you think she's going to feel?"

"I can't imagine," Terry said. "But I want to be there when she wakes up. Come on, let's go back."

Jack nodded but didn't stand up with him. "You go. I've got some things I need to do."

***

Tina looked at her father in surprise when he said Jack wanted to talk to her. She hadn't had anything to do with the reporter, and there was no reason why he should have come just to see her. Unless…

"Oh God. It's not Shona, is it?"

"I shouldn't think so or he'd have told me. You go for a chat, okay? Just try not to say anything which might land us with a lot of bad publicity."

Tina smiled cautiously at Jack as she joined him, already on the defensive, and he, in turn, realised he was going to struggle to put her at her ease.

"First of all, I've just left the hospital, and Shona's holding her own. And it's thanks to you that she is. If you hadn't told Carol what you'd told Shona, I hate to think what would have happened."

"I only told her the truth."

"I know you did. The thing is, Terry's at the hospital with Shona, and he's saying—well, never mind what. Will you tell me exactly what he told you?"

"Why? So you can finish the whole thing off in the newspaper?"

"No. We've put that story to bed. We did what we said we would. There'll be nothing else going into the paper about it, at least not as far as I'm concerned. The court case will have to be reported on obviously, but that's a long time in the future. I want to make sure the right people are actually going to court."

Tina gave him a considering look. "If you're not interested in writing any more about it, why are you here?"

"Personal reasons."

"So you and Carol are an item then?"

"An item? God, that makes me feel old and past it. I'd prefer to say we're in love with each other."

"Wow. You are a quick worker, aren't you?" Tina said with admiration.

"I take my chances when I get them. You'll be the same when you get older. Anyway, enough about that. Are you going to tell me what Terry said to you?"

She smiled at him and nodded, visibly relaxing. Something told her she could trust this man. That he only had Carol's best interests at heart.

"He said his wife came home from work—she worked at the hospital—with Shona. She'd been nursing a girl who didn't want her baby, and she'd begged Mary to take her for her, didn't want her to be taken by strangers. Terry knew it was a bad idea, that they should have gone through the official channels, but there was no guarantee they'd be allowed to adopt her, and the girl had threatened to kill the baby if Mary didn't take her."

"And that's all he said?"

"Yes, why? That's the truth, isn't it?"

"No, it isn't. But it does mean that Terry may not be going to jail with his wife."

"Are you going to tell me what happened? I've trusted you—it works both ways, you know."

Jack saw no reason not to tell her the truth now. Like she said, trust went both ways, and she hadn't said a word to anybody about that visit from Terry at the time.

"Mary stole Shona. She took her from the nursery and walked out of the hospital. She'd been trying to persuade Carol to have her adopted, and when Carol wouldn't agree, she took her anyway.

"When it looked like Shona was going to reveal what Mary had done, she tried to poison Shona. I don't know why, I'm not a psychiatrist, but I suspect she'll end up being committed on grounds of diminished responsibility rather than for the actual crime. That's up to the courts now."

"God!" Tina gasped. "Poor Shona! It's going to be hard for her when she comes round."

"She'll have Carol there and, hopefully, Terry. Mind you," he warned, "the police might want to talk to you about that meeting with him."

"That's okay."

It was that response which convinced Jack he'd done the right thing talking to Tina. She was the sort of person who loved being the centre of attention but never to the point where she might end up in trouble, whether it was with the law or her parents. In that respect, she was a lot like Mary—self-preservation at all costs— and just the mention of the police would have been enough to make her change her story if she wasn't telling him the truth.

***

Peter was in shock. At the moment, all the attention was on Carol and Shona, mother and daughter reunited, but at some point, the question of who her father was would crop up, and yet somehow it didn't bother him anymore if the truth came out. How could he care about that when Shona—the child he'd never known about—had almost died? Hadn't he been the one who'd wished Tina was more like her just a few weeks ago?

Tina tracked him down in the lounge, trying to keep himself busy. He wanted to go to the hospital, make sure for himself that Shona was still alive and would recover from what Mary had done.

"You okay there, Dad?"

He nodded, carried on stocking the bar.

"Bit of a shock for you, I suppose, finding out Shona is Carol's daughter."

"We all knew the girl would turn up at some stage."

"Yes. You didn't think you'd actually know her quite so well, though, did you? So it looks as though I've got a half-sister then, doesn't it?"

He froze for a moment, then shrugged. "It's not common knowledge yet, Tina. I'd like to keep it that way."

"So would I. But the fact remains that she is related to you. Don't worry, Dad, I'm not going to blow this wide open, but you know Carol told her about your affair ages ago, so it won't take long for Shona to put two and two together."

Peter genuinely hadn't thought of that. If Tina was right, it was going to mean another conversation with a different girl whom he'd have to ask, yet again, to keep quiet. And just when he'd thought that things were getting simpler.

***

Shona opened her eyes slowly, painfully, saw Terry sitting beside her bed and smiled her relief. She'd known he'd come eventually, just as soon as Mary called him.

"Hi, sweetheart, welcome back," he greeted her.

Her attempt at a smile was reward enough for him. He looked over at Carol.

Shona followed his gaze and frowned. "Where's Mum?" she croaked.

"I'll explain everything later," he promised. "You need to rest now, get your strength back."

"Carol?"

"Yes, love. You gave us a right fright, you know."

"I was really ill, wasn't I?"

"You were. Yes. And like your dad says, you need to rest now." Terry threw Carol a grateful look, and she shrugged. However much she wanted to call him 'this man', it would do no good. Not until Shona knew the truth.

"Do you fancy a coffee?" he asked.

Carol would have refused except Shona might find that suspicious, so she nodded curtly and followed him off the ward.

Terry's was getting to be a familiar face in the cafeteria, albeit with a different person every time. The woman behind the counter smiled at them both. "It looks as though you've both had good news today."

"We have. My...our daughter has just woken up."

Carol glanced at him sharply, and he flushed. Couldn't she just be grateful that he'd acknowledged she was Shona's mother? He wasn't trying to cause any trouble here, but he wasn't quite ready to let his child go yet. She supposed in a way she could understand that, even empathise with him, but as soon as they were seated at a table where they couldn't be overheard, Carol laid into him.

"What was all that about? She isn't *our* daughter, she's mine, and that's an end to it. The sooner you realise that, the better for everyone concerned—especially Shona."

"None of this was my doing."

"You weren't there. You knew what your wife was like, and you weren't there to protect Shona."

Terry considered her for a few moments before he spoke again, and then it was with a certain amount of diffidence.

"If you thought I was so evil, you'd have already called the police, but you haven't. You've allowed me to stay with you while we waited for Shona to wake up, which tells me this verbal attack is a reaction to what's happened."

"If that's what you want to believe, it's up to you," Carol said. "I was only thinking of Shona. The last thing she needs is to come round and find neither of the people who raised her at her bedside."

"And now?"

"What do you mean?"

"She's awake now, so how long are you going to wait before you tell her the truth?"

Carol stirred her coffee and shrugged. "Do you want the honest answer or the one I think you want to hear?"

"Let's go for honesty. It's been sadly lacking for years."

"I want to know you were telling us the truth—that you knew nothing about her being stolen—before I do anything. If it is true then I can't condemn you, say you can't ever see her again, can I? But I warn you. If it isn't—if I find out you lied to us—you'll never see her again."

It was more than Terry could have hoped for, but he still had to push for more reassurance. "So you are going to let me carry on being part of her life?"

"I can't stop you. She's an adult. She'll make up her own mind. I'd say it depends on how she reacts when she knows what happened. For all I know, she may never want to see me again either."

"You've done nothing wrong."

"She knows a lot about me. She knows who her real father is, and that's going to be a big problem. In some ways, I've been as daft as you have."

Chapter Thirty

Six Months Later

GLADYS PATTED HER newly cut hair and caught her son's eye in the mirror. "What?" she asked sharply.

"Nothing."

"You're worried about me and Ethel being on our own, aren't you?"

"No, I'm not actually. I think the pair of you will be absolutely fine just as long as you realise you have to listen to the carers and not try and do everything for yourself."

"I'm no fool, lad, and I'm certainly too old to start playing at being a nursemaid. All Ethel needs is company, and she'll get plenty of it moving in with me. I think it's an ideal solution all round."

Jack certainly wasn't arguing with that, especially not on his wedding day.

***

Shona laughed when she found Carol sitting at the kitchen table with a cup of coffee in front of her.

"So how many hours have you been sitting here?" she teased, filling the kettle to make another cup.

"I couldn't sleep. Decided to get up early. It's a big day."

"It's been a big year!" Shona replied with a sigh as she sat opposite her.

It had been a long, slow recovery for Shona, both physically and emotionally. There'd been all the shock of knowing what

Mary had done and then the confirmation that she was Carol's daughter. As Tina had pointed out to Peter, she'd known who her father was, but unlike her half-sister, Shona had thought long and hard about what she should do. Peter hadn't needed to ask her to keep quiet; she was happy enough with the family she'd found and didn't want to see Tina deprived of either her mother or her father.

As for Terry…that had been totally different. It wasn't Carol who was keeping her away from him; it was Shona who'd cut him out of her life, refused to acknowledge his messages, wouldn't see him, wanted nothing to do with him.

That was the one thing which worried Carol on this day. She'd got her life back, had her daughter living under her roof and was marrying the man she loved. As time had passed, she'd allowed herself to realise that Terry had, as much as her and Shona, been a victim of circumstances. He'd lost everything while Carol had gained, and she worried Shona would eventually regret cutting him off. He'd raised her, risked imprisonment so he could be at her bedside. Carol just hoped she hadn't made a mistake inviting him to the wedding.

It had been Jack's idea. He had a feeling the only chance there was for Terry and Shona to heal the rift between them was whilst he and Carol were away on their honeymoon. As long as Carol was around, Shona didn't want to know about her previous life, but with her out of the way, Terry would be able to talk to her, hopefully reason with her, put his side of the story to her yet again because she certainly hadn't listened to him the first time.

***

Valerie looked at the dining room and nodded her satisfaction. It had been a foregone conclusion that Jack and Carol would have their reception at the hotel. It wasn't going to be a big affair; both had said family and a handful of friends. Nevertheless, Valerie was determined to make it a memorable day for them.

Tina bounced through the door and hugged her mother. "It looks brilliant, Mum!"

There was a new contentment about Tina these days. Valerie believed it was because of her new boyfriend and the fact she'd finally moved away from Kelly and Tracey and had a new circle of friends. Peter just thought his daughter had finally grown up, found the thing in life she could do and was gaining confidence in her abilities. Either way, she hadn't objected when Carol began to train Shona up as a chef or when Peter told her Shona would be going to catering college. Maybe she would have if they were paying for the course, but thanks to Mike Land's generosity, Shona could fund herself through it and still have a comfortable nest egg behind her.

***

Terry had thought long and hard about his wedding invitation. Part of him was desperate to see Shona, but he knew full well she wasn't the one who'd invited him. As gestures went, he had to give Carol and Jack credit for giving him this chance, maybe his only chance, to talk to Shona, and for that reason, he'd finally accepted.

That had been a month ago, and now the day was here, he was wondering yet again if he'd made the right decision. What if Shona cut him dead, refused to even acknowledge him? She was going to be the only person he knew there apart from the bride and groom, and he'd feel a complete fool if he was left sitting alone for the entire day. But wasn't it worth looking a fool just for the chance of seeing the girl he'd brought up as his own again? And if she did refuse to speak to him, at least he'd see her looking beautiful, not the desperately ill girl who'd been lying in a hospital bed. As memories went, it would at least be something.

Carol and Jack had deliberately kept quiet about Terry coming to the wedding. It wasn't that they were worried about Shona's reaction so much as they thought a 'surprise' attendance from him would have more impact. Maybe faced with seeing him, Shona would realise what she'd lost and give him the chance they both thought he deserved.

***

The sun was shining when Carol and Shona left the house, the younger woman quick to point out that it must be a good omen.

"Oh I don't need omens, not with the way my life's turned out," Carol replied gaily.

"Are you sure I'll be able to cope with the meals while you're away on your honeymoon?" Shona worried.

"Of course you will. And you'll have Val to help you. Just keep the menus simple, things you've already helped me with, and you'll be fine."

They'd deliberately arranged the wedding around the college terms to make sure Shona wouldn't be taking too much on, and despite all her worries, Carol knew how good she already was. If she'd had any doubts at all, she wouldn't be leaving Shona in charge of the kitchen.

Jack was waiting at the registry office, his welcoming smile revealing there'd been a hint of anxiety at the back of his mind. Beside her, Carol felt Shona freeze and knew she'd seen Terry, but Carol said nothing, going to stand with her fiancé as her daughter glanced around wildly for a means of escape.

All too soon, he was standing beside her, smiling at her, touching her arm.

"Shona."

Her instincts were screaming at her to ignore him, but she couldn't. This was the man who'd raised her, looked after her, been there whenever she needed him. No matter what happened in the future, she couldn't walk away.

"It's good to see you," he continued, "and especially to see you looking so well again."

"Thanks. Yes, I am. Well and happy."

He winced at that, and she wondered if she'd been unfair by saying it.

"Have you been to see—Mary?" she asked.

"A couple of times, yes. She's not doing too well, it's been… hard for her."

"It hasn't been easy for any of us," Shona snapped but then backtracked. "I'm sorry. It must be difficult for you too, having to go and see her. I know I wouldn't do it."

"I wouldn't want you to. As for upsetting? No, it makes me angry. She sits there with people fussing round her while the rest of us—you and me and Carol—are left alone to try and get over it all."

Shona bit her lip and touched his arm gently.

"I'm sorry," she said. "I didn't want to see it from your point of view. So far as I was concerned, it was both of you who lied to me. I know you told me you didn't know I'd been stolen, but you still didn't want to tell me I was adopted, did you? It was as though you were trying to cover up for her."

"I thought she could tell you more about it than I could, that's all. If I'd known the truth—"

"If you'd known the truth, none of this would have happened. And I mean none of it. Carol would never have met Jack, I wouldn't be working in the hotel now—I'd still be at uni, wondering if I was doing the right course. So stop blaming yourself. There's a lot of good things have come out of it as well as the bad."

Terry drew a deep breath. Was she finally going to forgive him? Allow them to be friends at least? Before he could ask, they were called into the registry office.

Carol noticed with satisfaction that Terry and Shona were sitting together.

It was going to be all right.

About the Author

I was born and bred in Yorkshire, close to the Dales, and now live in Leeds. I am married and have two sons.

I've been writing for most of my life. It's what keeps me sane, although I have to admit it isn't always easy, helped as I invariably am by our two gangster cats, aptly named Bonnie and Clyde.

Most of my inspiration comes from life, although not necessarily mine. I'm well past the heroine stage now! Like many other writers, one of my favourite pastimes is people watching, so, if you ever see a strange woman sitting scribbling in a café, beware! It could be me…

By the Author

The Write Way
(Bradford Writers Circle,
edited by Sheila Kendall and Julie Pryke)

Mission Accomplished

Deadly Chains

Tangled Webs

Beaten Track Publishing

For more titles from Beaten Track Publishing, please visit our website:

https://www.beatentrackpublishing.com

Thanks for reading!

Lightning Source UK Ltd.
Milton Keynes UK
UKHW011408071119
353072UK00001B/18/P